To Follow Elephants

To Follow Elephants

Rick Hodges

Stormbird Press

Stormbird Press

Stormbird Press is an imprint
of Wild Migration Limited.

Cover design by Stormbird Press

Typeset with Antique Olive and Kazimir.

National Library of Australia Cataloguing-in-
Publication entry:

Hodges, Rick, 1965–Author

To Follow Elephants

ISBN 13: 978-1-925856-13-2 (pbk)

ISBN 13: 978-1-925856-14-9 (ebk)

1. Ecofiction 2. Africa 2. Wildlife 2. Adventure

*The publishing industry pulps millions of books
every year when new titles fail to meet inflated sales
projections—ploys designed to saturate the market,
crowding out other books.*

*This unacceptable practice creates tragic levels of
waste. Paper degrading in a landfill releases methane,
a greenhouse gas emission 23 times more potent than
carbon dioxide.*

*Stormbird Press prints our books 'on demand', and
from sustainable forestry sources, to conserve Earth's
precious, finite resources.*

*We believe every printed book should find a home
that treasures it.*

For Dad

1

The morning she sensed the approach of the dry season, First Grandmother led her family across a river. She was headed for a place she knew many sweet and green things to eat would be growing, treats that even the youngsters could reach with their short, wobbly trunks. She was a good leader, and her herd was large and healthy, with 30 or more of her sisters and daughters and many of their young sons not yet old enough to go out on their own. The older females trumpeted with delight when the matriarch signaled it was time to go, for they had vivid memories of the taste and smell of the ripe fruits and green leaves in the place First Grandmother was leading them, and they urged their new babies to follow, pushing them gently with their tusks. The little ones hoped their journey would bring them to see the mountain where the Spirit lived, and where she created the very *first* First Grandmother, and her nine daughters, that they had learned about in the stories First Grandmother had told them.

They would have many questions.

"First Grandmother, where are we going? I haven't seen this place before."

How many times had she heard that question in her long life?

"We are going to a special place," she said, "the place where we were first born. Where all elephants were first born."

"Why are we going there?"

"The soil that gave birth to us is food for us too."

She could see they didn't understand, but First Grandmother remembered her own confusion when she first took the same trail up the mountain as a young one. Instead of speaking, she stopped and dug her tusks into the soil at her feet, loosening it a bit to touch and smell with the tip of her trunk. Then she lifted the sample to her mouth for a taste. She watched the little ones imitate her and laughed.

"This is not the soil we will eat," she told them, "but we are getting close."

As they moved up the mountain, she felt cool air sliding down from the summit, which was made of a cold white rock she had never noticed anywhere else— and had never seen up close, since it was too high for an elephant to reach and nearly always surrounded by clouds. Then the wind shifted, and several young mothers stopped in their tracks and lifted their trunks in alarm. They had detected a strange, threatening scent. First Grandmother lifted her trunk and detected the odor—a woman! But she quickly recognized it as the friendly one who follows elephants everywhere, yet at a respectful distance. She turned into the breeze and saw the friendly woman, with dark skin, walking up the mountain on her two legs, following the family as always. There was no threat. First Grandmother led on.

In a broad clearing, she stopped to let the young ones rest a bit after the climb. Elephants don't like climbing mountains. They aren't built for it. She felt it in her own old bones. But it had to be done. The little ones frolicked and mouthed the soil, anticipating eating dirt as First Grandmother had promised, while the adults scanned the edge of the clearing and sniffed the air for threats. She noticed a few of the younger elephants eyeing her and imitating her as she turned her head and raised her trunk in different directions.

After ascending into more forest, they reached another small clearing. She watched as the young ones emerged and stood still, gazing in amazement at the huge opening in the side of the mountain, flanked by rocks larger than their mothers. First Grandmother remained still, remembering the first time she had seen this place as a youngster, back when the hole was a bit smaller.

Then the youngsters seemed to understand all at once, and they ran into the hole with the mothers fast behind them. They all tasted the salty, mineral-rich soil they gathered from the walls of the cave. First Grandmother ate some that had fallen to the cave floor. She could feel the nutrients coursing through her body. The mothers dug into the sides of the cave with their tusks to free up more dirt, and the little ones dug eagerly into the clumps that fell to the ground.

When they were satisfied, the mothers went back outside but the little ones continued to explore and enjoy the adventure of the cave with First Grandmother.

"This is the place where we were created," she told them in the dim light. "This is where the very first First Grandmother bore her nine daughters and led them out into the world, the ones who were the first mothers to all the elephants. They are the daughters who summoned nine bulls here to create the nine families of elephants that live today, including ours.

"This is where you come from."

2

Wanjeri lay in her bed and cried for three days when her mother died. She cried only in her bedroom, quietly, never in front of her other family members who came to her house to show their respect, and never ever in front of friends or at school.

It was a day longer than she cried for her father, but perhaps the crying for her mother was also crying for her father, since he died on Tuesday morning and her mother died the following Thursday evening.

Her mother and father had both been generous and kind people who seemed never to get angry with her. Wanjeri was their third child, though when her mother died, she was pregnant with what would have been Wanjeri's younger brother or sister. So Wanjeri mourned for the baby who had also died. Her private mourning conformed with Kikuyu custom, unlike the Luo, who wailed and shrieked as they walked behind the bodies of their loved ones on the way to their graves. Wanjeri was glad for it as she would feel uncomfortable making such noise. If she had been born a Luo and did not show the expected level of emotion at the death of her parents, they would suspect her of being an ungrateful daughter. Some of the elders might even whisper she had caused their deaths through witchcraft. Even in the city, some people still thought like that.

Still, though she was not a Luo, there was some whispering, and Wanjeri caught wind of it soon after her mother and father were buried. They had both died of AIDS, it was said. She knew it was not true, and she promised herself she would push to the ground any girl in school who said it to her face. None did. But they looked at her in a different way and talked to her less frequently. One girl even refused to drink from the same faucet, fearing that Wanjeri would spread the disease. When they did openly tease her, it was over small things, like the way she wore her hair in tightly wound strands with small ribbons. Her mother used to wind the strands together, but now her older sisters Wanjiku (named for her father's mother in the traditional way) and Nyambura (named for her mother's mother) twisted Wanjeri's hair, and they were not as precise as her mother.

Wanjeri's uncle Mubego soon resolved the problem when he took responsibility for the orphaned girls and their brother, Julian, and announced he would send Wanjeri to a boarding school in Kiratu. Her sisters, much older than Wanjeri, had nearly completed school and both would be married soon. Wanjeri dreaded leaving the city for such a small, boring town. "Think, girl!" Uncle Mubego exclaimed when Wanjeri whined about the school. "Most girls your age are working on farms planting yams and beans! You have the privilege of schooling." Uncle Mubego was an officer in the Army and used to telling others what to do. She would have her sisters with her for a while longer, he reminded her. And, she added in her mind, she would no longer suffer evil looks from her old classmates.

The day before she was to leave for the new term in the Kiratu School, Wanjeri went to the dusty square behind her old school and found the girl who had spread the rumors about her parents. Without saying a word, she approached the girl with her right arm stretched out straight and caught her by the throat. She squeezed tightly enough to make the girl choke and cry and looked her straight in the eye. Then she let go and walked away, only pausing once to turn and see if the girl had received the message. Wanjeri was never much for finding the right words, but she had sent a message nonetheless, and it felt good. She could still sense the weight of the girl's larynx against her fingers hours later.

The Kiratu Academy was small, with only 21 girls and another ten or so boys in another hall on the other side of a hill. But because there were so few students, they all learned together under one teacher, making her class larger than at school in Nairobi. Her sisters, Wanjiku and Nyambura, both studied in the same room, though they were near graduation and had more advanced lessons and books.

Wanjeri had seen elephants before, of course, but only at Nairobi National Park, the tiny game reserve just outside the city surrounded entirely by a fence. She was a city girl, and it stunned her to see the creatures roaming outside just a hundred meters from the classroom window, with no fence to be seen. She was even more surprised when the teacher glanced at the animals and then ignored them, continuing with the lesson. An older student explained it after school: "They can come here and roam free on the school's land. They don't bother us, and they are no danger. The farmers in this area hate them because they eat and trample their crops. The farmers build big fences and chase them with dogs, and the ones with guns will shoot at them."

"Do they live here all the time?"

"No, they only come in the long dry season. They stay here to be safe, but there is not much food so they must go other places to eat."

Wanjeri scanned the trees edging the horizon, but the elephants had disappeared during class.

"The teacher takes no notice," added her classmate, "but when a white teacher from overseas or a missionary instructor comes, they are terribly surprised."

I am terribly surprised too, Wanjeri thought.

From that day, Wanjeri wanted to know more about elephants. She regretted the days at the park in Nairobi that she had ignored them as she giggled with her sisters in the back seat of the car. She did not understand why the creatures meant something to her. They seemed so much larger, more alive and powerful, when she saw them walking the same paths she walked on the school grounds, even when she contemplated the smelly piles of dung they left behind for her to avoid stepping in.

For the next week, she snuck glances out the window

of the classroom, but saw no more elephants. Her marks suffered a little for not paying attention. But she devoted more time to her studies when the teacher mentioned that good marks were necessary for entrance to university. She had resolved to go to university to study a field whose name she had just learned—zoology.

* * *

"Do you think it's cold here?" a young English girl once asked her as she sat having tea with a group of fellow students.

Wanjeri almost spit out her tea. "Of course it's cold here! I've never been so cold! I grew up a few miles from the equator!"

The tea helped ward off the cold of London in winter. The energy of her talk and the thoughts of the steady heat of home warmed her a little more, like shivering. And she had learned the art of speaking her mind more directly, like her classmates. They appreciated it, laughing at her outbursts.

"Have you ever seen snow?"

Wanjeri enjoyed telling her classmates about her home, so she suppressed her irritation with some questions. She glanced at the snow outside the cafe window, still drifting down into the dark streets hours after it started, though it had turned wetter, almost to rain.

"No, I never saw snow until I came here, but we have it. At the top of Mt. Kenya."

"Do people climb the mountain?" asked another student, a young man she knew from biology class.

"Tourists climb it, and when people get old sometimes they climb it to get closer to God. They believe God lives in the mountain."

"Do you believe that too?"

Wanjeri grinned with the possibilities. She could tell these young London university students anything and they would believe it. But she could not bear the thought some would never learn the truth, so she did not abuse her power. Instead, she thought for a moment and then answered: "I went to Christian schools and they told me God lives in heaven. But all my classmates believed God lives in the mountain. Now I go to university to learn science, and most of my professors don't believe God lives at all, and they're from the country that brought us the Christian schools. So I would say I'm confused."

They laughed. She was now the center of attention and had signaled her willingness to talk openly about herself, unleashing the other student's curiosity. Wanjeri summoned her African politeness and continued to answer their questions forthrightly, hiding her growing discomfort. London had taught her two things about why she loved working out in the bush watching elephants all day—it was warm, and elephants never asked her questions.

"Are most people in Africa Christians or their old religions?"

"There are mostly Christians, and some Muslims, but some still believe the old religions. But many people believe both. They keep the old gods with the new one."

"How do they manage that? Don't the Christians want to stamp out the old gods?" The boy from biology again.

Wanjeri thought for a moment, and said, "It's like Christians who study the classics. The Greco-Roman gods, the mythology and the stories, mean something to them, even if they don't quite worship them." Her answer made biology boy nod in approval.

"Can you tell us any mythology from Africa?" asked a young girl, a fellow zoology student.

"Yes, but I need more tea first please." Her hands were cold, but the tea warmed them. She understood now why Londoners cradle hot drinks in both hands.

"Pardon me if I've turned you into a show," the girl said.

"Really, I don't mind. I like to talk about home. It makes me feel warmer."

It was easy for Wanjeri to pick a story to tell. It was the only one from the old beliefs she knew: God, whose Kikuyu name is *Ngai*, invited Kikuyu, the first man, to build his house on Kirinyaga, one of the old volcanoes that created the plains with its ash. Ngai lived within Kirinyaga, which is called Mt. Kenya today. Ngai gave Kikuyu a wife, Mumbi, to share the house. Kikuyu's farm on the slopes of the mountain was very prosperous, and Mumbi bore nine daughters, and they became the founding mothers of the Kikuyu clans.

Mumbi actually bore ten daughters, but the Kikuyu believe it is bad luck to count blessings one to ten, so to talk of the ten daughters, they say there were "nine in full" instead. Or perhaps it was because the tenth daughter did not marry that they only spoke of nine. Nobody knows the reason for sure.

The same girl interrupted the story: "Do you believe

it's bad luck to say 'ten,' Wanjeri?"

"I am a scientist. These are just stories to me," she replied.

"Ten! See? No problem!" Wanjeri added, to laughter.

She continued with the myth: To bring husbands for the daughters, Ngai told Kikuyu to build a fire to roast a sacrificial lamb. From the fire came the husbands, each the same height as their wife. The daughters and their husbands founded the clans of the Kikuyu. Most Kikuyu farm the soil around the volcano, but many are clever businessmen and craftsmen.

"And they name most Kikuyu girls after female ancestors," she said, "which means most are named after one of the original daughters who founded the clans, including my sisters and me."

"All the girls have only ten names?"

"Most of us, yes."

"Is yours one of the ten names?"

"It is."

Wanjeri and her companions finished their tea and drifted off into the snow, but the boy from biology stayed with her and walked her home. The snow had turned entirely to rain now, but it was still very cold, and it stung her face.

"You didn't say if you have ever climbed Mt. Kenya." he said.

"I've only been up a short distance. As I said, Africans go up the mountain, but never to the very top."

"Why not?"

"It's traditionally the place where God lives. So I

suppose some are afraid of what they might find there."
As she remembered the mountain, an image of a terrible
moment deep in her memory flashed into view until she
willed it away.

"And others are afraid of what they might *not* find
there," she added.

This made him laugh. They walked a little more
through the snow without speaking. Then he continued:
"What do you want to do when you graduate?"

"I'm going to research elephants."

"Sounds brilliant. Don't you know all about them
already though?"

"Only what I've seen for myself."

"Don't they teach about wildlife there?"

"Not nearly as much as they ought to. Especially at
the university level. That's why I'm here in this freezing
place where no elephant in his right mind would ever
come."

"Yes, it is strange that you need to come to Europe to
learn about elephants."

"I've noticed that." She laughed to assure him she
was not poking fun at the plainness of his observation.

"Is it more expensive to come to school here? I mean,
the tuition?"

"Oh yes. But my family is quite wealthy. My uncle is
paying for most of it."

"What kind of business is your uncle in?"

Wanjeri was silent for a moment. "I don't know.
Something not good."

3

It was First Grandmother's job to tell stories that would pass her knowledge on to her granddaughters and grandsons. One granddaughter would someday take her place and lead them all across the land to the right places at the right time of year. But her favorite story to tell was not of how to browse the hills for ripe fruits or nuts in the good days, or how to dig wells in the plains with their tusks to find water during the long dry season. Her favorite story was for the youngest ones, the ones born just a season before who still walked on playful, unsure legs and wiggled their trunks as they ran. Every youngster must be led at least once to the mountain and the caves that gave birth to all elephants and told the story of the first elephants who emerged from the earth. There were three of them now, the youngest a curious grandson who took a break from playing to ask her.

"First Grandmother, how did I come from the mountain?"

"My precious little one, it is good you want to know that, for it is so important. It was many, many grandmothers before me, when ..."

"How many grandmothers before you?"

"How many? More than all the stars in the sky, more than all the blades of grass."

The young one was very impressed by this number.

"Do you remember when we visited the mountain?" she asked him. "And we went to the great caves inside?"

"Yes, I remember."

"Well, before all the grandmothers, the Spirit that lives in the mountain looked on the plains, and the hills beyond, and the lakes and rivers, and the forests, at all the living creatures. She looked at the buffalo, and zebra, and wildebeest, and crocodile. She looked at the monkey, and the okapi, and the hyrax, and the lion. She looked at the hyena, the woman, the leopard, the cheetah. And she noticed that none of the creatures were perfect. None knew and loved the land like the Spirit, who lives in the land. None loved their children the way she did. So the Spirit decided to create a new creature, one perfect like She was.

"She took some earth from the mountain. From this earth, the Spirit created the first grandmother—the very first one. She made the first grandmother large, the largest creature of all, like she is the largest of all. She gave the creature great strength to do great things—to lift, and dig, and carry, and push, and fight the lion and hyena. She gave the first grandmother a long trunk that could reach high into the trees for the best leaves and fruits and into the air to smell the animals far beyond the scent of our sisters, and low into the ground or the ponds to bring forth water and drink it or spray it on ourselves or share with our little ones. She gave the trunk the strength to lift a young one, like you, but also the tenderness and dexterity to stroke your skin or clear the mud from your eyes. The Spirit gave her powerful tusks to dig the earth to seek Her nourishment in the caves. And the Spirit told the *first* First Grandmother all the good places for food and water and the paths to find them and the times to go to each and how to know when it was time to go. That is why we go to the caves where the Spirit took the earth, and we eat some of the earth. It gives us nourishment directly from the Spirit.

"When the first grandmother was complete and had the knowledge the Spirit gave her, she asked the Spirit for children, for the Spirit had given the grandmother a strong, strong love for children. The Spirit told the first grandmother she shall have nine daughters. But the first grandmother said, 'If I am to have nine daughters, I must first have a mate, but there are none other like me.' And the Spirit told the grandmother to make a sound, the deepest, longest sound she could make, so low that no other creature could hear it. And the grandmother made this sound, and it traveled for many miles beyond the mountain, and in two days a grandfather appeared, and they mated joyfully, and she gave birth to nine daughters.

"And when the nine daughters desired to have children, the first grandmother knew to tell them to make the low sound to call fathers to them, and nine fathers appeared, and they mated joyfully, and they each gave birth, and in this way the first grandmother became a grandmother, and passed her knowledge to her daughters.

"And those daughters became the next grandmothers, and they had children in turn, and that is where you came from. And that is why you are the most precious creature on earth. You come from the Spirit, who created you to be the perfect being from the soil of the mountain and to care for the perfect beings who come in the time after yours, and give to them the knowledge that the Spirit gave."

This made the little one feel very good.

"Will I become a grandmother?" he asked.

"No, little one, you are a father, so you will go out on your own when you are older and live among the other creatures, and only when you hear the call of a mother who wants a child will you come back to a group of mothers."

"Will you give me knowledge?"

"Little one, I am giving you knowledge right now! But you will learn more as you grow older. You will never need to know all the things I do, because you will not lead a group of mothers, but you will learn what you need to know. When you eat from your mother's mouth the food she has chewed for you, you are learning the right things to eat from their taste. When your mother and her sisters take you to the bare earth and pound it to dust and spread it on your back, or to the mud to roll in, you are learning how to protect your skin from the sun and the bites of insects."

"Grandmother, where did the grandmothers before you go, the ones that numbered as many as the stars?"

"When a grandmother becomes old, she goes to the marshes to eat the soft plants, for her teeth have ground down and she cannot eat hard food any more. There, she dies, leaving her bones for all to honor. There are many other ways to die, but a grandmother tries to lead all away from death until their teeth wear down too and they can go to the marshes. Tomorrow, we will go to the marsh and honor the grandmothers of the past. Then you will see the river for the first time in your young life and cross it to reach good foods you have not tasted before."

The young one was excited by this idea, and he had trouble sleeping that night in anticipation of seeing the river and tasting the food.

4

It was heaven to come to the beach house with June and her boys because this was one of the few towns in Maryland where open drinking was allowed on the beach. Mrs. Pearson detested having to hide a flask under her towel.

As Keith slapped each wave that came to the shore, Owen ignored his brother and dug in the sand. He watched as Keith ran screaming from imaginary sharks and sat in the shallow surf to let the receding water of each wave creep through his shorts and down his legs.

Owen kept digging. When he reached the water table a foot down, he could crouch inside and the rim of sand edging the hole would hide the top of his head from view. As the water at the bottom soaked the sides and the hole began to collapse, Owen simply expanded it. Then he created a castle wall out of the rim, with notches at regular intervals to spy and repel invaders. He refused all of Keith's pleas to join him in the water to hunt for sharks. After rebuilding one part of the wall so he could step out without smashing it, he worked on fortifying the exterior of his creation.

"Digging your way to China?"

Owen looked up from his collapsing hole and squinted in the sun. Mrs. Pearson had left her perch with his mother under the umbrella. She rarely showed much interest in Owen's sand projects, so Owen wasn't ready with an answer. "No," was all he mustered.

The wind blew her jet black hair into her eyes. Her body was beginning to show signs of her age through her one-piece swimsuit, but her eyes remained as youthful as ever. She could probably be more attractive if she worked on her hair and used makeup better and found a nicer suit. To Owen, who was too young to notice such things, Mrs. Pearson was his mother's peculiar friend, like an aunt he rarely saw who always had witty things to say he didn't quite understand.

"So it's a fort?" she asked.

"Yeah."

"Who's the enemy?"

"Keith."

And that was enough information for her. Mrs. Pearson headed back to the umbrella for another gin and tonic. "You couldn't get Owen out of his hole, huh?"

June was settled under the umbrella in her chair with a copy of *I Am the Cheese* propped open over her stomach.

"Nope. I established that it's a fort, though, and Keith is the potential invader."

"It drives Keith crazy that Owen doesn't play with

him in the water. And he won't let Keith play in his hole either."

"I guess you'll have to get up and get wet, June."

"Fat chance. The water's too cold, and I just put tanning oil on. Get me a drink too, please, while you're at it."

Owen conducted a ceremony to mark the occasion of his fort's completion. He circled the hole clockwise three times and then jumped in, dizzy. He ignored the screams for help from Keith as he was devoured by sharks. The saturated sand at the bottom gripped his feet up to his ankles, and he sat in it. It felt good inside. It was cool, shady, and quiet.

"Keith! Not so far out!"

Keith came out of the water to Owen's hole and peeked inside. "It's a pool!" Keith declared. He began to dig a trench from the ocean to the hole to guide more water into it. "No, it's *not* a pool, Keith! Leave it alone!" Keith gave up and ran back to play in the waves.

Mrs. Pearson's tote bag beeped. "That's my pager." She went back to the house to return the phone call.

Owen imagined his hole was a cave that led under the ocean to an underwater city protected by domes. He started digging a cave through the wall, but stopped after six inches for fear of collapse.

Back from the house, Mrs. Pearson stood next to June's umbrella and finished her drink. June looked up from her book to make sure the children were out of earshot. "You were on the phone a long time."

"It was my contact. About Kenya."

June continued to hold the book to her face, but her

eyes stopped tracking the words across the page. She fixed them on the page number, 91, and waited.

"My contact couldn't find out that much. There's some kind of blackout surrounding him. The military is handling it, and they aren't talking to diplomatic types."

"What do we know?"

"All indications are it's true."

"How long will he be ... what's the ..."

"No information on that, which is very strange. It's why my contact thinks there's more to the story."

June took a deep breath and put the book down. "Why didn't we take him? The U.S.? To try him here?"

"Technically, it's a crime against Kenyan law. I think what would happen is that we'd take him and prosecute him once his sentence was served over there, but I don't understand all the legal issues."

The water drenched Owen's head and wrapped its way around the sides of the hole, smoothing it and leaving a residue of tiny salt bubbles on the surface. It was too much water to be the work of Keith—it was just the incoming tide. So he kept his seat in the swirling sand at the bottom of the pit instead of leaping out to defend the fort from his brother.

The afternoon sun had dropped low behind them. It peeked underneath their umbrella and illuminated June's face. She shaded it with her hand to protect her eyes and hide her tears.

"The State Department wanted to negotiate a way to get him out of there, but our military people and their military people won't say a word about any of it."

"Is that the best thing?"

"Is what the best thing?"

"For him to get out of there?"

Mrs. Pearson took a big sip of her drink. "I could go over there. Use my U.N. credentials, try to figure something out."

"Only if you think it will do some good. But you don't have to tell me about it if it doesn't."

Keith screamed. They both looked up, but it was just another imaginary shark—he was busy slapping at incoming waves again.

"It's so completely out of character for him, June. I don't understand it."

"I don't know what that means any more—character."

"So do you want me to go over there?"

"Yes. But don't tell me when you go. And if you don't like what you find, tell me you went on vacation instead. Tell me you went to Europe for a big meeting. Just tell me anything else. I don't know if I can handle it if ...."

Owen heard Keith scream again. He jumped out of the fort to check. Keith was fine—just playing. But the light had changed since he had hidden himself in his fortress. A fleeting cast of darkness was coloring the sand as the direct rays of the sun disappeared. It was the first warning of night's approach, and it made Owen uneasy. The world had changed, just a bit, since he left it for his sandy hole, as if someone had rearranged his room while he slept. The Earth seemed to have shifted on its axis after hitting a bump in the ether of space, just enough for Owen to sense it but not enough to make sense of it, like the bright spots he could see when he closed his eyes after looking toward the sun. The feeling moved from his eyes to his stomach. It felt like getting carsick by reading a book in the back seat of the station wagon.

He felt hot and clammy, then cold. His legs shook. His knees buckled under him and he dropped to the sand. Clutching his belly, he rolled to his side. The urge to run from a terrible danger seized his limbs, yet his body would not cooperate. He threw up, and finally his mother noticed something was wrong. He did not remember her carrying him to the beach house, but when he woke up on the couch, his stomach felt queasy, his legs ached, and his skin felt tight. But the cloud of dread that had threatened to cover his head and smother him was gone.

***

"It's physical only. It's an abnormal fear reaction without something to fear. It doesn't mean he's afraid of anything. It only means his body thinks he is. Do you understand what I mean?"

"I think so. Owen, honey, does that sound like what happened?"

"Yeah, I guess."

The doctor pulled a stool up to sit directly in front of Owen. His eyebrows were grey and oversized, and he gave Owen a serious look. "You're sure there wasn't anything you saw that made you afraid? And nothing you stepped on, or bit you, or stung you on the beach?"

"No. It just happened when I got out of the hole."

"It could have been the blood rushing out of his head when he stood up," offered June.

"I don't think so. Not all of those symptoms. It's a panic attack. And he's likely to have more."

Owen swallowed.

"When?" asked June.

"At any time. Something might trigger it, like a small fear, or a sudden change in scenery. Or nothing at all. We won't know until he has them again. Tell me something—have you seen this happen before?"

"Maybe a little bit. I thought he was getting sick, but it never lasted long. Then I thought maybe he was missing his father." June didn't want to bring up Owen's father now, but she let it slip.

"That could be a reason. How about you, Owen, have you felt like this before?"

"Yeah, I guess. I get dizzy and ..."

"Can we do something to prevent it?" June interjected.

"There are some medications, but they haven't been very successful with other people. Maybe when they do more research. I don't want to try them on a child though. There's also evidence that exposure therapy can help."

"What's exposure therapy?"

"It comes down to facing your fears. It works well sometimes with irrational phobias, such as fear of spiders—the patient looks at spiders, then holds one, to learn to control and think through the fear impulse and learns that spiders won't really hurt him. But there's no particular fear for Owen triggering this, so he couldn't be exposed until we know what it comes from. If it comes from anything."

The doctor turned back to Owen. "Do you have any questions about all this, Owen?"

"What ... causes it?"

"We don't really know. It's probably a faulty circuit in the brain. It doesn't mean you're a coward, and it doesn't mean you're crazy. Just think of it like an allergic reaction or something."

"Okay."

"We do know it runs in families sometimes."

Owen saw his mother clutch her cheek and stare into space, lost in thought.

5

Wanjeri thought being alone for days on end in the bush would be hard to bear. She talked to nobody except during her daily radio check-in and the occasional Masai who visited her campsite. But soon she learned to listen to the rich sounds of the plains and the creatures that kept her company. And then she began to love that there were no other people.

She kept her camp simple and easy to pack up because the elephants might suddenly storm away. She slept in the Jeep at night for convenience and safety, and in the daytime she sat under a tarp draped from the back. The tarp gave her shade in the dry seasons and shelter in the rainy seasons. The elephants knew her odor well, and their eyesight was poor anyway, so they did not react in fear when she left the vehicle and revealed herself as a dangerous human. Still, these elephants were not used to people watching them as much as the animals that roamed the tourist areas were, and it took Wanjeri months of following this group before she could ease the Jeep close enough to observe them in the open without the aid of her telescope. In the morning, when the elephants often moved on, she would strike camp by stowing her equipment and chair, rolling the tarp up, and checking under the hood for snakes or lizards that had curled up next to the warm engine for the night.

Her job was to observe the elephants for most of the day and record everything she saw in a journal. The work would satisfy the last requirements for her university degree and earn her a small stipend. After she graduated, she would stay on as a field researcher and earn a little more. The journal would become part of the scientific record. She knew much of what she observed was nothing new to the world of elephant research, but it had to be done to prove she was a capable observer and to fill out the scientific record a bit. Of course, there was always the chance she would see some kind of elephant behavior nobody else had seen before. She hoped for a moment like that, but she wasn't sure she would know it if she saw it. Still, it helped to sustain her through the hottest, most tedious days.

Then came the day in late March when dark angry clouds appeared. The air smelled dense and fresh, and Wanjeri knew the rains were near and so did the elephants. They would move on to fresh new growth in their favorite spots soon, too far for her to follow. This would probably be her last day of observation of this group. A more experienced observer would track them.

March 27

5:54 am—Sunrise. Female P2 (matriarch) not

first to stir today, unusual. Female J3 active first, touches her offspring Male Y4 and several other juveniles with trunk in morning greeting.

6:02—Fem. P2 active. Most juveniles active.

6:21—Fem. J8 nurses offspring Fem. B6. All of group active.

6:55—Fem. B6 finishes nursing. Joins another juvenile (Male K4?) in mock threat play.

7:02—Most adults now tusking and stripping bark and leaves from same baobab trees they have worked on last five days.

7:19—B6 persists with play after companion moves to feed with adults, but gives up. Second-year juvenile Male T2Y takes chewed bark from mouth of mother, Fem. T1, who does not resist like previous day. Feeding behavior continues for several minutes until T2Y stops.

8:02—T2Y experiments with stripping bark with left tusk, but does not eat it.

8:39—Audible stomach rumbling.

8:51—Matriarch and several adults move 50 meters west to bare ground, stomp earth to create dust and rub it on their bodies. Two juveniles follow and roll in dust.

9:04—New break in right tusk apparent in Fem. J6, approx. 15 cm missing.

9:29—Matriarch moves to water source, 100 meters beyond. Entire group follows close behind. All drink. Water fairly low but more plentiful than previous seasons at this location. Most only drink, but several juveniles briefly enter water and play.

9:54—Audible stomach rumbling.

9:56—Stomach rumbles may be vocalizations. Difficult to distinguish.

10:03—Juvenile T2Y excited after play, bumps his mother's rump repeatedly as observed on previous days. Matriarch intervenes to discipline him with strike of trunk to his head. T2Y makes mock threat display but quickly drops it and discontinues behavior.

10:15—All juveniles in water except Male E3, who continues previously observed reluctance to enter water.

10:17—Audible stomach rumbling.

10:32—Three Masai approach observation area, entire group moves to the other side of the water, beyond campsite range of observation.

This was Masai territory. Masai men sometimes came to visit wildlife observers. They were looking for supplies to buy or trade and sometimes for information on the location of game animals. The elephants had a healthy respect for the Masai, but they did not fear them as an immediate threat. They simply walked a safe distance away, and would likely return when the Masai left. Though the Masai were keepers of domestic cattle, and feasted on their milk and meat (and even blood drained from live cattle), they sometimes hunted for game, and most of the young men still tried to fulfill the rite of the passage to manhood by killing a lion. But the Masai avoided elephants and never attacked them like farmers did to protect their crops.

Wanjeri greeted the Masai warmly despite their intrusion on her work. They had lived in this place almost as long as the elephants, it seemed, and since their presence affected the elephants' behavior, she entered them in the journal. Soon she learned to think of the Masai as just another creature roaming the landscape as much a part of the ecosystem as the rest. The Masai lived almost exactly as they had lived for a thousand years or more, in the same place. Few people on earth could still say that. Was it fair to think of them as unnatural intruders on the elephants' territory? Were people not just animals, Wanjeri pondered, at the tip of a different branch in the great family tree? Was it self-awareness that set people apart, or intelligence, or their sheer dominance of the Earth? If the Masai could claim a place in the landscape, was it too late for Wanjeri?

She had plenty of time sitting under the tarp to do this kind of thinking.

When the Masai left, she checked in on the radio. The message surprised her: the next researcher due at her station, a more experienced observer who would track the group in its migration, was sick with malaria. Would Wanjeri stay on for a few more weeks and track them?

She packed everything in 10 minutes, ready for the moment the dust became wet with rain and the matriarch rallied her daughters and granddaughters and their daughters and sons to lead them out to sweet green grass and ripening fruits.

6

The cool rich smell of moisture was filling the air, and the sky over the hills darkened with the season's first rains as First Grandmother led the herd away from the grove of trees that had hosted them for the dry time. The path to the rich fresh grasses, which First Grandmother knew better than any other grandmother or mother, led first to the marsh containing little more than thick mud formed from the last remaining water stirred by the elephants to cool themselves and coat their skin. A few older grandmothers and grandfathers from other herds, content to remain there and wait for the rains and eat the soft plants, grazed at the edges. On the southern side, over a patch of higher ground, lay the bones of several elephants. Some were bleached white from years in the sun; a few were darker. They were the last of grandmothers and grandfathers who died in the last season, most still remembered by the adults in the herd.

The elephants stopped here, and many laid their

trunks on the bones gently, as a mother would her child. One lifted a tusk in her trunk and carried it around the pile of bones. The young ones watched with First Grandmother.

"Are these the other grandmothers, the ones that number as much as the stars?" asked the youngest one.

"Yes, these are some of them. They have gone back to the earth of the Spirit."

They watched together, for a long time, until the sun receded and they could see better in the softer light. Then the little one spotted the woman.

"First Grandmother, why does that woman always follow us and look at us? Is she hunting us?"

"Ah, yes, you noticed her. No, she is not hunting us. If she were, we would circle around the young ones for protection and perhaps challenge her and chase her away."

"Does she want to chase us away like the other women?"

"Ah, you mean the women who make noise and yell when we seek food near their houses?"

"Yes, Grandmother. They throw our own burning dung at us too!"

Grandmother laughed at his observation. "Yes, they do that too. They fear we will take their food, or they fear us because we are larger. Women want to protect their children, and their males, just as we do. They are like any other animal. They mean no harm."

"How can you say they mean no harm when they throw our own dung at us, and sometimes rocks!"

The little one realized that he had spoken too directly, without enough respect for a Grandmother, and he lowered his ears and trunk in shame.

"It is alright, little one. You are surprised at the things I say to you. Please understand. They mean us no harm just like the lion means us no harm. They may harm us, but it is the meaning that is important. Like the lion, it is just their nature. Women and their males are not perfect beings like us. They were not born of the nine daughters in the mountain. They do not have the knowledge to know better. They do not think about what they do; they cannot."

"I understand, Grandmother."

They looked out at the woman, who was watching them quietly. The wind shifted and they caught her scent. She smelled sweet and salty, like most women, but without the threatening musky odor that some of them carried.

"First Grandmother, you did not tell me why she watches us and follows us."

"I am sorry, my little questioner. Women sometimes hunt us, but this one does not. Sometimes women look at us because they seek knowledge. You see, as I said, women are not perfect beings like us, but they are closer to perfect than other creatures. They are clever—clever enough to know they are not perfect, and that we are. They know they do not have the knowledge we have. So sometimes, some of them watch us, and follow us as we seek the best places, hoping to gain knowledge the way my children learn knowledge by following me."

"Will they ever get the knowledge we have?"

"I don't think so."

"Perhaps we should try to give her the knowledge, in case we lose it someday and can no longer find the best food and the water to keep us alive in the dry time."

First Grandmother was impressed by the young elephant's foresight. "That is a wise idea, little one. But I don't think we will ever lose the knowledge since we pass it to our children. And I don't think women can ever learn it anyway. They do not have the intelligence we have. Do not worry, we will always find the best food and places for water, and the race of elephants will never disappear."

7

Owen had never seen his mother cry. It scared the hell out of him. But by then, he was getting used to the feeling of being scared.

By the time he got to high school, Owen had almost no memories of the real Karl Dorner. He only possessed the images his mother had manufactured before Owen began to invent his own. She would gather Owen and Keith every Sunday morning, because that was his favorite time of the week, so she said, relaxing and reading the newspaper (the big fat Sunday version of the *Baltimore Sun*). The brothers cared little for newspapers, so Mom perched herself on the sofa with the paper, and jazz on the radio, while Owen and Keith sunk each other's battleships in their pajamas on the floor. For them, "Daddy" was not the name of a person, but the title of a photograph. Daddy hung on the mantle behind her, in full 8x10 glory, completing the altar of worship. She was always fully made up by seven each Sunday before she woke the boys, with her brown locks in one perfect unifying curl just above her collar, even later when she stopped getting the boys dressed and dragging them downtown to Old Saint Paul's Church on Charles Street following the newspaper ritual. Instead of church, his mother preached her own sermon about their father. Like a real minister, Mom usually took inspiration for her homily from something she saw in the newspaper. This is the strange hot country where your daddy lived when he was stationed overseas before you were born, or these are the kind of communistic people that your daddy is protecting our country from, or your daddy might want to remodel the den like this picture when he comes home. The morning sun would warm them through the big bay window and she would hide from it behind her newspaper as Daddy looked down with steady approval on his wife, who grew a little more desperate and confused every Sunday, and his two clueless sons.

As the boys graduated to comic books and television, their mother stopped dressing up on Sunday mornings, opting for a presentable heavy quilted housecoat and silk slippers. The stories she told changed too: Your daddy is coming home later than we thought. Your daddy is on a secret mission and he could walk in the door at any minute, or not for years. Your daddy is involved in some very difficult business in a very tough world. Their mother wrote a few letters to Daddy, but they came back, unopened.

Owen and Keith's comic books migrated to the bottom of the pile in their closet, and they played war games with the neighborhood kids, Kenny and Danny and Fred, and sometimes Danny's little sister, Paige. Danny always tried to relegate Paige to the role of a M*A*S*H nurse, but she refused and shot bullets with her finger just like the boys. For each battle, Owen and Keith took turns playing Daddy. He was no longer a man in a picture on their wall, but a character to play in war games, like John Wayne or G.I. Joe. Then Owen and Keith stopped playing games and Keith started chasing girls.

Owen became consumed with shyness and couldn't bring himself to talk to girls. He could feel the fear grip him whenever he thought about it. And stammering and sweating through an attempt to talk to a girl, just to be laughed at, made the feeling even worse.

Then one day Owen found his mother in tears on the sofa, holding the photograph of his dad that had hung on the wall overhead for as long as he could remember. The photo had left a light-colored rectangle on the wall behind it. Her resolve had finally broken, and she hadn't ever shown him how to handle something like this. He tentatively held her by the shoulders.

But then he wondered why she was crying, and before thinking, he blurted it out: "Is he dead?"

His mother turned and hugged him. She was back to being the comforter, the parent, and Owen was relieved.

"No, he's not dead." She sniffed and wiped her face with her sleeve. "It's just that your father ... he's going to be gone a lot longer than we knew."

"Why?"

"He's doing something very important. A military mission." Owen was afraid to ask her to say any more.

"He's going to be gone a long time," she said again.

"I wish you had known him better. I wish he had come back before all this. He was a good man."

"He is a good man," she corrected herself.

"Owen, you're a lot like your dad," she said, wiping her tears away. "You look like him, see?" She showed him the photo. He did.

"And you have his confidence. You've got courage."

Owen had never ever thought he had anything like confidence or courage. He was pretty sure he had none of either. He held his mother silently. If he was going to have something like courage, he thought, it wasn't going to come naturally. He was going to have to decide to have it.

He decided, then and there, to have it.

But his body would not follow.

Owen had never experienced another strange attack as bad as the one on the beach years ago, but he had come close. He had managed to avoid situations where he could feel his fears would overwhelm him, but he could not avoid them all.

It happened once when he was waiting for the bell to ring to release him from school for the day. It was something he did every day, but this day he felt the waiting in his body. It began at the bottom of this stomach, like that day on the beach, and soon it consumed him in a shivering, cold sweat, as if he were waiting to die in the electric chair rather than to get on the school bus. He could barely breathe. The fear that someone would notice his condition only compounded the feeling of dread. Finally, the bell rang and he could walk off the sweat and the cramps. But the next day, the fear it would happen to him again at the end of the day drove another "attack." The anticipation of being consumed with fear consumed him with fear.

Reading a book his teacher assigned him in English class one day, he stumbled on a term that described what was happening when he feared the fear—"self-fulfilling prophecy." Still, knowing the term for it didn't help him control it. He couldn't break out of the pattern.

It would happen any time he was waiting for something. Since his day at school was filled with bells about to ring, the attacks could creep up several times a day. Usually, he went home feeling lucky if it only happened once.

Soon, Owen's grades went down, and he started staying home sick more often. He didn't talk about it with his mother, even when she tried to bring it up, but it seemed she already knew what was happening to him. She made an appointment for him to see a doctor again. She didn't mention what kind of doctor, and he didn't ask, but when they arrived and saw "Psychiatry" on the door, he felt relieved she had brought him this far. It was a strange feeling for him, to feel hope instead of anxiety, and a sense he could be in control.

The doctor gave him some pills, which is exactly what Owen expected him to do. But he also suggested Owen go to see another doctor who would help him by confronting his fears, just as that first doctor had suggested after his attack on the beach.

Owen thought that was an awful, terrifying idea, and when his mother tried to take him, he insisted she cancel the appointment. Besides, the medication—a tiny blue pill he took once a day—seemed to help, at least sometimes. But the attacks still came. More pills, new pills—the attacks still came at least once or twice a week, until Owen just couldn't bear to cause an embarrassing scene in the middle of class that none of his classmates could understand or cared to. The rest of his day he spent worrying about whether it would happen. He was ready to drop out of school, but the idea of giving up on college made his anxiety worse. Owen stuck with school, but spent most of his time at home shuttered in his room.

Then one Monday, Owen couldn't bear to leave his room to come to breakfast, or go to school. He spent all day there, and most of Tuesday, ignoring his mother's gentle pleas for him to try to leave, until the empty, exhausted feeling finally wore off and he pulled himself to the living room. She went along with the charade that he had been sick to his stomach, but when she asked him to come with her back to the doctor, he knew it wasn't a stomach doctor. He refused to go.

After a week of begging off school and listening to his mother's more insistent pleas, Owen finally went back to school. He managed to go into the school building by vowing to simply get up and walk out the front door immediately, as if he had never arrived, if he felt an attack coming. And it worked well enough to let him finish school, though his mom arranged for him to do much of the work at home, in his room. He kept track: the longest he spent shuttered in his room, not counting bathroom visits, was 70 hours. He managed to hide the fact he wet his pants once rather than open the door, or at least his mother pretended not to know. The time spent shut in his room was much like a long, drawn-out attack. Once he got himself together, he felt fine and could function normally and go anywhere, until the next time he felt the warning in the pit of his stomach.

With graduation nearing, Owen was actually keeping up with work enough to get his diploma. He had always been a smart kid and zipped through the material. Owen didn't go to his graduation ceremony. He spent it in his room. He decided that just making it through school was enough. The school mailed his diploma and his mom bought a nice frame for it. He put the diploma in his sock drawer.

Owen spent the next month of summer mostly in his room as his mother worried in silence about him, afraid that pushing him to do something with his life would make him worse. The pills didn't help as much anymore. He put them in his sock drawer with his diploma.

Once, his mother broached the idea of sending him to some kind of special school, like a college but not quite the same, she said. He didn't listen to the details. He was sure it was more like a mental institution. For him, it would be one regardless.

She tried to keep him engaged with the outside world by bringing daily newspapers to his room.

It worked, but not the way she expected.

One morning, she came home to find him at the kitchen table with paper in hand. She hadn't seen his face all day.

"You didn't tell me everything about daddy."

He realized he was clutching the newspaper tightly

against his chest. He spread it out on the table to smooth the wrinkles and slid it toward her, waiting as she read the article as fast as she could and got to the part with her husband's name.

"You were young. If you want to know ...."

"I mean you didn't tell me the truth about him."

"The truth? The truth is, I don't really know the truth."

"What do you believe though?"

"I just ... can't say."

Suddenly he was angry, so angry he startled himself as much as his mother.

"What do you mean you can't say? What's that supposed to mean? You don't know and you don't care?"

"I do care, Owen. I just don't think you ..."

"What? You forgot about him. You stopped telling us anything about him. You just forgot!"

"I didn't ever forget him, Owen. I just didn't talk about it. It was hard, for me and for you and your brother."

"You didn't think we'd find out?"

"Find out what?"

She took a deep breath. "I wasn't ever sure," she said. "It wasn't like him at all. I just wasn't ever sure. I tried to find out a little, but I couldn't. Mrs. Pearson tried to help. But I wasn't sure."

She put her hand on his shoulder, but he pulled away.

"I didn't want to upset you," she said.

"You always use that as an excuse for not telling me things!" His words rung louder in his ears than he expected.

Owen picked up the newspaper and went back to

his room. June said nothing. She was anguished about Owen's questions, but also thrilled that he had left his room.

He studied the newspaper again. The front page was covered with stories and photos documenting the opening of East Germany from behind the Iron Curtain and the crumbling Berlin Wall. People from all over the world were gathering in Berlin, pounding on the wall with hammers and sticks and celebrating.

He turned the page again to the story about forgotten victims of the Cold War. It listed Americans who had died or languished in prisons around the world following major wars and minor battles in the simmering confrontation between East and West. He understood some of it, though much of the history had happened before he was born.

But there was one name there that he knew very well.

Some of the people celebrating at the wall, the article said, had come from all over the world. They spontaneously jumped in cars or airplanes, arriving in Berlin just in time to become part of history, watching, and helping, the Iron Curtain fall at their feet. One young man said he had come with nothing but his clothes to be there. He was clutching a small chunk of the wall that had been hammered off.

Owen's head was suddenly clear.

He thought about the doctor who had wanted him to confront his fears to solve his problem. It seemed like such a crazy idea at the time. You don't face something you are afraid of, you get as far from it as you can. But now he knew that wasn't working out at all. He was lonely in his room. He was tired of his room, and if he never dared to conquer the fear, he'd spend the rest of his life in his room. There could be no compromise, no living with it any more. All that was missing was learning exactly what his fears were and where they came from, so he could go straight at them.

Owen went to the phone and called his brother at his college dorm. Keith could help him with the money and arrangements to book an international flight. Owen did it all before he could change his mind or Keith could ask too many questions about why—or warn his mother.

Then he took the pills out of his sock drawer and popped one in his mouth. He was going to need every bit of help he could get.

8

The first elephant Owen encountered in Africa nearly gouged him in two.

The bus driver had finally stopped for a bathroom break since taking to the road running south from Nairobi Airport early that morning. The "bathroom" consisted of a twisted mass of wiry, thorny acacia trees. Owen found a private spot at the edge of a dense forest further up the road, away from the other passengers and safely out of reach of the long thorns defending the acacias. Then the elephant appeared, its bulk emerging from the trees with no warning, as if the creature's rough gray hide spawned from their bark. Owen saw a flash of white tusks, and he cried out in surprise. Ears erect in alarm, the beast turned and trained its tiny eye on Owen. The eye grew larger, and Owen felt a tusk run straight through his guts and out his spine! He grasped at his stomach, but there was no wound. The animal had turned to flee instead of goring him, smashing and snapping its way through the stubby trees, as other passengers yelled and clapped to repel the animal.

The elephant's trumpeting echoed against the distant hills as its rump disappeared into the forest.

Though he felt safe back on the bus, the jitters from the adrenalin would not quite leave him. Owen recalled the elephant's eye. Perhaps it was fear rather than rage he saw in that elephant's gaze. It didn't matter now—the feeling of terror lingered with him.

Oh, no. This was not a good place for it to happen. Not here, not now. He wished he could stop the bus, get off, and put his head between his legs for a while. That usually helped.

Owen had never been so far outside his comfortable territory, so reliant on himself, than in this place. What exactly had he done, jumping onto an airplane with no plan and flying to the middle of Africa? A week ago, he couldn't bear to leave his room. The airline flight had been surprisingly easy (with a double dose of the pills). Perhaps he was conquering his demons after all. Or maybe he was just finding new things to fear, like huge elephants jumping out from the trees.

The elephant's eye persisted in his mind's vision, and Owen's stomach ground and twisted. He swallowed the feeling back, but every mile he traveled beyond the angry elephant was another mile closer to Kumbata, the little town where he would meet a man he knew well but had never met.

So he tried his best to lose himself, and that stupid elephant, in the world outside himself.

Owen studied the brown and black backs of heads

that filled the bus. Aside from a few women with hair wrapped in brightly colored cloth and tight-fitting white skullcaps on a couple of the men, every passenger's head was bare, with shortly cropped hair. Directly in front of Owen, a pair of earlobes, cut open and stretched to excruciating length, lay tucked neatly over the tops of the ears as casually as a strand of hair. One short young man who had entered the bus from a roadside stop sported a black suit and tie, but the rest wore simple button shirts or shabby T-shirts over their thin frames. Some men wore T-shirts with completely unfashionable or incongruous messages, obvious castoffs from wealthier places, like the older man in a pink shirt beckoning everyone to "Ask Me About Mary Kay." Owen considered getting up and asking him about Mary Kay, just to hear what he had to say. The thought made him laugh a little, and that made his stomach feel better.

Not a single man or woman wore shorts in the hot weather. Nor did Owen, but only because he had packed his bag in such a hurry and it was nearly winter back home. No matter—while he loved to wear shorts, here it seemed childish, and he was a man now.

Owen studied his reflection in the window. He was pleased that his face looked older than his 18 years. He hoped it reflected an inner strength beyond his age. His face was lean and tight, matching his body, and he had mostly avoided the scourge of acne. His beard was still thin, but he had the sense not to try to grow it out yet. He might have to now—he had not packed a razor.

Though his brother Keith was the older one,

Owen had always felt himself the more mature and responsible, at least until he had retreated to his room. Having no father around makes a boy grow up fast. Since yesterday, though, when he boarded a plane to Africa with nothing but a small bag, a bottle of pills, a newspaper article and a rash idea, he couldn't shake the feeling he was acting like an impulsive child. But it was too late for such thoughts—he was hurtling through Africa on a windy bus. Wise or not, he had committed to his mission and to facing fear.

Outside the window, the landscape had changed little since the bus had emerged from the modest suburbs of Nairobi. The land was flat and dusty, with the only hints of green covering a few hills framing the horizon. Owen could hardly imagine that there was ever a wet season in this place, as the guidebook he had hastily bought in the airport said was coming soon.

The guidebook also had many useful words in Swahili, the language of the whole area, and he had tried to learn a few. But the only ones he remembered now—because heard them over and over—were *jambo,* "hello," and *mzunga,* "white man" or "stranger."

Short, scrubby trees, hardly more than large shrubs, held fast to the dry soil. Further out, between the road and the hills beyond, itinerant ostriches and animals resembling cattle roamed about, though they were too far to discern. Owen did spy a giraffe, which was easy to recognize even at a great distance. It was so strange to see a giraffe roaming free. His first impulse was to believe it had escaped from a zoo.

He turned his gaze to the roadside. Goats gathered

in tight groups, sometimes meandering into traffic as a young boy struggled to corral them. More than once, Owen thought the bus was certain to hit a goat, but somehow bus and animal avoided each other at the last second.

And everywhere, there were people. People to shoo the goats off the road, people to sit in the sun next to a collection of fruit for sale lying on the ground, people to walk barefoot along the road or hundreds of yards beyond among dust and nothingness with the giraffe, children in front of half-moon huts to wave at the bus crying "how are you!" as a single word: "howayoo!" It seemed there were people everywhere in Africa, and most of them were walking. The rest were stuffed onto the bus, and the other overfilled buses it passed, sometimes with just inches to spare. It was not unlike Baltimore or any other American city, except for the complete absence of a city.

Some people walked along the road, but he could spot some much further away, toward the distant hills. They walked in places miles from any dwelling or road he could see, remote places that Owen would never think of going to on foot, even if his car broke down. Yet they walked as though they were strolling down the block for a cup of coffee. And, Owen began to notice, some walked without shoes.

Owen slipped a newspaper clipping from his shirt pocket. The paper was damp from sweat. He had read it over and over in the last week, since he first saw it. He could almost recite it from memory now, so many times had he scoured the words for clues, hints and nuances.

But there was nearly nothing to go on. It was written to chronicle how life was changing for millions of people in Europe, like the ones in the picture hammering with glee on a high concrete wall in Berlin. It was not written to help an 18-year-old American kid find his father in Kenya. Yet the impact of those small hammers in Germany, which barely dented the hard concrete, had sent Owen halfway around the world.

The Cold War was over, and the newspaper article catalogued its prisoners of war—people suspended in a global stalemate, one whose stakes were so much higher than the value of their tiny lives. People like Karl Dorner. Owen read the fragment from the article again:

> Capt. Karl Dorner—a U.S. military advisor to Kenya, Capt. Dorner assisted a local rebellion in 1974 against the American-aligned government of this East African country. Currently held in a prison in Kumbata, Kenya, Dorner could face treason charges if he comes home. Details of the strange incident have remained murky, and U.S. officials may prefer that Dorner stay in Africa rather than dredge up sensitive or embarrassing secrets in a messy trial.

The bus slammed on its brakes and Owen dropped the paper. He scrambled to grab it from the aisle floor. When he looked up, he saw the reason for the sudden stop. A man with his face obscured by a cloth held a knife pointed at the driver. Owen eased back into his seat and stuffed the newspaper deep into his pocket.

The bus driver hit the brakes again. The man with the knife was talking to the driver in a language Owen did not understand. The bus turned right, onto a narrow dusty path. It was a good place for a robbery—yes, the man would rob them all, and then let them go, he thought. Owen felt for the travel wallet he had bought at the airport that was stuffed into the front of his pants. He could live without the cash until he found a bank. He took the money out and put it in his pants pocket, leaving his passport in the wallet. Owen's brother would be mad enough he had "borrowed" his passport; it would be worse to lose it.

The path narrowed. Branches slapped the windows as they moved, and dust swirled all around. Some nervous passengers closed windows to shut out the dust. Soon the path widened, and the bus stopped and opened its doors. Out of the trees came another man, taller, with no shirt or cover over his face, which seemed set in a permanent scowl. He came onto the bus and sat down near the front as if he were just another passenger. The bus lurched forward again, moving deeper into the brush.

Then Owen felt it happening again. Only the slightest worry, an insignificant distress intersecting with another, could set it off, and this situation was much worse. It always began in his stomach and moved to his limbs. He tried to breathe it out, like he learned from the doctor, to carry the shaking and sweating and nausea away every time he exhaled, and he closed his eyes to concentrate.

But he could not close his eyes for long because he needed to know what was happening. So he opened his eyes and watched the taller man gesturing and talking to the driver, obviously giving directions through the path between the trees, while the man with the knife stood right next to the driver, watching the passengers warily.

Owen tried a new tack—he would think his way to serenity. It was only a knife. There were dozens of people between him and the weapon. The rag over the man's face made him look like a kid playing cowboy. The crazy elephant had scared him more than this clown. It still didn't work.

Then he remembered the pills. Quietly, Owen reached into his bag and tipped a pill into his hand. He swallowed it and breathed deeply.

He felt better just knowing the pill would soon do its work. The pill, and the breathing, and the talking himself out of his own feelings brought him enough peace to keep it together. He pondered the situation: He had actually stepped onto an airplane, left the country, and come to this strange place where he knew nobody and where buses could be robbed at knifepoint, and he was making it. It was a miracle, really. His confidence grew, and exhilaration at feeling like a normal person again replaced the stomach-wrenching anxiety.

The tall man yelled something, and the driver jammed on the brakes. The dust settled, revealing a small clearing all around. The man with the knife waved Owen and the other passengers off the bus. Everyone spoke in a language Owen did not understand.

On the way out the door, Owen passed between the seated man—the apparent boss—and the man with the knife. Their demeanors were complete opposites. The armed hijacker was intense and rangy and pushed the passengers out of the bus with his free hand. The boss looked mean, but he acted cool and calm. He stared closely at every passenger as if he were searching for a face. Owen wasn't sure whether getting off the bus was good news or bad, or whether they would end up in the hands of the serene master or his nervous assistant with a knife, so he suspended his thoughts and just followed the other passengers out. He watched an old man coax down two dusty boys who had been riding on the roof.

The fresh air outside felt good, and so did walking. Owen breathed deeply and let the dry air burn off the layer of tepid sweat covering his face. The pill was taking effect.

The boss and the driver remained on the bus while the one with the knife stood guard at the door. The passengers sat in the shade of the trees, talking in frantic tones. Owen asked a black lady wearing a yellow robe from head to toe what was happening, gambling she knew English, as most people seemed to speak it here. "They are letting us go and taking the bus," she said. He sighed with relief. They hadn't even taken anyone's money. They just wanted the bus? The kidnappers seemed confused and began arguing with each other.

With everyone out, the knife man hopped on the bus and it continued along the trail. After traveling a few dozen yards, before the driver had even switched to second gear, soldiers suddenly leaped out from the trees and forced their way into the bus while it was still moving. Then it stopped. More soldiers came running out, holding rifles. The bus door opened and the knife man, the boss, and the driver all emerged, each held by the neck by a policeman. The soldiers threw the three to the ground, shrouded in swirls of dust.

The passengers watched. A few hid in the trees in panic, but Owen and the rest just stood still. Owen felt a hand clutch his arm. The lady in yellow, with a smile more gaps than teeth, beckoned him to go with the other passengers as they gathered behind a group of soldiers, some helping a passenger who had fainted. A pair of Jeeps drove past from the direction of the road. Soon the bus driver joined the passengers. The soldiers—or were they police?—helped the driver stand up and tended to his head, which he held in his hands. It was over.

Owen saw a soldier/policeman drag the robber who had held the knife by his arms and stuff him into the back seat of a Jeep. Perhaps the blood dripping from his mouth and nose had something to do with his inability to walk for himself. The other bandit, the tall one, walked unaided to the vehicle, unmolested by the police except for his hands tied in front of him. He got in the Jeep the same way he had boarded the bus, with no hint of distress or anxiety. The Jeeps sped away.

The passengers all got back on the bus as if it had been nothing but a routine stop. Aside from more animated conversation and the unsteady walk of the man who had fainted, it seemed almost as if they were used to things like this. Their calm helped Owen keep a lid on his stomach. He closed his eyes and the stress slowly left his body.

After just a few miles back on the road, the motion of the bus sent him into sleep. He rested his head on the window and dozed as best he could. Sleep, he had found, was sometimes a way to calm and control his restless nerves. Sleep was like the ultimate calming drug. When he was asleep, nothing bothered him, and he only had good dreams. And this short but terrifying incident was a good reason to seek that sort of calm.

While he slept, the hills and trees gave way to modest buildings and shelters built of nothing but logs supporting tin roofs, and more people. When he woke up, everything felt normal again.

The bus reached the center of a small town and slowed to a crawl. Owen looked for road signs, but there were none, so he walked to the front of the bus, pushing politely past several people standing in the aisles, and asked the bus driver if they had reached Kumbata.

Before he could speak, the bus stopped at a small building made of cinder blocks, and finally he saw a sign: "Kumbata Bus and Taxi Station." The bus stopped and everyone got off. Owen followed.

He stood and looked around for a moment. Here he was, in the middle of a strange country with strange languages, strange people, wild elephants and bus robbers, and he had survived it all. He had made it so far, so fast. But he hadn't reached his goal yet.

With his bag over his shoulder, Owen went inside the station, which had no glass in its windows and no door whatsoever, just an open entrance way. Several people sat sleepily on benches, taking little notice of him. Behind a wooden desk in the back sat a man who looked like he might be in charge, so Owen asked him.

"Can you tell me how to get to the Kumbata Prison from here?"

The man looked up at him slowly as if he had never heard a question asked of him before.

"The prison? You want to go to the prison?"

"Yes."

The man stared at him for a moment before replying, "You go to the right as you exit, then right again. Follow the electric poles. Not far."

"Thank you."

"Why would you want to go to …?"

But Owen was out the door before he could hear the question or see the man pick up the phone and talk to someone in a hushed voice.

He almost stepped on some fruit laid out on the ground for sale with an old lady with short hair sitting behind it. She asked him, in English, if he wanted to buy any. He thought maybe he should because he had to walk and didn't know how far. With only $92 in cash he had grabbed before boarding the plane, and $7 spent on the bus trip, he needed to save money, so he resolved to use his feet instead of a taxi to find the prison. Walking seemed to be a popular option in this country. He stopped and picked up a bunch of tiny bananas, half the size of those he ate back home.

"Fifty shilling," the lady said. Owen had no Kenya money. He hadn't thought of that. He didn't know what to do. He pulled out a dollar and showed it to the lady, and she immediately took it and nodded her head in appreciation, her smile showing a few missing teeth. He guessed from her reaction, and how several other fruit sellers pushed their products toward him and said "One dollar!" that the dollar was probably worth more than 50 shillings.

He came to the second right turn. It was nothing but an empty road, with no sign, leading into the same scrubby, thorny trees where the elephant had been. He stopped for a moment and looked around carefully before taking to the road. His shoes were almost white from dust now.

The bananas were delicious—sweeter and firmer than any he had tasted back home. He ate them as he walked, flipping each peel into the brush.

He hadn't gone more than a quarter mile when a Jeep coming from the other direction came his way, stopping in front of him and blocking his path.

In front sat a driver and another man, both in blue uniforms and with handguns strapped to their chests. They were dressed like the men who had intercepted the robbers on the bus. They were young men with deep dark skin and serious, but not quite threatening, faces. In back sat a much larger man in a much more important-looking uniform, all white, with a few ribbons here and there. He wore dark sunglasses.

Still sitting, the large man spoke to Owen: "Hello, my friend. You must be lost. There is nothing of interest down this road."

Owen had thought about this moment on the long plane trip. He expected that he couldn't just walk into a prison in a faraway country and demand to see someone. But in his imagination, the people he had to talk past wore nice suits and sat in offices. He wasn't ready to meet guys with guns on a dusty road as he held a half-eaten banana in his hand.

Before he could reply, the big man spoke again.

"Are you a visitor to Kenya, young man?"

"Yes, sir." Owen never called anyone "sir" but it just came out of his mouth. "I'm from America."

"I could tell! Well, welcome! I am Col. Mubego and I am happy to welcome you to our country." He gave Owen a broad smile that revealed a golden tooth. The smile and friendly words quickly put Owen at ease. "And what is your name please?"

"My name is Keith Dorner," he lied, using his older brother's name—the name on the passport he had in his pocket.

The smile disappeared from Mubego's face.

"Well." He paused and looked Owen up and down. "Well."

"I'm looking for the Kumbata prison."

"Are you now?" Mubego lifted a walking stick he was clutching in his right hand and tapped it against his hat a few times, as if to goad his brain into thinking harder.

"Julian!" he barked.

Owen watched as a fourth man, much younger and thinner and without a uniform, jumped out of the seat next to Mubego and got in the very back, sitting in the rear bed facing backwards.

Mubego motioned to Julian's former spot with his stick. "You're not a tourist, then. I might be able to help you in your journey. You can be my guest. Please sit."

Half wanting to accept the man's help to get to the prison, and half thinking he had no choice, Owen got in the Jeep.

"It seems fate has brought us together on this road," Mubego said. "I happen to be the warden of Kumbata Prison."

But, Owen thought, we're headed away from the prison.

9

"We don't need carpet," Manish said. "We already have carpet. What do you want to put down more for?"

Manish's wife, Ishana, kept covering their bedroom floor with scraps of red and green oriental carpet, and after a few days of complaining that she had covered perfectly good wall-to-wall carpet, he got used to it. It did feel a little more like home. He wasn't in the apartment very often to see it anyway, and when he did come home, she had usually turned out the lights already. He would sit alone in the living room and eat samosas she had made or a sandwich he brought home from the 7-11. Then he would stuff his earnings for the day in the shoebox beneath their bed and slip under the blanket beside her.

Given his wife's tastes and a lack of cash, the apartment had come to be decorated in a style balancing intricate south Asian traditional art with empty walls and open space. Their teenage daughter, Adya, had papered nearly every square centimeter of the walls of her tiny bedroom with posters and magazine cutouts of various movie and pop music stars, about half of them Indian and half American. Michael Jackson held a prominent position in the center of the largest wall. Down the hall, the walls of Manish and Ishana's bedroom were nearly bare. Ishana was a practical woman. Her walls were as empty as her clothes were colorful. Everyone saw her clothes when she went out, but nobody came to see her walls, so why bother? Only the carpets covering the floor sported anything that smacked of luxury.

But, of course, there was a big television in the living room for Manish. He got a great deal on the TV, along with a VCR for 15 bucks, through his brother Billy (his adopted American name that he insisted everyone use, but that Manish thought was silly). Billy's girlfriend, a chubby white girl with stringy brown hair who always wore sunglasses and clung to him like he was a grand prize she won from Africa, had some murky connections to get deals like that. Ishana bought a few Bollywood movies from the Indian store on 85th Street, and sometimes Adya watched the musical numbers, but Manish preferred American movies. He owned his favorite—"Indiana Jones"—along with the "Star Wars" movies, a few classic westerns, and a copy of "Beverly Hills Cop" Adya gave him for his birthday that she watched more than he did. He rented more tapes almost weekly, consuming the vast library of American films that were cheaper and easier to find in New York City than in Kenya. He even asked Billy about getting a portable television with a built-in VCR to watch while he was driving his cab, but Billy told him he had a friend who had a friend who lost his hack license for watching

TV in his cab, even though the friend said he only watched while his car was idling. So Manish resisted the temptation. But he could still talk about movies with the people he picked up in his cab.

"Have you seen 'Die Hard?' Do you think it was good?"

"Haven't seen it."

"What about the last 'Star Trek?'"

"I'll wait for the rental."

The movies, whether watched at home or talked about with fares or with fellow cabbies in taxi lines at hotels, counteracted the aching dullness of driving 12 hours a day. This did not work for Adya.

"I want to go back home," she announced after a day at the mall. "I want to go back to Sarit Centre." She cocked her hip expertly, stretching her tight jeans to the limit.

She couldn't have picked a worse time to talk about going back to Kenya—Manish was counting the cash from one of his best days in the taxi since the family had moved all the way to New York last winter.

"You have dozens and dozens of shopping malls to go to and talk to your friends or whatever you do there, and all you want is the Sarit Centre, a silly little mall in Nairobi? Don't they have better stores at the malls here?"

"That's the problem, Daddy." How quickly she had mastered the American teenager roll of the eyes at the absurdity of adults. "All my friends are at Sarit Centre. I don't care about the stores."

"You're not shy. You'll make new friends." He had

made $623 in one shift—unbelievable. He went to the bedroom to get the money box from under the bed, and Adya followed.

"I don't want new friends. American girls aren't friendly. They walk around with their noses in the air. And I haven't met a single Asian boy."

"What about that Indian girl from your class?"

"Her? She's three years younger than me and she dresses in saris even though she's fat."

"Now who is walking around with her nose in the air?"

"Daddy, I just want my old friends, and I don't care if they're fat."

Ishana said nothing. She gave no hint she was listening carefully while she washed the pots. She knew Manish was attached to this country, and had been long before they moved, probably because of the movies he loved. Her husband's feelings mattered to her, and his happiness and success she considered integral to her happiness and success. But Ishana often longed for the steady warmth and smelly chaos of Nairobi. She wondered, too, if Adya noticed that her mother wore a sari sometimes and was not as thin as she used to be.

She was surprised, and thrilled, that Adya had mentioned she was looking for Indian boys. On the other hand, Adya had not found any Indian boys, and a 16-year-old girl was not likely to wait to find one for long. She pondered the idea of arranging marriage, but she knew Adya would reject it outright, having had enough of a taste of modern life in both Kenya and America, even though her parents' marriage had been arranged. Ishana had long ago fixed in her mind she would have married Manish anyway, but she was afraid to know if he felt the same way. So she remained silent.

The next morning was sunny and mild, a perfect September afternoon—bad cab weather because people wanted to walk instead—so Manish thought he was lucky when he picked up Delilah that day. She would probably have walked too, but she was struggling to carry a box.

Delilah still clung to a girlish beauty, though not enough to hide her true age. Her bright blonde hair lay squarely against her cheeks, and she carried herself with an earnest elegance, like a woman who has found herself a little lower in social station than she expected. Through the rear-view mirror, Manish saw a faint smile that connected her lips to her eyes, like squinting in the sun, which he would soon learn was her everyday expression painted fast to her face.

"I only need to go eight blocks, honey, is that okay?"

He pulled away from the curb. "It's okay—business is slow today."

"It's just this box."

She offered another five dollars to carry the box up to her apartment, four floors by the stairs. She sat in the nearest chair, handed him a twenty and asked him if he could come back tomorrow to lift some more heavy things and move furniture. She had just had knee surgery and walking up wore her out. Nobody in her building was both strong enough and friendly enough to help her, she said. He figured it was just like a fare, but without paying for gas.

The next day he moved a few things around while she

watched from her sofa and smoked, directing the action by pointing her cigarette around the room. She was all business, and paid him $20 for a half hour of work, so he was surprised when she asked him to come back the next evening for a drink.

That night, Manish did not watch a movie. He lay next to his wife and listened to her breathe. He thought about Billy's white girlfriend. It was not such an uncommon thing for a man to have interests beyond his wife, especially one with fair skin and light hair. He had never touched such a woman before, and he was very curious about it. Would her hair feel smoother? Would she smell different? Would her flesh feel like cream the way it looked? To have experiences beyond a man's wife, as long as it did nothing to weaken the bonds of family, was certainly the tradition, the expectation even, in places like New York. And closer to home as well—what about the prince of Zanzibar who built a palace with 99 rooms for his 99 wives?

So he went to Delilah's the next day. They sat on the couch and talked about her life and his cab and movies and carefully avoided any talk about his family while he wondered what her interest in him was. She was not ugly or undesirable, but he was just an Indian cabdriver nearing middle age. Was she that lonely? Or was there something special she saw in him that only a woman like her could detect?

"I've lived in this city almost all my life, but I still feel like a Southern girl," she told him, mixing her drink a little seductively with her finger. "My parents were all the way from Alabama. Never go to Alabama, you wouldn't like it. I've never been myself."

"I don't know where that is. If somebody asks me to take them in my cab, I can call you for directions."

She laughed a high, cackling laugh that startled him, but then she pecked him on the cheek. "That's so cute. Alabama is a long, long way away."

She had a jazz station on the radio, and she slipped off her shoes and stood up, holding out her hand for him. They danced, slowly, close. Then she whispered in his ear.

"You've got to go now. But come back tomorrow night and I'll have a surprise."

He figured he had lost $100 or so in cab fares that evening, but he could make it up. He went straight to the bathroom to shower so Ishana wouldn't smell the cologne he had worn.

The next night, Manish knocked on Delilah's door, and she answered wearing a slim, black, sleek silk nightgown, sexy but not overstated. "Surprise!" He liked it. He liked being courted and fussed over and surprised. He had never really been on an actual date, let alone knocked on a door with a blonde woman in black lingerie behind it.

She led him to the couch again and then put on a pouty face. "Manish, I have a problem."

"What is it?"

"I feel really bad asking you, but I have nobody else to turn to. You're my only friend in this city."

"What is it?"

"My landlord is cheating me. There's nothing I can

do. This building is rent-controlled, but he gets around it by accusing people who don't pay more of selling drugs, and then he can kick them out. If I don't pay him another $500 by tomorrow, I'll be living on the street, and I can't afford another place."

Manish said nothing, so Delilah kept talking.

"It's just this once, because he only wants extra rent from the past year. I can pay you back, not all at once, but I'll pay you back."

"If I drive tonight, I could earn enough. I would lose the money anyway by being here with you."

"You're my only friend in this city." She kissed him. "You're my hero."

Manish could still feel the tingly, scented kiss on his lips when he walked down the front steps of Delilah's building.

"That your cab?"

Manish looked for the source of the question. It was an old man in a white T-shirt, his face barely visible in the declining light. He was sitting in a lawn chair perched in a strip of earth bordering the building, alongside an open window to a ground floor apartment. He nodded his chin toward Manish's cab again.

"That your cab there?"

"Yes." Was he parked illegally?

"You come visiting Delilah?"

"Yes."

"You know she's a rent whore?"

"Pardon me?"

"She is a rent whore. She suckers cab drivers outta

their money, 'cause they got a lot of cash. Soon, she's gonna tell you she needs money for the rent. I see the cabs come in and out of here about once a month. She's livin' pretty on the cabbies." And he laughed.

Manish gripped the wheel hard all the way home. First, he was angry at the old man for saying those things about Delilah. Soon, he became angry at Delilah, because everything the man said made sense. His anger at Delilah soon subsided, though, replaced by anger at himself. He was ashamed for falling for her tricks, for daring to believe she would want a simple, dark-skinned cabbie from overseas, for thinking it was possible for him to betray Ishana and Adya and remain a good man at the same time. He had fallen hard for the temptations of this city, its casual immorality, and for the irrational lust that drove him to pursue a white-woman trophy.

He went home and watched "High Plains Drifter."

The next morning, before Adya went to school, he got up instead of sleeping in and ate breakfast with her. He counted the cash in his box from the last week's earnings, calculating how much more he would need to earn to cover airfare for three. As he counted, Manish pondered the things he could do with his life that would be more meaningful than driving around and watching movies. Then he said, "I think we should think about going back home to Kenya."

Adya grabbed him and kissed him. Ishana said nothing, but she smiled.

10

"We can't do it now," said Julian.

"It is no problem."

"What if there are difficulties?"

"That's why I'm here. So it's done right."

Mubego and Julian were going back and forth as the Jeep sped Owen back to the heart of Kumbata town. They spoke in Swahili so Owen could not eavesdrop. When they reached the main road, the driver looked back at Mubego and waited. The Colonel tapped his stick and pointed forward, and the driver turned toward the bus station.

"We are headed for my house. You can be my personal guest. Eat and drink whatever you like."

"Thanks," replied Owen. His guest?

"We have to pick up another guest first."

They stopped in front of the station. "He should be out in a moment," said Mubego. Julian jumped out of the back and stood next to the door of the station, waiting.

"Tell me, Mr. Dorner—how old are you?"

"I turned 18 yesterday." He had forgotten about Keith's passport and his brother's age already. Too late.

"Congratulations! You look younger than that. But that's good. It will serve you well when you are my age. But you are still young. I think we need to find you a babysitter."

"How old are you?" Owen asked Mubego.

Both of the men sitting in the front of the Jeep turned slightly, startled at the forward question. It was not the kind of personal question they would ever dream of asking Mubego. Also, they wanted to hear the answer.

Mubego handled it with grace. "That is an excellent question, young Mr. Dorner. The fact is, I am not sure. All I know is that when it was time to fight the British for our freedom, I was old enough to fight. That was 30 years ago, so I must be older than 30." It was part cryptic answer, part joke, and everyone in the Jeep except Owen was used to hearing Mubego talk this way.

"Oh," is all Owen replied. He ran his fingers through his hair. The wind on the open-air trip had blown it all around. Now that they had stopped, the sun was coaxing sweat from his scalp.

"So, when do we go to the prison?" he said.

The question made Mubego laugh a big belly laugh. The others started laughing too.

"You, Mr. Dorner, are not at all a surprise. You speak your mind. Yes, you're just like your father," said Mubego.

Owen wiped sweat from his forehead. "You know my father?"

"Of course I do. There are only 37 prisoners at Kumbata. I know him quite well. I've known him a long time. Even before he ..." But he stopped.

"So I guess you know I came to see him?"

"Why else would you be here?"

"When?" Owen asked.

"When what?"

"When can I see him?"

"Oh, that will take a little time to arrange."

Owen doubted it was that hard for Mubego, but he saw no other choice but to wait.

"Paperwork and permissions and things like that. It will take time."

"Manish, my friend!" Mubego suddenly turned and spoke to a brown-skinned, black-haired man coming out of the bus station.

The man stopped, startled, and for a moment looked like he would panic and run away. But then he saw Julian and the other men, close enough to jump out and grab him, and his body resigned to the futility and he relaxed his muscles and switched to a different mode.

"Hello Colonel, so nice to see you, Colonel," he said, punctuating it with a nervous laugh.

"I'm always intrigued when you come to my town for a visit, Manish. I wouldn't want to be a bad host."

"No, sir, you're always a good host."

This Manish fellow had the blackest hair Owen had ever seen, and deep brown skin, almost as black as Mubego and the other Africans. Other than his coloring and a large round nose, his features were not much different from Owen's.

"I think you should join my other new friend here as my guest at my home tonight, Manish. I don't want you to get into any trouble while you're here."

Manish looked relieved. "Yes, sir, that is generous of you."

Mubego motioned to the front of the Jeep with his stick. Manish ended up squeezed between the two men in front, and off they went.

From the corner of his eye, Owen studied Mubego. He had taken off his sunglasses. He was well groomed, with slight touches of grey around his temples, and had a broad nose. His composure was confident and disciplined, but not boring. He also spoke English quite clearly, with a faint African accent, but not enough that Owen had to listen carefully and ask him to repeat words, like with some Africans in the airport and on the street. A solid gold upper incisor flashed in the sun whenever he spoke or smiled, which was often. He managed to appear tough, yet agreeable at once. When he spoke an African language to his soldiers, Mubego's voice seemed clipped and harsh, like he was giving orders, but his English always sounded soothing.

Owen could not see anything of Manish but the back of his head. He wondered what Mubego wanted of this man, but this time he held his tongue.

It was a long ride to Kumbata and the Jeep was open to the air. But the heat, the famous heavy African heat that Owen had expected, actually wasn't so bad. The flat dusty plain and bright sun Owen had seen in photographs of Africa looked hot, but they deceived. This place was high above sea level, and so far Owen found the dry air ranging between bearable and comfortable, certainly better than the steamy summers of Maryland.

There was something else—something pictures in magazines couldn't convey. He noticed it on the bus, and he noticed it here whenever the Jeep was still. The odor of unwashed bodies was everywhere. Sometimes it was thick and rank, like a homeless man bundled with all his stinking clothes on a downtown street, but often the smell was almost sweet, fresh from skin rather than stale clothes. It was the smell of people who apparently did not use deodorant (and would probably find the idea silly). Like the air that carried it, the smell of deep brown skin all around him was bearable, and perhaps even comfortable. But sometimes, when his nose caught a sudden strong sample of the musky odor, it triggered an instinct deep inside Owen. Like catching the odor of a predator stalking him, the smell shot straight to the most primitive part of his brain and primed his body to flee, like the feeling that gripped him when he had encountered the elephant on the bus trip.

Owen watched the people walking along the side of the road. Why were so many people walking? It was just like what he saw on the bus ride—people walking everywhere, even far from a town. Maybe they were just too poor to own a car or ride a bus. Or maybe they walked because that's what you do when your car breaks down in a place where nothing but your legs and your wits will get you home. No gas stations or phone booths along the road; no highway patrol to change your tire for you. No room in the overstuffed cars for hitchhikers either.

Owen had not yet visited the mountains, or the coast, or come close enough to a river to see the rich greens that East Africa offered. Nor had he seen the wet season wash away the dust and swell every plant's leaf and every animal's belly. He had seen only brown earth, brown grass, brown animals and brown people. In the dry season of the high plains, the dust and heat had painted all the brick and tin shacks and people's clothes the same color.

Kumbata turned out to have the same two colors Owen saw everywhere else—the sun-washed gray of nearly everything on the ground and the striking blue of the cloudless sky. The streets consisted simply of the countryside jammed into a smaller space, with the usual shanties built of sticks supporting bits of metal and plywood, running for many blocks. Only a solid cinderblock bank, painted white, and a low-slung hotel rose above the pattern.

Owen had passed through several villages on the bus. Some looked many years old, like the ones filled with primitive round huts of mud or modest cinderblock structures. Others looked like they had just sprung up yesterday, with ramshackle shelters constructed from scraps of sheet metal or old bricks stacked atop each other. Kumbata looked both ancient and brand new at once, as if an old town had suddenly doubled its population.

In the meager spaces in front of the town's buildings, people were conducting every imaginable useful business that Owen could count. People were hammering metal into something, fixing car engines, brewing tea and selling fruit and old clothes laid on rickety wooden stands or just out on the dirt. With his car backed halfway into a pond, a young man washed his car with the muddy water. A girl in a clean crisp school uniform walked down the street. She looked just like a Catholic school student back home, except for the books balanced on her head, just like Owen had seen African women carry pots in pictures.

The Jeep slowed as they emerged into the center of the town, a dusty square. A concrete clock tower facing the square looked solid enough to withstand a nuclear blast. Owen looked at the time on the clock. He had no watch, but it couldn't possibly be 8:25 right now. Across from the tower stood a feigned reminder of home—a restaurant with golden arches, the name "McMoody's" painted over the front door next to a hamburger. The glass front gave Owen a glimpse inside; it looked bright, clean, and popular.

"This is Kumbata," Mubego announced. "We live here, Julian and I, though this is not where I was born," he added. "I am from Nanyuki. It is a Kikuyu town."

"What's a Kikuyu town?" Owen asked, prompting the Colonel's deepest and heartiest laugh yet. The others in the Jeep laughed too, even Manish.

"Please excuse me, but it is funny the way you said it! Kikuyu is not a kind of town, Kikuyu is my tribe. My family, you see."

His laugh sounded like a grandfather watching a child play, and it put Owen at ease. As he was about to apologize, Mubego held his hand up to stop him from speaking, his way of saying no apology was necessary.

They stopped at a building a few blocks outside of the town center, but still on the busy road. The wall surrounding it, with an iron fence lining the top, gave it the look of a fortress.

Or a prison.

11

Owen noticed her arms first. Sinewy and slim, with deeply tanned skin that glowed, even in the fading daylight. Her bare arms seemed a little too long for her body. A narrow chin and jaw framed fleshy lips, and straight black hair draped simply but elegantly over eyes that tilted ever so slightly, making her look a little sad, a little sleepy. Her skin was deep black and her eyes were thoughtful and bright. She was sitting on the ground in front of Mubego's house, and she managed to look perfectly natural there with no chair or even a cloth under her.

As he stepped out of the Jeep, she looked him over with unexpected boldness and smiled.

Her clothes confused Owen. She was the first black woman he had seen in Africa wearing khaki pants and a white blouse. He thought she might be from America until she spoke. "Hello, *Jambo*," she said. She kept her eyes, dark irises framed by white, then again by dark skin, locked on him. She couldn't be more than a few years older than he was, in her mid-20s perhaps, but it was a world of difference.

She was the first African woman, perhaps the first African at all aside from Mubego, who hadn't immediately treated him like a guest arriving at a hotel.

With Owen's bag in hand, Julian shut the Jeep's door. "Perhaps you will meet my ugly sister sometime. She studies elephants, but when she is watching them, you can't tell her from the elephants."

"And when I'm out there I see my brother, who goes out dancing with and kissing hippos."

Owen was perplexed for a moment at this sudden unusual talk from Julian, and then he got it. Julian's sister stood up and play-slapped his arm as he dropped the bags on the ground. "This is my sister, Wanjeri," he said. "She is very pretty, but also the ugliest of my sisters. Wanjeri, meet Owen Dorner from America."

She gripped his hand. With the mention of his name, Wanjeri's smile faded and she seemed to ponder something, and she forgot to let go of his hand. Her hand felt rougher than Owen expected, and warmer.

"Nice to meet you," he said, breaking her out of her spell.

Julian's demeanor—the first time he had seen the young man act playful instead of stern—put Owen at ease, as did Wanjeri's presence. He looked around. Mubego had already vanished into the house.

"My sister hates to be indoors," Julian said. "She thinks she's an animal." He walked past his sister and she smacked him playfully.

"He is right. I hate to be indoors for too long. I even sleep outside sometimes when I am in town."

"Out here?"

"No, I wouldn't sleep in the front. It's too dangerous. In the courtyard, behind the wall." She pointed to a high wall attached to the side of the house.

"You said your name is Dorner?"

"Yes. Do you know that name?"

"No." But he could see something in her face that said otherwise. He smiled nervously. Never mind his recent 18th birthday that made him officially an adult—she made him feel like the teenage boy he still was. He had felt his confidence growing since the day he got on the plane, but she put a dent in that.

"I have been to America. It's very big."

"What brought you to America?"

"I helped make a wildlife film, and I went to the first showing."

"Wow." Stupid thing to say. He couldn't seem to do better.

"My contribution was small, just research. I was never near a camera."

"You know a lot about the animals?"

"I do. But I had to go to America to make a film about them. Many children here grow up never seeing much wildlife and never appreciating it. The city children especially." She spoke with great confidence, but also some formality, like she was presenting a paper at a scientific conference.

"Does that surprise you?" she asked.

"Yes. It does." He couldn't conjure more words than that.

"I wish more Africans knew more about their own heritage and the animals all around them. But they are used to seeing animals all around them, so many of them don't care."

"I think so, too." He instantly felt silly speaking as if he knew anything at all about it.

"Wanjeri!" Julian called from the door before she could answer. "Come in."

Julian gestured to Owen to follow her inside.

"She would stay out here day and night with the animals if we let her," he said.

12

First Grandmother told the little one that, in the dry seasons, they would travel at night to stay cool—but he and all the other little ones must stay close because of danger.

"What danger is in the dark?" he asked.

"There are many dangers for a small creature like you, but the grandmothers will protect you."

He already knew many of the dangers. He had smelled the sour smell of lions, which mixed with the smell of dried blood and dead flesh. The smells unleashed an instinctual fear in him that, along with the rest of the herd, caused him to want to run away. And often when the air brought a fearful odor to their trunks, the elephants scanned the area with their noses and ears and eyes, and sometimes formed a defensive circle around the young ones. When they heard lions or caught sight of them, the herd would flee and, if they were on a trek to new ground, find another path around the threat.

But it wasn't until he first saw the bones that he understood. He had seen the hyenas and vultures and marabou storks gathered around the last remnants of a dead animal after the lions had finished with it and lay, bellies fat, sleeping nearby. But he had never seen exactly what was in the middle of the crowd of hungry animals as they fought for scraps until he grew a little taller. Then, one day, as the herd crossed open grassland between groves of trees, he saw a fresh kill. It had bones.

The bones, with fragments of the skin of the zebra that had given up its meat to the lions still stretched across them, were like the bones of his ancestors he had visited with First Grandmother. They were not as white and they were not yet scattered, but they were bones. The little one understood at that moment that bones were inside all living things, including his own body, and that the death of a lion's prey was the same death his ancestors had succumbed to, and that would come to him someday, especially if he came too close to a lion.

The realization frightened the little one. At first. But then he felt comfort knowing his ancestors would remember and honor him when they found his bones, just as the grandmothers had shown him with their ancestors' bones.

He was thinking about this one day as the herd gorged on ripe fruit high in the trees and he caught the scent of the woman who watched them. He soon found her with his eyes, next to the big rock she moved around in. When all the low fruit was gone, First Grandmother came to him and reached higher in the tree, passing the morsels to his small trunk.

"First Grandmother," he asked, "Do women have bones?"

"Why yes, of course. All things that are alive have bones. Why do you ask?"

"The woman is watching us again."

"Yes. She means us no harm. She is not a lion."

"I know. But do women ever eat elephants?"

"Yes, there are women who will hunt and eat elephants. But we stay far from them."

"Does the woman's rock have bones?"

First Grandmother almost dropped her fruit. "What do you mean? What rock?"

"The rocks that the women move in, to make them faster."

"Ahhh, those. They are hard like rocks, yes. But they are not rocks. Did you notice, little one, that they smell like fire? And they growl like lions, or even elephants?"

"Yes, I have heard and smelled them. I just thought they were another kind of rock."

"Yes, they are another kind of rock, but one that moves with women inside them. And like rocks, they do not want to hurt you. Only the women inside them could mean you harm."

"But not this woman, who follows us?"

"No, not her. We stay far from those who would hurt us, and far from their moving rocks."

"Do lions hunt women?"

"I think they might, but I have never seen it. I don't know."

The little one was very surprised to learn that there was something First Grandmother did not know. He had heard other grandmothers tell him they don't know something, but usually they told him to go ask First Grandmother, so he thought she knew everything. He did not know it was possible for her not to know something. But it would not stop him from asking her more questions.

"The women—why do some hunt us, and others yell or throw things at us without hunting us, and others only follow us?"

"Women are strange creatures. They move about in rocks after all!"

This made the little one laugh.

"Some women want to harm us and others are our friends. And some women even harm other women."

This was shocking to the little one. A creature that would harm its own kind? He couldn't imagine why.

"What makes women hurt other women? Why would they do that?"

"Do you remember what I told you that day when we went to visit the ancestors' bones? Women do not have the knowledge. They were not created from the soil of the mountain by the Spirit, and they did not have nine grandmothers to tell them not to hurt each other or first grandmothers to pass that knowledge to their daughters."

The little one felt very lucky that he had a first grandmother to pass on the knowledge to him. He thought he might never learn everything there is to know though. There was so much. If only the elephants could pass their knowledge on to other creatures, like women, the same way they teach each other.

13

Mubego's house was grander than the ones in town, or those lining the road on their approach. It was clean and well kept, and perhaps freshly painted. This house had two levels and a hint of oriental design, though with a little ornamentation and a front porch, it would have passed for one of the plain brick row houses of Baltimore.

Inside, the minimal furniture and decoration did not show wealth, but the space between them did. The home was spacious and clean, nothing like the seemingly endless rows of tiny huts and hovels Owen had seen lining the road on the bus ride.

A man in plain white clothes brought them tea at the massive wooden table in the dining room just inside the front door. Mubego excused himself and went to the back and the man in white showed them to the bathroom. Manish jumped up. When Manish came back, his face was clean. "You will like it, my friend. A toilet, and hot water."

Indeed, there was a toilet, and hot water. It was a western toilet, not a hole in ground or even an elaborate, fine porcelain hole in the ground like the one Owen found, to his shock, at the bus station in Nairobi. There was more—an actual toilet seat on the toilet, and no dirt on it, and a sink with the promised hot water coming out.

Manish politely stood up when Owen came back to the tea, and again when Mubego rejoined them.

"You are Mr. Owen Dorner, citizen of the United States," Mubego announced. "Not Keith. You are here with a 30-day tourist visa, which you obtained on arrival to Nairobi airport, but in your brother Keith's name." He sat with them at the table, waiting for Owen's reaction to his knowledge of Owen's every move.

"Yes," was all Owen could say. It seemed there was no hiding things from this man. Was this an interrogation?

"Please relax, you are not in any trouble. I am just gathering information to help you. Mr. Dorner, I will need to see your passport, or rather, your brother's."

How did he know he was Owen and not Keith? And how did he know Owen's real name? It didn't matter now. He was caught. Without a word, Owen gathered the passport from his back pocket and handed them to Mubego, who put the documents on the table without looking at them.

The tea man brought Mubego a cup and he helped himself from the pot after heaping sugar into the cup. He drank a sip and then settled his large frame into the chair with a satisfied sigh. To know things—to know secrets—was a display of his power.

Owen glanced at Manish, who was holding his teacup firmly with both hands, eyes lowered, as if he were wondering what new trouble he had become attached to. Manish's posture showed he was more used to giving deference to powerful men than Owen was.

"Why would a man travel on his brother's passport rather than his own?"

Mubego looked at Owen sternly. Nobody else dared speak. Owen began to sweat a little. He could be in really big trouble. He felt the pill bottle in his pocket.

Owen had taken his brother's passport because he didn't have one of his own and didn't have time to get one. But would Mubego care?

Then Mubego broke the tension. "It's no matter. If you want to be your brother, be your brother. I won't make it my concern. I will even call you Keith if you like."

Owen breathed again. It seemed to him Mubego liked to play tough guy and then soften up, like he was toying with people. "No, my name is Owen."

"Besides," continued Mubego, "you want to get *into* prison anyway, right?"

Everyone laughed except Manish.

"Julian, we have two guests for the evening," Mubego announced. "You are guests in my home and are welcome to anything you may need. I have some business to attend to. Please excuse me." Mubego passed the passport back to Owen, stood, and went out the door.

"It's cooler outside," said Julian, directing them to a back door. "I'll have more tea brought to you."

The courtyard behind the house shielded sturdy

green plants with broad leaves and gentle shade within high tan stucco walls. This small oasis contrasted sharply with the gravelly ground and dusty road outside. The occasional truck groaned past, leaving a trail of diesel exhaust and dust visible over the wall. Owen recognized the bright green banana trees sporting short stubby bunches of tiny unripe fruits. At their feet grew a flawless green lawn—a lawn in this desert! Near the back, in the best shade, sat a tidy little structure: a solid cement table with a little fabric roof and some wooden chairs. Owen and Manish sat.

The tea man came again with a pot and a plate of fruit and pastries. Once it was served, Owen noticed Julian standing just inside the back door as if waiting, like the servant, for when he was needed by the guests—far enough to leave them to themselves, but close enough to hear. Manish had chosen a seat facing the door, with one eye on Julian.

"So, you met your first elephant on the way here."

Owen stared at Manish, speechless. How did he know about the elephant? Manish answered the unspoken question.

"I was on the same bus. I saw that from the window."

"You were on the bus? You saw the elephant? It almost killed me."

"No, it wouldn't kill you," Wanjeri said. She had appeared in the courtyard without either of them noticing and without a sound. "It was just a warning. It's the dry season," she said, "and elephants will come close to the road for food or water. That would never happen in the wet season. It is best to make noise to warn the animals you are there. The ones you will find near the road only charge you if they are startled."

"Were you on the bus with me too?"

She chuckled. "No, but I have seen that happen with elephants many times. To me, even."

"I saw so many people walking on the road when I was on the bus," Owen said. "How do people walk around out there without any kind of protection from wild animals?"

"Protection from the elephants? Elephants don't eat people," she said.

"Are you sure about that?"

Manish laughed, and his white teeth showed brightly against his reddish-brown skin. "Those people know how to handle themselves. Just like the people on the bus when it was robbed."

"Your bus was robbed?" Wanjeri looked genuinely surprised.

"Just some hooligans with knives," Manish told her. "The police came fast and that was that."

"Excuse me." She stood and went back inside.

Owen thought about her name. "Wanjeri." What could that name mean? He mused on the possibilities—what would it be like to be with a woman like that, so set apart from his own world? She had gone to school in England, so she had just enough knowledge of his world to relate to him, and she spoke his language, yet he knew almost nothing of her world.

And she was easy to talk to. He felt none of the crippling shyness that talking to girls at home caused in him. Of course, at first he hadn't thought of Wanjeri that way. She was a black African girl, and an adult woman, not a teenager like him. That he could ever be involved with her hadn't crossed his mind. Still, he was 18 now, just a few years younger than her. It seemed suddenly possible.

How different it would be to live here with someone like Wanjeri, in this place? They would live in a snug house like Mubego's—no, a smaller one, closer to town. They would be the strange couple, the mixed-race couple, of both worlds, and her family would come to their house and her mother would cook big meals of rice and strange meat served on a huge plate and they would eat it sitting on the floor, like he had seen in magazines. His friends would visit from America, and Wanjeri would take them out on safaris, and they would camp out in the open and see stars they had never seen before. And he would sit with his arm around her with her delicate head snuggled on his shoulder, and they would stay warm by the bonfire in the middle of the camp. He would run a safari business, with Wanjeri as guide, and they would go on long trips out in the bush for days. She would teach him her language, and they would meet other tribes and speak to them as real people instead of tourists. They would have the most beautiful light-brown children in the world, and after a few years spent at home when they were young, they would take the children out to the bush and they would grow up with lions and baboons and elephants.

The fantasy of such a radically different life than what he expected fascinated Owen and gave him a strange warm feeling in his belly. Then his mind turned to his father, and his stomach turned to stone and the warm feeling disappeared.

He had constructed fantasies about his father too, of course. But these he had stewed over and refined so many times they became nearly a complete record of a life never lived, and felt almost real. He saw himself going on fishing trips to the woods upstate, to get beers with his brother and hang out like other people at pubs, to the car show to admire, and then buy, his first car. But these fantasies did not intrigue him, not any more. They brought longing, and a feeling he could only describe as regret. They were times he would never have with a dad he had never known. He could never get those times back, but perhaps he could stop the feeling of sinking into a deep hole each time he pondered a past that had slipped by, no longer possible except in his mind.

Owen stopped daydreaming and noticed the sun was rapidly setting and Manish and Julian had gone inside, leaving him alone to his silent musings.

14

The Tea Man—his name was never mentioned, and Owen began to call him "The Tea Man" in his mind—led Owen to a large room with two simple beds, one with Manish already in it, sound asleep. His bag was at the foot of the bed.

Owen lay down and closed his eyes. He heard the door close. It turned out Manish wasn't asleep yet.

"I presume you haven't been in Kenya for long?"

"Just a day," Owen replied.

"Well, then, I can tell you that you have nothing to worry about. The safari guides will take you out in a car, and you are perfectly safe."

"I'm actually not here to see animals."

"No? You're not the Indiana Jones type?"

"Not really."

"You Americans, you're all the same. Always overdressing for the wrong occasions."

Owen opened his eyes and glanced down at his shirt.

"I didn't have much time to pack my bags."

Manish giggled. "No, I didn't mean you! That's from the movie! *Raiders of the Lost Ark*. The Nazi says it. I forget who he says it to, either Harrison Ford or the girl."

"Okay, I get it. So you like movies?"

"We Asians are crazy for movies. Any Indian you see loves movies. I mean the Indians from India, you know, with the dot on our heads? Not feathers in our hair." He laughed and poked his forehead with his finger. "India makes more movies than Hollywood each year—did you know that?—and I think there are more cinemas in India than America too, not counting the movies they show outdoors, which is a lot. There are only a few theaters in East Africa, but I saw plenty in New York."

"You've been to New York?"

"I lived there. For a short time. I drove a cab. How about you?"

"I'm from Baltimore."

Manish fell silent for a while, as if in serious thought, before continuing.

"When I was in New York," said Manish, "on sunny days like this one was, I would go to the multiplex and see two or three movies sometimes."

"On a nice sunny day you went to the movies?"

"Sunny days, in the spring especially, nobody wants a cab. They want to walk everywhere. Bad for business, so I park the cab instead of wasting gas looking for fares. Cold, rain, snow—that's when you make money. On those days, I maybe rent a video for VCR before I get home and watch it before bed. It helped me sleep after all the driving."

Owen looked down at his shirt again. He *was* a little overdressed.

"Yes, I'm a cab-driving, movie-watching Indian, and I'm proud of it," he said to Owen, a little louder, perhaps so that Julian could hear. "Quick, give me some curry!" he said in his best silly Indian accent. Manish giggled again at his self-deprecation. Then he stopped laughing. "How old are you, really?"

"Eighteen. Yesterday."

"Happy birthday, young man! You look younger."

"I was seventeen three days ago, so ..."

Manish chuckled. "You're not using your brother's passport because you needed to be older, are you?"

"No. I just needed one fast."

"Why?"

"I had to come here. Because I'm 18 and a grown man now."

Manish sat up in his bed. "It doesn't matter why, anyway. Mubego already knows, whatever the reason. He's already got a file on you, for certain. I don't know why you are here, but I already could tell it's not to see animals. You wouldn't be here, you'd be in some awful tent in the bush. Don't worry about it though. As you can see, the Colonel is very hospitable, even when you make trouble for him. Besides, we all must appear to be something we're not sometimes."

"What kind of trouble are you making for him?" asked Owen.

"No trouble at all for him, not while sleeping in his house." Manish lowered his voice. "Mubego and his nephew—Julian there, that's his nephew, Wanjeri's brother—they like to bring people here. This isn't my first time here as you probably gathered. When he brings you here, you might be a guest, you might be a prisoner, or you might be a friend—or all three."

"What do you think I am?" asked Owen.

"I don't think he knows yet."

Owen rolled to his side and yawned. But Manish wasn't finished talking. "What was that he said about you trying to get into the prison?"

"I'm just here to look someone up," Owen replied.

"You know someone in the prison?"

"Someone I haven't seen in a long time."

"I've been in Mubego's prison. Maybe I know your friend."

Owen fought the urge to ask if Manish knew his father and everything about him. It was all too much, too soon, for him to digest. He evaded again: "What about you? Why did you come all the way from India?"

"I've never been to India. I was born here. There are many Indians in Kenya. They call us Asians but we're all born here and we're all Indian."

"I had no idea. Why so many?"

"We came when the British were building the railroad up from the coast, back in the 1890s. We came to work. If you ever ride the rails, remember that many Indians like me built it. Not me, you see, but my grandfather worked on it."

"He must have some great stories to tell."

"My mother does. My grandfather died of malaria

when she was three years old. The railroad was just 11 miles from completion. But my mother's uncle survived to the end, and he told my mother stories about her father."

Like Mom told me stories, Owen thought.

"In India, my grandfather was a cook," said Manish. "He was the best cook in his village, and that is saying something in India. I'm telling you my friend, if you want the best food in Africa, eat Indian food. Have you had Indian food?"

"Sure. It's good."

"Yes. Perhaps you have been to one of the 14 Indian restaurants all in a row, on the lower East Side. You know that street? I have eaten at all 14. You must come to my house, and my wife will cook you the best food you can imagine. Better than any of those 14."

"Why did you come back to Kenya?" Owen asked.

"Oh, too expensive and my family was homesick."

"That's too bad."

"No, it was a good decision to come back home, I was homesick too. I had things to accomplish here. Important things."

"Did you just come back to Kenya today?"

"No, no, I live in Nairobi with my family. But this is your first time here?"

"Yes."

"So you experienced our roads. Rest assured, they are much worse than they were when I left for New York."

"A few of our roads are as bad as this," said Owen. "But I guess this country doesn't have as much money to spend on things like roads."

"Oh, my friend, this country has plenty of money. It's not money that is the problem."

"Plenty of money?"

"Certainly. It's a matter of where the money goes."

"Where does it go?"

Manish lowered his voice again, this time to nearly a whisper. "It goes in the pockets of certain politicians. Tax money, international aid money, bribe money. All in their pockets."

"Corruption?"

"Corruption and waste. Did you know if you get elected here, the government buys you a new Range Rover, so you can drive these roads? Instead of spending the money on the roads so nobody would need a Range Rover to get over them in the first place. It's crazy."

Owen lowered his voice too. "This is a democracy, right? Why don't people get fed up?"

"You mean angry?"

"Yes, angry. Why don't they vote out the politicians?"

"Because they spend the money on other things."

"Like what?"

"They invest in the right people."

"Oh, I get it. Not that much different from back home."

"Except you don't get thrown in jail for complaining." Manish lowered his voice. "Don't tell anyone I said this, but things weren't so bad when the British were here. They built these roads, and they kept them up. Like they built the railroad. And I'm not the only one who thinks so. I don't want them back, mind you, but shouldn't we do better on our own?"

The house had grown quiet, but someone made a noise somewhere and it spooked Manish.

"We shouldn't talk about this now," Manish whispered. "We can talk about movies. I could talk about movies all day. Don't mind me, my friends, just an Asian talking about movies."

Owen pondered it. A Kenyan pining for the British—things must be bad. He knew from reading the newspaper article it wasn't long after the British left Kenya that the U.S. Army sent his father over here. What was the country like when his father arrived? And what kind of trouble had kept him from leaving?

"I don't know why you are here," Manish said, "but I'm glad you are. I would get a little less hospitality if you were not with me."

"How did Mubego know you were there at the bus station?" asked Owen.

"Him? He knows everything that's going on, like I said. He knew you were coming too, I'm sure. He knows as much as he can, and when he doesn't know something, he'll work on it until he does," Manish said.

"You want to drive that man crazy? Don't tell him something."

15

Though it was not his first time climbing the mountain to eat the soil that nourished the herd, it was still just as hard on the little elephant's short legs as the last time. It was harder, though, going back down. The little one saw the effort his older brothers and sister, and the mothers and grandmothers, also put into climbing, and that made him feel less small and weak.

Sometimes the woman who followed them climbed the mountain with them. He wondered if it was hard for her to climb the mountain too. Other than this woman, it seemed women rarely came up the mountain.

When they reached a clearing near the bottom of the mountain, he noticed that today, the woman who sometimes followed them was nowhere to be seen. But the little one saw other women, and their males, at the bottom of the mountain, looking at the elephants. The women stood in a group near a grove of trees. Instead of walking or moving along past them as most did, these women stood still and stared. It scared the little one for a moment, until he saw they were like the woman who follows them—not hunting, just looking.

"Why do those women look at us?" he asked First Grandmother.

"They look at us for the same reason as the woman who follows us everywhere—just for the joy of seeing us. They know we have knowledge that they can never learn, so all they can do is look."

"What use is looking at us? Shouldn't they be looking for something to eat or a place for water to drink and bathe in?"

Instead of responding, First Grandmother stopped in her tracks. She held her trunk high in the air as elephants do to smell the air.

"Stop," she said. "Stop and look and listen and smell. From here, on this mountain, you can see and hear and smell many things for a long way. Sometimes it is good to just look at things and enjoy them, just as you enjoy eating the ripe bananas I reach up and grab for you, or to smell the water as you approach the marsh after a long walk on the dry plains."

He stopped and put his trunk in the air as she instructed.

"Do you smell that? I smell pineapples," she said. "And the women over there. I hear them making the noises they make, like monkeys but soft. I see the green hills beyond us that we will walk toward to find our next meal."

"I smell the pineapples too. Where are they?" he asked.

"That is why you use your eyes with your nose. They are that way, toward the setting sun. But those are pineapples we cannot reach because of a high fence and angry women, so we will not try, as we have plenty of other food. But it is still good to smell them, isn't it?"

"Oh, yes." He stuck his trunk out in all directions, but the sweet pineapple odor filled his trunk no matter where he pointed it.

"Sometimes it is good to enjoy what you can see and smell and hear just because that is why the Spirit in the mountain made you from the soil. For no other reason."

"Yes, it is good, First Grandmother."

"I'm glad you think so. And that is why the women do it, too—just because they want to look at us. That is why the woman who follows us looks and smells and hears us, too. Perhaps the women who look at us all the time wish they were elephants instead of just women."

The little one thought that idea was amusing.

"Remember, little one, if you smell and look and listen enough, you can find your own knowledge and someday, perhaps, you will know even more than I do, even if I tell you everything I know."

The little one thought that idea was even more amusing.

Rick Hodges

16

Owen stared past Manish at the bare, pale yellow wall behind him. The moon was shining directly on the wall through the bedroom window. The bars in the window cast lines on the wall. He looked at his watch: 1:30 a.m.? He hadn't set it to local time. He found a clock in the room, on the wall. It said 8:30. He was seven hours away from home. He had never experienced jet lag. Then he realized it wasn't the moon shining; it was the sun.

Owen lay awake, his mind reviewing all he had done in such a short time and his body adjusting to the time difference. So many things to discourage him, or repel him, or scare him away, yet here he remained. What a bus ride! An angry elephant and a hijacking at knifepoint! Was this what people encountered every time they rode a bus in this country? Yet he had continued on without running in fear into the bush. (Or was it that the bus still felt like the safest place, all things considered?) Maybe this crazy trip would work. He rolled to his side. He had fallen asleep in his clothes, and he felt the bottle of pills in his shirt pocket. He pulled it out and swallowed one, just in case.

He was so close. How far from his father had he been on that road when Mubego intercepted him? A mile? A hundred yards?

He put the pill bottle back and fished the article out of his other pocket. "Karl Dorner—a U.S. military advisor to Kenya, Dorner led a rebellion in 1974 against the American-aligned government of this East African country. Currently held in prison there ...." The first time he had read it, Owen took it as good news, almost as if his father was dead and now had come back to life. Then he decided that this Karl Dorner was certainly the man in the photo above the mantel at the house he grew up in, and so he read it as wonderful, perfect news.

Then he read it as terrible news. The father Owen had imagined—strong, heroic, loving and faithful— was now replaced by the father he actually had, but knew almost nothing about. The camping trips with a flashlight under his blanket, the intimidating stares that would have made bullies scatter, the voice in his head that urged him on in weight-lifting sessions—all his fantasies that replaced the man he missed would be washed away. The man his mother considered dead had risen and killed off the man Owen had carefully constructed in his mind, and this real man was labeled a traitor. It would have been easier to crush the paper in his hands and throw it in the street and let the better man live in his imagination instead. That's what his mother would choose, which is why he told her he was going on a camping trip, instead of to Kenya to end up lying on a stranger's bed reading a damp scrap of newspaper.

Did she really believe he was going camping? Outdoors? With just a few pills to help him after weeks of refusing to even leave his room? No matter, he had made it here, and things were working out so far, and that was that.

So Mubego was warden of the prison. Owen would need his permission to see his father. Would he grant it? Owen thought of his mother and brother. He should find a phone to try to call one of them. He had given his mother a quick call on the way to the airport, leaving her a message on the machine with the camping trip cover story. Don't worry, he had told her, he'd be away from a phone for a few days and couldn't contact her. The pills were working, he said. They had freed him from his room and he wanted to go out into the world and enjoy what he had missed. Now he wondered if she ought to know the truth about where he was and why. She would be worried. But the truth would probably worry her even more. He saw her face, ragged from the strain of raising two boys without a father around but with his image to maintain. He saw her digging in the garden early last spring, pushing bulbs into the soil, willing them to take to the still-frozen ground and sprout despite planting them so late.

Confront your fears.

Quietly, Owen stood up and, pillow in hand, found his way through the house to the courtyard. Wanjeri wasn't there. She had already awakened, perhaps, though he saw nor heard anyone else in the house awake yet. He found a soft spot and lay down to try to catch up with as much sleep as he could. He thought about his room at home, and with his eyes closed, he imagined that the cool stone walls of the courtyard were the walls of his room, and fell into sleep.

But his restless mind, imagining the worst that could happen, wouldn't give up so easily, even in sleep. Owen dreamed of strange animals, baboons or leopards, climbing the walls from the outside. Then men with masks and knives, like the ones who robbed the bus, climbed over. Then an elephant smashed his way through the walls, waking him. He retreated back to the room.

***

Awake again, Owen could feel the African sun warming the room quickly, even from under the bed, where he had tucked himself safely.

He heard Manish talking in a hushed voice on a phone next to his bed. "I can't leave now."

"I'm at his house! I'm using his phone!"

"I will find a way to deliver the message. Just don't move until I contact you again."

"What else could I do? I'm at his house. Don't worry, he doesn't know I'm using the phone."

"Once they know the Asians will join the general strike, that won't matter. And Mubego will have bigger problems than me. With our help, they can shut down the whole country."

"You know me. I play the jolly Indian. Even Mubego isn't sure."

Owen shifted his way out from under the bed to the top of the thin mattress, quietly so Manish wouldn't notice. Manish turned his head and saw Owen on the bed, awake.

"I have to go." He hung up, gently, still wary of waking anyone else in the house.

"You didn't tell me everything," said Owen.

"I could say the same about you, my young friend with the same last name as Karl Dorner who wants to visit the prison he's in."

Owen sat up. "Do you know him?"

"Like I said, I've been in Mubego's prison before. I heard them say your last name. Are you his son?"

"Yes." Manish already knew anyway. Owen reasoned that he might as well learn what he could from this man who had already been in the prison with his father, the place he wanted to be.

"Ah." Manish stood silently for a moment, and then he brushed his black hair back across his head and shifted gears. "May I ask a favor? Can you not mention anything of what you just heard?"

Owen was starting to feel in over his head. Was it time to give Manish a reason to trust him by doing the right thing? Or to make some sort of deal? He chose.

"I won't say anything. But can you help me?"

"Certainly. What do you need?"

"I don't know yet. When I do, you can help me."

"Is Mubego going to let you see your father in the prison?"

"He says he will, but it will take time to arrange."

Rick Hodges

Manish chuckled. "That's his way of saying he will take as much time as he likes."

"Oh."

"If he wanted you there, you'd be there already."

"Why were you in Mubego's prison?" Owen asked.

Manish sat down on Owen's bed. The sun was warming the room rapidly, and Owen saw tiny drops of moisture on his head, under his jet black hair. "This country is good, for an African country at least. But it could be better. I work for people who want it to be better. That's as much as I should say."

"Why is my father in Mubego's prison?"

Manish looked up, surprised. "You don't know why?"

"I know a little of the story. I don't know how much of it is true. I've never quite believed it."

"Probably not much of it is true at all, I would guess. But I don't know why either. I was only in the prison a short time and I barely spoke to your father. It's not smart to know too much. But you will find out, soon enough."

Owen nodded.

There was a knock at the door. Julian was calling them to breakfast.

"I do know your father is a good man."

17

The little one was impatient to grow as tall as his older siblings and the grandmothers. He wanted to reach the tops of the trees for the best leaves and ripest fruit. He wanted to be brave, like his older brothers who played by banging their newly grown tusks against each other. He couldn't wait to grow tusks for himself.

First Grandmother had brought the herd to an open plain with rolling hills visible in the distance. Those hills, she said, were their destination—but to get there, they must walk close to a path where many women traveled to their own places. They traveled both on their feet, in their strange way of moving on just their hind legs, like baboons sometimes did, and in their moving rocks.

First Grandmother led them swiftly so they would not spend too much time near the path of women, but it was enough time for the little one to see. He saw so many women moving along the path, more than he had ever seen in one place before, more like wildebeest than women.

Though First Grandmother wanted to protect the herd from the danger of getting too close to this great column of traveling women, the little one noticed a very large elephant standing calmly near the women's path. It seemed content and fearless, and it towered over them.

"Why does that elephant not fear the women?" he asked.

"He is a grandfather," she explained. "See how big he is? See his big tusks? The women fear *him*."

"Why is he not with a herd?"

"Grandfathers go away from their herd when they are older. That is why you never see grandfathers unless a grandmother is ready to mate."

He thought about it. Yes, he did not see grandfathers in their herd, only younger males.

"You too will go out on your own some day and see the world and not be afraid of women," she added as she moved to the back of the herd to urge another youngster to walk faster and keep up.

He could not imagine ever leaving the herd and his grandmothers and brothers and sisters. He decided he would stay with the herd forever instead.

He watched the women move out of the corner of his eye as the herd crossed the plain toward the hills. The talk of grandfathers brought a new question in his mind, and when First Grandmother reappeared with the other youngster in tow, he asked.

"Do women have grandfathers?"

"Yes, they do. All animals have them."

"Do their grandfathers go out away from their herd?"

"Sometimes."

They had come closer to the big bull elephant standing near the women's path. He could see more clearly now the women who were walking, and the rocks others sped along in as fast as wildebeest at full speed.

Suddenly the big male trumpeted. The sound filled the sky. The little one looked and saw several women moving quickly away from the big male. Perhaps they had come too close and he was warning them away.

He was impressed that this grandfather was big and fearless and did not run from women.

"Will a grandfather fight a woman?" he asked.

First Grandmother never ever tired of his questions. It was her purpose to answer.

"Yes, sometimes. But only to defend himself when they attack him or come too close. Grandfathers, like grandmothers, never fight a woman or other animal unless there is a reason."

"Do grandfathers fight each other?"

"Yes, they do."

Her answer surprised him, and she could tell.

"But never to kill each other. Do you see your older brothers playing by hitting their tusks on each other? They are practicing to fight. They will not kill each other, but yes, they will fight when they are ready to mate. They feel great power when the time comes."

"But they are elephants, and elephants have the knowledge. We should not fight each other."

"I cannot explain that to you, little one. It is only

something you will learn for yourself someday."

No, he thought. I will never leave the herd and I will never fight either, not even when my tusks grow.

18

The sun was already hot and high when The Tea Man served breakfast at the courtyard table. Owen took off his shoes and walked in the prickly lawn to the shady part and took a sip of the best fresh-squeezed orange juice he had ever tasted in his life. He drank it down and asked for more.

Manish sat at the table, waking himself up with the help of his tea. Owen avoided looking at his watch so he wouldn't calculate how many hours he had slept, or not slept. He was weary from thinking and worrying and wondering, and from jet lag. And he was beginning to be weary of sitting in this courtyard drinking juice instead of meeting his father.

Owen spied Julian standing in the doorway, the same as the evening before, close enough to hear anything he said to Manish.

The cement table was still cool from the night's chill. From this vantage point, the trees hid the walls, giving the illusion of Mubego's house springing from a clear spot of amply watered jungle. It also hid the growing despair outside the walls, among plant and animal alike, caused by lack of water. Owen wondered how these people managed to live in the strange dry country he saw on the bus and from Mubego's Jeep, so different from the vivacious forests and green lawns of Maryland watered by rain year-round. Here, plants were yearning for the rainy season to return and soak the dust again before the sun desiccated their flesh. Goats and dogs and, oh yes, how could he forget? Elephants. All pacing the sullen ground. The people of Kumbata and the small strips of land beyond tried to extract a little extra from a land ill-prepared to grow much more. Mechanics who could fix any vehicle with almost nothing to work with labored on the roadsides to keep hot, battered trucks running long past their natural life spans.

"Sure is better in here than out there." Owen realized he had said it out loud when Manish answered his thought.

"Yes, this is a very comfortable home. Is that what you meant?"

"I meant ... everything."

"Everything?"

"The plants, the juice."

"The wealth, too. The luxury." Manish said, eyeing Julian.

"Yeah, that too. It feels funny sitting in here, like it's not part of the rest of the country. Like it's ..."

"America?"

Owen nodded with his lips glued to the glass of juice,

the sticky liquid perched on the edge of his tongue, teasing.

"If you ever feel homesick here, go to one of the better hotels in Nairobi or an expensive game lodge," said Manish. "Or a nice Indian restaurant. Clean, modern, air conditioned. It's like the U.S.A. in a bottle."

"I'm not homesick. I like change sometimes." How quickly his outlook had changed since, only days before, he lay locked in his room and his safe routine. He was ready to be brave and free and make up for lost time spent huddled alone.

"This is more than change, my friend," Manish replied. "Going from America to the Third World is like falling through the ice into the cold water. Even I feel it, and this is my home country."

"I'm handling it."

"Because you can go back whenever you want." Owen looked at Manish, who was looking right back, his eyes bright white against his deep brown skin and helmet of black hair. "You can escape like that," he said with a snap of his fingers.

"I could. But I don't want to."

"It looks bad out there, especially in the towns," said Manish. "But life isn't as bad as it appears to your eyes. People have different ways of getting by here."

"How?"

"They are resourceful. They waste nothing and use their wits." Manish turned to see if Julian was still listening, but he had disappeared. Still, he leaned in closer to Owen. "Or they get a government job and take kickbacks and bribes and such things. And live in nice houses with walls to block out the suffering."

"Aren't the walls to keep out crime?" Owen asked.

"Certainly. But there's not much difference here between crime and everyday suffering. Don't worry, you should be safe without walls if you keep your wits about you."

"I've already seen crime up close."

"You have?"

"On the bus here. When the bus we were on was hijacked. Remember?"

Manish's face hardened. "Yes. That must have been terrifying for you."

"It was terrifying, but also strange how the police were there so fast. We were out in the country."

"Yes, that *was* strange," said Manish.

"I don't remember seeing you on the bus," Owen said.

"I didn't want to be seen," Manish replied. "I think perhaps ..." He looked up at Julian, who was walking toward them.

Owen spied Julian too and changed the subject. "How do you keep this so green?" he asked Julian.

"Remember, this is the dry season," Julian said. "When the rain comes, we collect water that runs from the roof in a cistern. Now, we let it out." He gestured to the water trickling from hoses concealed under the trees. "We do not spray the water like in other countries. This country must save its water, not let it evaporate."

"My friend loves our fresh juice," said Manish. "Could you ask to bring him another glass?" Julian hesitated a moment as if he would reply, but then turned to go back inside. Manish waited for Julian to leave.

"My wife wants me to come back home," Manish said. "They told me on the phone. At least she knows where I am this time and that I am safe."

"You can't leave?"

"No, I can't leave without asking Mubego, and I dare not ask Mubego. I'm his until he releases me or puts me back in his prison. Besides, perhaps you could use my help."

"Don't worry about me," said Owen.

Manish shrugged. "To have a conscience is a burden. It troubles me you will be lost here without someone who knows this country."

Before Owen could respond, or even think about what Manish said, Julian appeared with The Tea Man, who was carrying more orange juice, another pot of tea, and bananas the size of Mubego's fingers. Manish opened the top of the teapot and proclaimed: "Ah, dessert! Chilled monkey brains!"

Owen stared. Manish held fast to a goofy, show-biz smile, teeth crooked but white against his deep brown skin, and then dropped the smile when Owen showed no sign of recognition.

"You don't know it? That is from *Indiana Jones and the Temple of Doom*. The worst of the three Indiana Jones movies. It was supposed to take place in India, but it did not resemble India much. For instance, they do not eat monkey brains over there. They eat some strange things, I can tell you, but not brains. My grandmother is from over there, and she still remembers things. There are people who catch rats for farmers, and for payment they take the rats to roast and eat!"

"I forgot, you've never been to India."

"Quite true. I was born here in Kenya, and my father and mother too. Many Asians live here in Kenya. The British brought my ancestors over to build the railroads, but we stayed and opened the best restaurants in the country and many other successful businesses. Lions ate many of the workers on the railroad. My grandmother says her brother was eaten, but my father told me he was just a drunk and fell asleep on the tracks and got run over by a train."

"I'll rent that movie next time I'm within a thousand miles of a Blockbuster," Owen said.

"Sure. A good movie. Hey, you can use my card if you want. No good here, but I still have it. They have some movie rental shops in Nairobi, but try to find a working VCR."

Someone was coming. Owen hoped it was Wanjeri.

Instead, he saw Julian backing into the doorway, wheeling a man in a wheelchair to the courtyard.

The man in the chair was painfully thin, with a slightly twisted body and neck. He didn't speak or move on his own, except to glance at everyone else, one by one, scanning their faces. Mubego followed him through the doorway.

"This is my brother, Mr. Abasi Mubego," said the Colonel as Julian placed the chair at the table.

Abasi said nothing. Manish and Owen said nothing. Owen realized Abasi could not speak. To answer the unspoken question, Julian broke the silence.

"Mr. Abasi was in an accident," Julian explained, using a formal way to talk about his uncle to strangers.

"Abasi doesn't talk anymore," Mubego said. "He was injured, in his head, but we have high hopes he will speak again. We won't ever give up on that," he said, glancing at Abasi.

"I'm sorry," said Owen, but Mubego ignored it.

"See, young man, I told you elephants were mean creatures," said Manish. It seemed Manish meant for Mubego to hear it more than Owen.

"An elephant attacked Mr. Abasi," Mubego explained. "He drove Wanjeri to see the elephants when she was a girl and one nearly killed him. Wanjeri still likes them despite what they did. They are mean, dangerous creatures."

Nobody knew what to say, but Mubego signaled that it was acceptable to ignore his mute brother by changing the subject.

"Did you both sleep well? Not too loud?"

"Yes" they replied together. Did Mubego overhear Manish on the phone?

"My friend Manish here doesn't snore too much? Very good. Now we can make arrangements for you, young Mr. Dorner."

Arrangements! Finally. Owen glanced at Manish, still in limbo, waiting for some arrangements of his own.

Mubego was wearing a more formal uniform than the day before, a crisp white jacket that had a higher, stiffer collar with a more military bearing. Under the rapidly increasing sunlight, Mubego's bright, rigid clothing revealed a greater share of both his heft and his deeply dark skin. Though his shoulders and neck still filled out the uniform with impressive muscle, age had added fat to his neck and belly. Still, his frame carried the extra weight with ease, like a warrior's body carrying a victor's spoils.

That was when Owen noticed Mubego's gold tooth, an upper incisor. It reflected the sunlight. What a dazzling symbol the tooth must be in a country where most people, Owen noticed, wore empty holes in their mouths in place of lost teeth.

"I am arranging for you to visit your father," Mubego announced.

Mubego's brown cheeks sagged slightly over the corners of his mouth as he clutched his teacup.

"If you are to see your father, however, it will require the permission of the Deputy Minister of Justice in Nairobi. It may take a few days to obtain a decision from him. If he approves, I would be glad to assist you."

That was easier than expected.

Only two days after landing in Nairobi with nothing but the name of his father and a remote town, Owen found himself drinking tea with the prison warden in his courtyard. It was either the best customer service on the planet, or something else was going on that he didn't understand.

It seemed Mubego liked to toy with him a little, but he hadn't stood in Owen's way. Perhaps he needed to remind Owen of his power, like a bull who snorts at every passerby to make his presence known.

"The question is whether your father wants to see you."

Owen had given no thought to that.

He had not dared to imagine what his father looked like now, or how he would talk, or what he would say. But not once since he first saw the news article did he consider his father might refuse him altogether. Why?

"Do you know my father well?" Owen asked.

"No one knows your father well."

19

Uncle Abasi had driven her places before, but never this far. Wanjeri was almost old enough to drive herself around, but not quite. Her parents had died barely six months ago and she was still adjusting to life under the care of Uncle Mubego. He had let her try driving in a Jeep on the plains, but navigating the hazardous roads was another matter to be left for when she was old enough.

It was the wet season, and to find elephants—Wanjeri's new fascination—she would have to camp overnight so she could go far enough from town to find a group of the creatures that was staying in one place instead of in transit. She had read every book she could find about them at school and asked her teachers everything they knew. She had learned that adult males would wander alone here and there, but she wanted to see a complete family group of adult females and young elephants led by a matriarch, the oldest and most experienced female in the herd.

Abasi told her he knew a good place near Mt. Kenya to see elephants. Uncle Mubego was happy to delegate taking a silly schoolgirl to see silly animals to his brother.

They took Abasi's Mercedes. The place he knew was just off the road. Wanjeri brought oranges and sausages for lunch, and she handed Abasi pieces to eat as they drove. She looked out the window, eager to see a stray elephant or a group, but it was hard to spot anything through the thick green of the bush in the wet season. She wondered if either her mother or father had liked elephants as much as she did. Is that where she got it? Neither had ever mentioned it. It made her sad that they were gone and she had no chance to share her new interest with them.

Abasi didn't talk much. He never did. He was like Julian, in his appearance and demeanor. He rarely spoke his mind, and he listened a little too much to his brother, Mubego. Everyone did. Others had to listen to Mubego, but people in his own family were entitled to speak up against him, she thought. Julian and Abasi seemed to believe the opposite—that family members must be obedient to their elders. Wanjeri did not speak of her defiant feelings with others, but she did not let go of them either. Besides, Uncle Mubego was simply her caretaker, not her father. As an orphan, she felt freer to go her own way.

As he drove, Abasi sometimes took a sip of some kind of whiskey from a brown bottle he often carried. She recognized the smell. It mixed with the smell of Abasi's sweat, making a sour-sweet perfume that filled the car, even with the windows open. It made her sick a little. After many sips, the car began to swerve, but she was used to the deadly way that everyone drove on this highway. Her only worry was getting home on time if he drank more.

He did drink more. After stopping, he fell asleep in the parked car, but Wanjeri didn't care, because they had found elephants.

They had pulled off onto a road between a flower farm and open space, near a place Abasi said elephants sometimes came to raid vegetable and fruit farms for food. She spotted them behind a grove of trees far from the road and yelled for Abasi to pull over. Grabbing her sketch book and pencils, she left him snoring in the car, climbed a crumbling fence, and moved as close as she dared, about 50 meters, and found a spot with a little shade. She counted them—nine, including three smaller ones that were likely, she reckoned, just two or three years old. She sized up their health, their tusks, and notches or marks in their ears, just as she had read about biologists doing. She sat for an hour and sketched two of them while they waved their ears lazily in the shade of the trees. They seemed content and well fed.

Wanjeri wished there were a way she could tell them they had nothing to fear from her, and she would protect them if need be, so she could go closer and even touch them. She wanted to be around them more and learn how to read their language, how they communicated with each other. She had read all about their intelligence, and she wanted to be a part of that, to converse with them, to learn all about them—especially the matriarch, who she had read was the keeper of the herd's memories and knowledge of the world.

The sun faded rapidly, and the elephants moved away from her, toward the mountain. That allowed Wanjeri to pick out the matriarch—she was the one leading them all away. She wondered where they could be going when this spot seemed so pleasant and safe for spending the night.

Abasi was still sound asleep in the car. She would have to spend the night here. She was prepared for it— uncles pass out and cars break down—so she pulled a blanket out of the trunk and lay on the grass next to the car, under the stars. She let the sound of the doves' calls put her to sleep.

When she awoke, it was still very dark, and someone was lying on top of her.

Abasi was groping her breasts with one hand and reaching into her pants with the other. Wanjeri had never been touched like that before, yet she felt a strange confidence as she reached next to her and found a rock, which she smashed against his head.

When he awoke several minutes later, he put his hands in the blood on his head and said, "Did I fall?" She told him yes, he had fallen, and helped him back into the car where he fell asleep again. Those were the last words anyone heard him say.

20

Walking back to his room in Mubego's house after breakfast, Owen spied a row of photos and mementos on a wall. On display in the center hung an oval-shaped warrior's shield made with animal hide painted with abstract designs. Framed photos, nearly all showing Mubego standing with people who looked powerful or influential, surrounded the shield. He read a label on one of them: a photo of a much younger Mubego with the president of Kenya. Another photo showed him younger still, dressed in a plain green military uniform rather than the fancy one he wore today, standing among trees with several other black men dressed the same, and one white man.

Owen studied it more closely. The white man had short-cropped hair and a smile that softened his determined, focused features. There was the face again in another photo, hair a little longer and cheekbones more prominent over a thinner frame, with Mubego and a beautiful young black woman, the three of them seated in the same courtyard Owen had enjoyed that morning. Owen thought he knew this man's face, but he was interrupted before he could be sure.

"You have a visitor, Mr. Dorner," Julian said, gesturing for Owen to follow him. Mubego overheard from another room and appeared behind Julian.

"*He* has a visitor?" Mubego asked.

Julian and Mubego moved aside for Owen to go to the foyer. There stood Mrs. Pearson.

"Owen, it's so nice to see you're doing well. You're so far from home!" And she presented her pale cheek for a kiss.

She looked exactly the same no matter how much she aged—jet black hair up in a loose bun, under a sunhat, the better to protect her fair skin from solar assault.

Mrs. Pearson was just the person who could track him down on such short notice. She still did work for the United Nations and she probably had all the connections and documents necessary. She had shown her diplomatic passport to Owen once. It was filled with stamps from across the world, and she had a head full of stories to match.

Mrs. Pearson always seemed to belong wherever she went, and everywhere she went, everything seemed to belong to her.

But why was she here?

As Owen obliged with a kiss to her cheek, she extended her hand to Mubego.

"*Hujambo*, Col. Mubego, it's so nice of you to have me in your lovely home. I hope you remember me—we met many years ago at a conference in Dar es Salaam. It's Barbara Pearson, from the U.N. Committee on Internecine Conflict."

Mubego shook her hand. Owen would remember this moment as the only time he ever saw Mubego caught completely off guard.

"Yes, of course I remember you. *Karibisha*! Welcome to my home."

Mubego waited until everyone was served with tea, for the second time that morning, before he queried her.

"So, you and Mr. Dorner are acquainted?"

"Oh, yes, I used to change Owen's diapers."

Mubego laughed, loudly, and patted Owen on the back.

Owen doubted she had ever changed a diaper in her whole life, but she had made her point.

Mubego told the Tea Man to welcome her to the courtyard for tea with his other guests. After they were all outside and out of earshot, he motioned to Julian to listen.

"This house is too full," Mubego said. "Things are getting too complicated. I don't know how this woman got here, or why. I don't know how this boy got here, or why."

"What should we do?" asked Julian.

"I need time to check into things. I need to get them all out of here for a while. And I need them to talk to each other, with you listening. I need a babysitter's help here."

"Yes, out of here. I could take them on a safari," Julian said.

"Very good idea! Take them all. Tell me what you learn. And bring Wanjeri as a guide. Let her tell them all about how wonderful those damned elephants are. Take a gun and shoot one if you want. We'll feed its heart to Abasi."

21

"It's true."

"What's true?"

"Pregnant women look radiant."

Barbara lifted her wineglass up to her husband's and smiled. With her bare legs folded under her and the warmth of the wine creeping from her belly up to her head, she did feel radiant.

"You know you can't drink, right?"

"Why did I go and marry a scientist?"

"There was a study just published. They found out that alcohol hurts the baby." Henry reached for her glass, but she pulled it away.

"I know, sweetie. This is my last drink until the baby comes. It's my drink to celebrate no more drinking." And she took one more long sip and put it down on the coffee table.

"Henry, I've made a decision," she announced.

"What would that be?"

"Now that we're going to be a family, we should all have the same last name."

"You don't have to do that. I really don't mind. I'm not a chauvinist about it." Henry had his hand on her stomach.

"No, I want to now. That you let me use my own name is enough for me. I'm ready to change. I know everybody at your office thinks you're married to a crazy feminist. And with a family it's just too confusing."

"Whatever you want, my darling." He nuzzled her neck and nibbled at her dark hair.

"I'm now officially Mrs. Henry Pearson."

* * *

At 34, she was older than most of the other women in the waiting room. She met Henry on one of those singles cruises for well-educated people—graduate-level and higher degrees only allowed on board—that sailed Lake Michigan from the Navy Pier once a month. Like many of the singles plying the deck that night, Henry and Barbara were already in their thirties and were only now thinking about marriage. There were other things to accomplish first. He was busy making advances in microbiology; she was writing books and articles on international relations in Europe in the 18th Century. But now she was finally married and settled and ready to have a child, and her age gave her the advantage of wisdom, she thought, and the resources to give her first (and likely only) child a comfortable life.

Surveying the waiting room, she pondered the future of all the children yet to be born to these mothers. The children might be friends, or schoolmates or lovers someday. They would all have the best medical care in the history of mankind. They would live in the most prosperous, most technologically advanced country and age in history. And her child would have two highly educated, healthy, caring parents. She rubbed her belly, fingering through her blouse the strange ridge that was once her navel, now stretched nearly flat.

She worried about their ability to handle a child at their age. But when she voiced her worry to Henry, he laughed out loud. "You have more energy now than most women ever have," he said. And it was true. Barbara had personality. She struck up conversations with complete strangers in restaurants, and she arranged successful parties with just a few days of planning. She settled on a sun-and-moon-and-stars theme for the new nursery and in one weekend of painting and stamping and stickering, it was done, and it was beautiful and original and full of energy. She was ready for a child.

Barbara and Henry had both begun calling the unborn baby "he" because it sounded right, but she soon came to know she carried a son. It was not the way she carried her growing belly or any old wives' tale like that; she just knew.

She was right. It was a boy. He was born early on a Saturday morning. But there was something about their son she did not know until he was born, something she never contemplated and never felt.

She felt nothing at first. Her head was still foggy from the medication, and even when she became lucid enough to understand, no emotions came forth. It wasn't until they brought Henry into the special nursery to see their baby son, laid in a tiny plastic box with tubes and wires connected everywhere, that she felt something. She felt shame. She had failed to deliver the child she wanted to give to him, and she could not hide it.

"Edward's Syndrome." It was an easy thing to remember, to tell friends and family, instead of some complicated Latin word. It was caused by an extra chromosome stocked in every cell of their son's tiny body. And the future was easy to explain too—the baby had a 90 percent chance of dying in the next week or so, probably today.

In the years ahead, she would work to erase by force of will nearly every memory of that day, but until she did, she relied on one good happenstance to salve the sting: she had seen her baby before they explained what was wrong with him. Otherwise, she might not have had the courage to look inside the little box. She might have expected some kind of genetic freak, but no, the baby was beautiful—tiny and fragile, with pliant skin and a soft tuft of hair at the top of his head. He wore a tiny diaper that still seemed a size too big, and a needle and tube in the vein of his wrist, anchored to a flat stick taped to his forearm. Attached to his foot, barely the size of Barbara's thumb, was a wire with a small red light at the end. It was connected to one of the machines next to his tiny bed-box that hummed and pinged and chimed in alarm when his breathing or heart rate dropped, which it often did. The baby's labored breathing and purple tinge was the only hint that his body would not survive long outside of his mother's.

Barbara was surprised that her baby did not really look much like his mother or father. Only his hair and skin tone gave him away. But then she noticed that the other newborns in the nursery also looked more like each other than their parents. She wasn't jealous of the other parents until she witnessed a mother clutching a baby, wrapped tightly in a thin blanket, to take it home. Then she hated the other parents—not for the blessing they enjoyed, but for not knowing that in having a baby, they had gambled on having one free of any random genetic mix-ups that could take it away again. These other parents had beaten the odds, but they did not appreciate their luck. She hated them for taking their blessings for granted, for beaming with pride in ignorance of what could have been had they lost the gamble. She hated them for not breathing a sigh of relief every time they picked up their healthy babies.

Two days later, when Barbara's baby died, she still hated the other parents, but now it was just for being there, in front of her, holding tiny babies full of breath. It was a simmering, colorless rage, too dissolute and confusing for her to cry about.

They named the baby Samuel and cremated him. The ashes were delivered to their door the next day; they came in a clay jar the size of a child's first drinking cup.

They planned to spread the ashes on Lake Michigan where they had met. But when the day came, she could not bring herself to go, so Henry took Samuel out on a boat with his parents. She could not imagine going out to the lake without thinking of that last glass of wine she drank while pregnant, though the doctors assured her it had nothing to do with it. But she sat at home, alone on the sofa, and thought about it anyway.

"It wasn't your fault," Henry would say, sensing her guilt. But his words did not comfort her, they only made her wonder if he really believed it. She knew it was probably not the wine, but she could not give up the feeling that something she did or something she was had caused it. She wanted to be responsible, in some small way. The alternative was to accept that the most horrible things in the world could happen to her, but she could do nothing to stop them. That truth was even harder to face.

She thought of having another child, and her mother and other relatives gently suggested it once they thought it was safe to broach the subject, but Barbara could not stop thinking about the new child's name. It could not be Samuel—this was the name they had chosen for their child before he was even planned. The new baby would always be the second try, the replacement baby with the second name on their list instead of the first. And her faith in healthy, happy babies wrapped in soft cloths and carried home from the hospital had evaporated. She knew about the great gamble, and even though the odds were still very much in her favor, the stress of waiting for the dice to tumble seemed too much to bear.

Barbara's absence from the lake when Henry spread the ashes was the beginning of the time they would grow apart, and the way they would grow apart. He seemed stronger, more willing to confront their grief, but to her this signaled only a willingness to get over it, and she would never get over it. She would carry Samuel with her forever just as she had carried the child inside her. He took her sullenness as blaming herself, but that wasn't it at all, and she resented having to tell him how she felt, so she didn't. She crumpled into her own quiet sadness, and soon he retreated from her. She thought they would recover after the first anniversary of his birth, Sept. 23, and then the date of his death two days later. Both their parents came to be with them and drew their feelings out. But it wasn't enough. It was too hard to be a family when there was someone missing from the room. Six months later, they were apart, and divorced soon after.

Barbara never bothered to change her name back. She had lost the heart for details. She lost interest in writing academic treatises about the ridiculous posturing of pompous diplomats representing declining royal families of Europe. She might have lost interest in everything she knew, but for her old friend who called about a job.

"I know of a great job for you at the United Nations in New York, arranging relief efforts for refugees," said June Dorner. "Lots of travel."

"I don't want to hand out bags of flour to starving people," she told June.

"No, it's none of that. You would do the big-picture things, arranging for the shipments, the finances, that sort of thing. Karl was detailed to the State Department in Africa for a while and he heard about it."

So, after a round of interviews, she became a functionary on the 14th floor of the U.N. building, saving the world a million pounds of sugar or a million units of antibiotics or a million *Nigerian* naira (about $5,000) in bribes at a time, immersed in work that empowered her to do good things without confronting the pain of the limits of her power. There were others at the U.N. who did the messier work. They would try, and often fail, to reach helpless mothers in remote parts of the world forced to watch their children die because they were born too poor or too far away from food or medicine. It was not her job.

22

Owen looked over his possessions as he packed them into his bag. Did he have the things he needed for a safari? He barely packed enough for an overseas trip, let alone a drive into Africa's wildlife-filled desert. A pair of khakis. Two polo shirts and two nearly new T-shirts, one plain white one and a blue one marked "Event Staff"—a gift from his brother after he worked as a volunteer at a concert to get in free. One pair of shorts, a few socks and underwear, and a small bag of toiletries. His old Orioles cap—a necessity. A Fodor's guidebook to East Africa he bought at the airport with corners bent from the quick skim on the flight.

The clothes seemed more precious now than when he threw them in the bag with little thought. They had become familiar talismans of home, a grounding from which to draw upon when he dressed. With hope, they would get him through a safari, too.

Julian's clothes—slick clean black pants and a silky pressed shirt—seemed entirely inappropriate for a safari, and that made Owen feel better about his.

"We must stop at my office to pick up supplies, if you don't mind," said Julian as he carried Owen's bag to the Jeep parked in front of Mubego's house. "We've hired Manish as the cook and he needs food. Oh, and we must fetch my sister, our official safari guide."

He loaded Mrs. Pearson's huge bag as she took her seat. Manish sat in the back with her luggage.

* * *

As Julian drove the five of them from the hills toward the valley, Wanjeri lost herself in the wonder of the plains again. How privileged she was to live in this place, near the gorge where the Earth was still splitting open in rebirth and where the first people evolved before they spread across the world. How fortunate to have studied in London where she gained a new appreciation of her home, unlike so many of her fellow Africans who took this beautiful wilderness, eclectic culture, and rich heritage for granted. Rarely did they bother to value the layers of time beneath their feet, and too readily looked upon Africa's array of magnificent creatures as mere bush meat, or as nuisances.

Wanjeri was proud to share this bounty with foreign visitors and Africans alike. A safari created an opportunity to teach them about the wonder of life in the African wild, and to teach Africans who should know better to embrace their country's diversity and interdependence and to see the connections between their lives and the lives of animals.

As the Jeep sped through the dry valley, Wanjeri

surveyed green flat plains, their foundation laid millions of years ago by volcanic ash that erupted from a gaping wound in the earth's crust. Jagged rock, minerals, and volcanic glass flooded the gaps between mountains, transforming jutting peaks into island *kopjes* that poked through the plains, until the volcanic pressure waned and the violent precipitation ceased. The grainy, ashen soil that remained held little of the rain that visited only twice a year. Only the heartiest of trees took root, most along the riverbeds. Without trees, the grass thrived, its browned tips baking under the African sun, yet sheltering roots that sustained life until rain returned.

When the rain came and the grasslands that covered half the surface of Africa turned green again, multitudes of animals migrated to feed on the great swaths—blue wildebeests, gazelles, zebras and buffalos with legs powerful enough to travel long distances, each with a stomach, or stomachs, evolved to wring nutrition from the fibrous leaves filling their huge bellies. When the grass was reduced to a mere shadow on the earth, the largest mammal migration in the world thundered on, but not before depositing a mountain of dung that fed the grass as payment for its bounty.

Behind these great herds of animals, and the grass that fed them, hid a predator that ate much less often, perhaps a meal every few days. This animal gorged on protein-dense food that required a day or two of solid sleep to digest. Lions, cheetahs, leopards, hyenas, and wild dogs let the grass-eaters do the work of extracting vital nutrients from the grass, then relied on their intelligence, speed, cooperation, and ferocity to snatch it for themselves.

Wanjeri considered the animal she escorted now—an animal who possessed the desire and free time to do nothing more than admire beasts eating, sleeping, mating, and traveling across a landscape dotted with small hills of granite and gneiss and the occasional tree. This animal, which would eat anything, moved about the plains in Jeeps.

Wanjeri's thoughts turned to her mother. She recalled her mother dancing around the kitchen in a bright red *kanga*, an inexpensive Kenyan sarong she wore out of pride rather than necessity. She was a fine cook who leaned over the hearth stirring vegetables in a large pot even though the family could afford someone to cook for them. She would have loved to see Wanjeri at home in this place and witness how much she had learned about the animals. How Wanjeri wished it was her mother who had driven her to see those first elephants near Mt. Kenya, rather than Abasi, her uncle. Wanjeri remembered much less of her father, a busy military man who was seldom in the house. When she tried to conjure his face, he always looked like his brother, Col. Mubego.

As an adult, Wanjeri still twisted her short hair into locks as her mother had once done. She smiled as she recalled her mother's sweet smell and the embrace of her warm, reassuring body.

Mrs. Pearson broke the spell.

"All those animals out there must produce great quantities of poop," she announced.

She had brought her own binocular. Mrs. Pearson made a point of saying "binocular," rather than "binoculars." When Owen said "binoculars," she was quick to correct him: To say "binoculars" was redundant, she explained, as the "bi" represented two eyepieces already. Owen knew she had only set herself up—when he saw the chance, he would say "binoculars," with the S, in her presence to knock her down a peg.

With her binocular, Mrs. Pearson scanned the horizon. The Jeep sped along the hard, flat road of the plains, the black wisps of Mrs. Pearson's hair not contained by the band at the back of her scalp rippling in the wind.

"I'm glad you came along, Mrs. Pearson," Owen said.

"Owen, if you don't start calling me Barbara I will wring your neck. You're not a kid anymore, you're 18, and looking at you is reminder enough I'm getting old, so stop reminding me."

"Sorry, it's a habit I can't break. You did change my diapers, remember?"

"Touché, little Owen."

Mrs. Pearson was the only person in the world Owen had ever heard use the word "touché."

"We're coming up on a place where we may see foxes," said Wanjeri. "Bat-eared foxes. I saw them last month at their burrow, with some kits. Slow down, Julian."

They all craned their necks hoping to see a pair, or a family, but there were no foxes.

The Jeep slowed as they reached the park entrance. A modest stone gateway, with no fence on either side, supported a sign, "Masai Mara National Park." Nothing more distinguished the flat grass plain outside the park's border from the identical landscape within. The park road became flatter and straighter and Julian picked up speed, bathing the passengers with hot, dry, dusty air.

Though he had brought Wanjeri along, Julian seemed eager to play the part of tour guide. His voice punctured the rush of the air as he called out the names of animals they passed. "That's a crowned crane. There is a cape buffalo. Don't worry, we will see plenty more of these later."

The air rushing through the windows and the open top of the Jeep felt good after the hot drive to the park. It even chilled Owen's damp skin. The wind also carried away body odor—Africa's official smell inside cars and buses. It didn't seem to bother anyone else. Owen was getting used to it.

As the Jeep advanced, specks in the grass looked up and smelled the air, clumps of grass hanging motionless from their mouths before they turned and fled to a safe distance.

"Where do they hide from leopards and things like that?" said Mrs. Pearson to Julian as a zebra's striped flanks heaved and its thickly maned neck rocked to the powerful gallop of its getaway.

"When they are small and the grass is still high, they can hide there. But mostly they run until whatever is chasing them gets tired."

"Or until the predator catches it," added Manish. "You know about the two men who encountered a lion? One says, 'Can you run faster than the lion?' The other says, 'I don't need to, I only need to run faster than you!'"

Owen obligingly laughed at the joke. Mrs. Pearson let out a knowing "hmmm."

Instead of his stomach tightening with the anxiety from the chance of lion attack, Owen chose to face and conquer that fear. He felt no panic. Had Africa helped him to figure life out already? Was he finally in control of his weakness?

They spied a zebra with a young foal just off the road.

"The newborn zebras can run the day they are born," Manish volunteered. "Their stripes help confuse predators. I learned this from listening to Wanjeri."

"Did you?" Mrs. Pearson said. "I haven't heard Wanjeri say much of anything yet. I thought you were our server, not our guide."

Owen winced. Manish was in the back of the Jeep so Owen couldn't see his reaction to her snide comment.

"The stripes help confuse the predators," said Wanjeri, repeating Manish's words to the letter. It was exactly the right thing to say to knock Mrs. Pearson off her perch.

Owen let out a small laugh at this clever retort. Wanjeri didn't seem to speak often, but when she did, it was worth the wait. Owen piled more heat onto Mrs. Pearson by lifting the binoculars Julian had loaned him to his eyes and saying, "I can see the zebra's stripes through my binoculars," enunciating the S at the end.

Nonplussed, Mrs. Pearson read from a guidebook Julian kept in the Jeep. "It says here zebras have white stripes on a black hide, not the other way around."

Julian slowed the Jeep and broke the tension. "Those are the wildebeest," he said. A small gathering of thin, muscular cows with sloping backs and curved horns sidestepped from the road, lowering their heads and twisting to face the Jeep. "They come north in July to the Mara from the Serengeti. They are also called 'gnus.' Listen and you will hear why." They listened, and heard the wildebeest grunting their names here and there, sounding like cows mooing, which to untrained ears sounded like "gnu."

Julian clasped both hands on the wheel even though he had stopped and turned off the engine. A small hill of smooth rock, like boulders stacked atop each other, thrust from the smooth land off to their right. "The wildebeest follow the rain. They have their babies here. Then they go back, into the Serengeti in Tanzania, the country to our south."

"The Serengeti is down there?" asked Owen.

"Yes. We are in the northern tip of it now."

Mrs. Pearson stood up on her seat to see better. "There are so many of them."

"There are one and a half million wildebeest, and a half million again of zebra," Wanjeri said. "And a quarter million Thomson's gazelle. And many other animals, too."

Owen stood and looked, too. "The wildebeest are interesting, but they're ugly." He said it softly to not offend Wanjeri. How strange, he instantly thought, for him to worry about whether insulting a wild animal would insult the guide. But that's how it felt—Wanjeri was showing these animals with pride.

When they had both scanned the horizon to their satisfaction and sat down, Julian started the car. "And now maybe we see simba, *Swahili* for lion."

Lions! Owen looked for a reaction from Mrs. Pearson, but all he could see was the back of her neck now framed with more unruly strands of escaped black hair. Julian turned the Jeep off the road and headed straight for the little hill of rock.

"Watch this," said Wanjeri.

The *kopje* stuck straight out of the flat plains like a pile of giant boulders dropped from the clouds. "Let's look here. This is a good place for *simba* to hide."

Julian was right. The lions, showing no fear of the Jeep, appeared from among the boulders minutes after Julian turned off the engine. Two lionesses and a younger lion bounded down the rocks into the grass. Owen noticed Manish and Julian surveying the area to ensure a lion did not approach the Jeep from the other side.

Both females plopped down on a flat rock. A cub persistently yanked on the adults' tails and ears until one batted at her and the other gently gnawed on her head. Without warning an adult lion leapt to her feet and stood alert. She stared directly at Owen.

Mrs. Pearson gasped.

With one chomp, the lion could easily bite Owen's head off. She was no pampered circus cat, but a wild creature covered in bald spots, scars and mange. Flies circled her head.

"I saw a *National Geographic* special once," said Manish, "and it showed a lion's claw had cut a hole in the side of a car like this one."

Mrs. Pearson shushed him. "You'll scare them away."

"Do they look scared?" he asked. Indeed, most of the lionesses looked sleepy, but their cubs were having none of it, clambering all over them.

"One has a collar on its neck." Wanjeri pointed to the one wearing a wide leather collar. "It is a radio collar for researchers to track her," she said. "They might track her by car, or maybe by airplane. I sometimes use a similar tracking system for elephants. They fit around the elephant's foot. They are bigger and sturdier to resist the elephant's tendency to rip them off with their tusks."

Owen noticed a dreamlike expression cross Wanjeri's face whenever she spoke of elephants. He was about to ask her more about her tracking work when Mrs. Pearson piped up.

"Why aren't they reacting to us?"

"These lions think vehicles are big moving animals that don't smell good enough to eat," Wanjeri answered. "If you were to get out of the car, then they could see you as a threat. Or as prey."

"Would anybody like to stretch their legs?" said Julian, who added quickly, "I'm joking. Do *not* get out of the car."

Owen noticed Mrs. Pearson shudder.

"Lions are the only social cats," Wanjeri said. "They live in prides, but the young males form their own groups of two or three, and then fight for control of an existing pride. If they win, they kill any cubs not of their offspring so that the females immediately mate with the new males."

"How awful," said Mrs. Pearson. "How can they do that?"

"A lion has no time for sadness."

Mrs. Pearson humphed again.

Owen scanned the area. "Where are the males?"

"Probably out patrolling their territory." Owen saw Manish and Julian continually scanning their surroundings and nervously glanced over his shoulder.

"I thought the males didn't hunt?" said Mrs. Pearson.

"Oh, they will hunt big animals. They help to take down buffalo or giraffe, and that feeds the whole group for days. But mostly they patrol to protect the pride from other males who threaten them and their cubs."

"Of course."

"I will tell my wife that males have a purpose," said Manish.

"Yes," said Mrs. Pearson, "but males also create the problem, don't they?"

"Oh, my wife knows that already," Manish replied.

Owen used his Orioles cap to swish away flies as they continued to admire the lions. After several minutes, a crowd of tourists joined them. The cats, now doing nothing more but brush the occasional fly with their tails, paid little attention to the excited banter and camera-clicking that sprung from the three additional metal boxes that weren't good to eat.

The tourists afforded Owen a mirror image of himself. But unlike them, he had not come to Africa to admire lions.

He vowed not to let anyone, or anything, distract

him from his mission, nor to wait for Mrs. Pearson to reveal, in her diplomatic but insistent way, why she had followed him halfway around the world. What did she want? He would confront her as soon as they were alone. She certainly came at the behest of his mother, who was bound to learn where he had gone. She was certain to worry about him, too, especially if she guessed his purpose. But what exactly did Mrs. Pearson plan to do? Try to drag him home?

Sweat trickled from Owen's brow. Maybe he *should* give up and go home. Enjoy a nice vacation and forget this crazy mission. His father may not want to see him as Mubego had suggested.

No, he was too close to give up now. He had to go through with it.

Julian drove back to the road and took them another two miles to a park station nestled next to another large *kopje*. He entered the station to pay the admittance fees while his passengers slumped on a bench drinking warm water from the bottles Manish handed out. Dozens of tiny multi-colored birds flitted about the solitary tree standing next to the hill. A few other tourist groups, clad in crisp new T-shirts and khaki suits covered with pockets, milled about with cameras tugging at their necks.

When Julian returned, Owen studied the rest of his party. What a motley group they made. Julian, with his perfectly kept short black hair and his narrow delicate face, wore a sly, worldly smile, and dressed like he was going clubbing. Wanjeri, a natural beauty with delicately twisted braids and slim but sturdy build, seemed equally comfortable in African and western clothes. Then there was Manish, an Indian who once roamed Manhattan in a taxi, now pulling water bottles from the Jeep. His helmet of jet-black hair remained unruffled despite the windy drive. Mrs. Pearson, who had moved from the cramped bench to perch on a rock, resembled the wife of a colonial prefect surveying the Queen's domain as she gazed out at the plains clutching a bottle.

Yet somehow, their little group worked out. Julian knew his way around, Manish endured humiliation to avoid imprisonment, or worse, and Mrs. Pearson contributed the requisite sense of entitlement. And Owen? He waited to fulfill his purpose. He pushed from his mind the discouraging things his father might say or any new barriers Mubego might place between them.

Manish unpacked the food. He was making money and being sociable, the two things he seemed to like best, yet he seemed nervous. He had never explained to Owen quite where he was heading on the bus that harrowing day, or why. Owen detected a shared restlessness—both men eager to return to their respective missions.

Owen wiped dirt from his face and examined his clothes—a polo shirt and Dockers. He looked like he was attending a church summer picnic. He felt even more out of place when two tall dark-skinned men, dressed in red garments draped over their shoulders and gripping spears in their hands, approached the tourists.

The men were trim and muscular, and as dark as burnt toast. One garment resembled a red plaid blanket. The other was solid red fringed with blue. One of them wore a metallic circular medallion on his forehead that reminded Owen of the round metal reflectors doctors wore on their heads in old movie scenes.

The men spoke to the tourists. One held his hand across his face until the portly white man attempting to shoot his photo took out his wallet.

"*Masai*," said Manish. "They charge $10 American for their picture. An outrageous sum of money for them, but a pittance for such tourists." Camera shutters clicked as a cluster of Asian tourists following a guide waving a flag handed the Masai men cash.

"Did you watch *Out of Africa*? It is about Kenya, set in Kenya. There are Masai in it," continued Manish. "They live in the wilderness with their cattle, but they earn extra cash from tourists."

"This economy depends too much on tourism," said Mrs. Pearson. "My office at the U.N. handled a program for a region to the north of here that financed improvements in agricultural export infrastructure."

"Do you know where all the U.N. money goes? Straight into the pockets of the bureaucrats," said Manish, waving his bottle. "None of it gets to the people."

Mrs. Pearson pressed her flat hand to her brow to shield her eyes from the sun as she stared at him. "Man-ISH, there are accounting reports, and I'm the one who filed them. This program escaped local corruption because I implemented the proper controls." She purposely pronounced his name wrong.

Manish opened his mouth to reply, but he spied Julian walking toward them.

As the *Masai* collected more ten-dollar bills from a group of blonde-haired, blue-eyed tourists, Owen listened to the "gnus" of thousands of bellowing wildebeest. All around, small birds chirped and whistled. The ground seemed to shift a little under the soles of his shoes. What a strange place, so different from his own world, and a challenge to his security and confidence. Lions ripping through steel car doors with razor-sharp claws. No hospitals, policemen or water for miles. People conversing in languages he didn't understand.

If only the other people around him showed the same unease in their eyes, or smelled faintly of dread, or crouched with their knees to their chins. That would make it easier for him to handle. Owen could rely on their validation of his fears and lean on them.

Mrs. Pearson sat content in the gentle breeze moderating the sun's heat, and Manish leaned on the Jeep and smoked a cigarette. The real tourists buried themselves in their field guides, recorded animal sightings and dispensed money for photos. None showed any sign of worry. Owen would have to cope alone with his fears. His anxiety would be met with no sympathy or understanding. It was just Owen, alone in this strange place with strange people. Even the zebras and wildebeest seemed unconcerned despite the lions hiding among them.

When the small party climbed back into the Jeep and continued east toward the distant line of hills, Owen closed his eyes. His skin turned damp and cold. He waited for his stomach to tighten and twist, and for tears to choke his throat while he struggled to breathe. The vehicle's motion over the bumpy road conjured recent memories of his bus trip, the charging elephant, and the robber with a knife.

Owen gripped his seat and focused on breathing through his nose, frightened that if he exhaled through his mouth, he would emit a cry like a small child awakening from a nightmare. He held on, the nausea rising up and down, punctuated by the bumps in the road his tightly clamped eyes could no longer anticipate. *Breathe in. Breathe out. Breathe in. Breathe …*

Slowly the nausea receded, and he knew it would be over soon. He was thankful Mrs. Pearson was out of his line of sight. If she saw him, she would know instantly what was happening. He would feel humiliated that he had not yet conquered his fears. Lions were one thing; feeling out of place and unsure of yourself was quite another.

He pulled the bottle of pills from his shirt pocket and took one, just to be sure. He kept his eyes closed until he felt the Jeep turn off the road—but then Julian stoked his anxiety a little more.

"Do you know what the most dangerous animal here is?" asked Julian. He pointed towards a grove of twisted acacia trees.

"Lion?" offered Manish.

"Buffalo."

Julian, who had spotted a group of buffalo ahead, timed his question for dramatic effect. A small herd of brown behemoths stood close to the road, a few eyeing the vehicle. Enormous backward-curving, crescent-shaped horns parted what looked like greasy hair down the middle of their heads.

"Buffalo kill the most people in Africa. They are large, and nervous. When they feel threatened, they attack and run. There are more buffalo than lions, and people are not sufficiently afraid of them. Therefore they are the most dangerous animal, on land. Some suspect it is the *kifaru*, but the hippo only kills people when they approach the river for water."

"But buffaloes don't eat lions," said Manish.

"I thought we would see dead animals and bones everywhere," said Mrs. Pearson, "and cheetahs chasing gazelles all over."

"Carcasses are rare to see," Wanjeri replied. "Large predators make a kill only every few days, maybe weeks. You have to follow the cat to see a kill unless you are lucky. Leopards catch things at night and hide them in trees. Then they devour the kill quickly. When the cats are satisfied, or larger animals chase them away as they sometimes do with cheetah kills, the hyenas and vultures eat every part of the animal, even bones, or carry them away and scatter them. They waste nothing. Even a species of eagle has learned to drop the bones from high in the air onto rocks so that they crack open and the eagle can eat the marrow."

Owen wiped the sweat from his forehead as his panic receded. Nobody noticed—sweating was normal in Africa.

***

At sunset, Owen joined Mrs. Pearson at the small folding table. He pictured hyenas crunching bones as he waited to see what Manish had cooked up.

The camp, the size of a softball field, rested inside a circle of low umbrella thorn trees—perfectly named for their shady habits and prickly branches. A small, simple wooden building painted dark red, labeled "Store," stood opposite the entrance, and ashes surrounded by a ring of rocks lay in the center. Several tourist groups had already driven in and claimed places for their tents. Most had Jeeps like theirs parked nearby. Owen could hear several languages and a few dialects of English trickling in from among the tents. A big truck pulled in and disgorged a group of tourists speaking excitedly in what sounded like Italian. The truck idled as they unloaded luggage and tents from the back.

A band of baboons marched right through the campsite. A small one sauntered near a camper's table, looking around and trying to appear innocent while edging toward the leftovers from dinner. It might as well have been whistling with its hands in its pockets, acting as nonchalant as a baboon can. Julian chased it off before it could grab any food, and it screeched and bounded toward its companions. Another pair of larger baboons shrieked and one jabbed and bit at the other until it ran out of the camp.

"You should not go outside your tent at night," said Julian as he set up one of their tents. "Dangerous animals. You are safe inside." Owen hadn't noticed until now—there was no fence around the camp. There was no barrier at all, only a few low trees to hide whatever animals lurked outside. He glanced at Mrs. Pearson. Her face showed no concern, but she was good at hiding things.

"No fence around the camp?" he asked.

"As Julian said, you'll be fine in your tent," she said.

"He told me the animals treat tents like cars. They see a tent and not anyone inside, so they don't bother you." She shrugged.

Could he learn how to handle stress by watching others handle it? He felt again for the pills in his shirt pocket.

Mrs. Pearson turned a page in the animal guidebook she carried everywhere and marked it with a pencil. "Good. I can add the olive baboon to my list. Maybe we'll see something else new. Julian lent me this book and I'm keeping a list of everything we see."

"I thought you told Col. Mubego you'd been here before."

"Yes, dear, but not out here in the bush. I never had time before. Just work work work."

A determined baboon stole a banana, creating mayhem when the others charged after it into the woods, chattering and squawking.

"The birds here are splendid," she said. "I never thought we'd see so many colorful birds. I looked them up in the book. Here is my list so far: the coqui francolin, Fischer's lovebird, lilac-breasted roller, helmeted guinea fowl and little bee-eater. Oh, we saw a black-headed heron too, let me mark him down. Red-necked spurfowl. Namaqua dove, a topi with a calf—that's not a bird. Blacksmith plover, brown parrot."

A group of young men with Australian accents wearing only shorts and boots built a fire in the ring.

"Vervet monkey. It goes under mammals," Mrs. Pearson continued, turning a page in her book. "Long-crested eagle. Yellow-billed stork, black grackle, Grant's gazelle, impala and waterbuck. And the lions. And look, we saw these things all over the place today. It's called the crowned crane. Their light blue eyes and spangled plumage make them so exotic-looking, but they aren't even rare. They're everywhere."

She held up the guide book with her finger and pointed to a stately bird which resembled a peacock topped with golden bristles. Owen recognized it. He had seen groups of them out on the plains when Julian pointed them out.

Owen chuckled when he realized the crowned crane bore a slight resemblance to Mrs. Pearson.

"And do you hear that bird sound?"

"Which one?"

"The *coo coooooo coo*. Over and over. It's called a ring-necked dove."

Owen listened, and it was familiar. He had heard it all day, in fact. It was the gentle, incessant song of the plains.

Manish came from the cooking fire behind their tent with a huge plate of brown rice mixed with vegetables and nuts. "This is called *biryani*. I hope you like it." She tucked her list in the book and put it aside. Owen watched as Manish carefully placed the large plate on the table in front of them. Having Manish, a dark-skinned person, serve him dinner made Owen feel strange. He rarely noticed when it happened back home. But this was a country populated almost entirely by dark people, and the incongruity of it all loomed larger. Mrs. Pearson didn't seem to mind. Was it because she saw nothing wrong with it? Or because she had been everywhere and was numb to the world's injustices?

Owen took a bite. "Wow, this is good. I didn't expect food like this in the middle of nowhere."

"I told you Indians are great cooks," said Manish. He lowered his voice. "Corn mush and mangoes and sausages are alright, but not as good as Indian food." Mrs. Pearson held her wine glass in her left hand as she ate with her right. They had put off dinner to scout for animals while the sun was still up, and it was now past eight with the sunlight fading. Mrs. Pearson's face softened in the low light. She was almost beautiful, but something held her beauty back. Not her sharp nose, or too-perfect hair—more as if she refused to reveal her full natural beauty, replacing it with studied grace and diplomatic dignity. Owen had seen her as warm, especially to his mother, and understanding, and even generous, but never quite real. He watched her chew the rice and down it with the wine as the light from the big bonfire in the center of the campsite steadily supplanted the sun's receding glow.

She waved down Manish with her upraised glass as he passed behind Owen. "Excuse me! Man-ISH! Could you get more wine please?" Then to Owen: "He really ought to watch my glass."

"He's not a waiter."

"He's getting paid to be one tonight."

"He is my friend first."

"A friend? How long have you known him?" Manish appeared with a bottle and filled her glass.

"I've known Manish as long as anyone else here but you."

"You met an angry elephant before you met me," said Manish. He filled the empty wine glass in front of Owen too.

"So, you're old enough to drink here, are you?" she said to Owen.

"Apparently," he said as he lifted the glass to drink the red wine. He was a little surprised at his boldness. But he was 18 and in a place of his own choosing, and he could do and say what he wanted, as long as his nerves went along.

"What happened with an angry elephant?" she asked.

"I got too close."

"Well, since there is no fence around this camp, you might get the chance again. You washed your hands, right?" she said to Manish.

"Always, madame," he said with exactly enough sarcasm.

"Our systems are more sensitive, you know—we haven't been exposed to all the diseases in the tropics." She was talking to Owen. "We can't afford to get a strange sickness out here. They would have to fly us out to a decent hospital."

"I've lived in the States, so I know how to wash my hands now, madame" said Manish, with more sarcasm this time. She still showed no sign she noticed or cared. "I'm civilized now," he added, but she still took no notice.

"Did you bring any white wine?" she asked. "I don't suppose it's chilled though, is it?"

"I might find a bottle in the camp store."

"Wine, not beer, please," she said to his back as he

headed to the tiny store on the other end of the camp.

"He is a good person."

"Wonderful. You tip him then." She smiled at him—to hedge her bet in case she wanted to say she was joking? But he knew her better than that. She was getting a little drunk and a little mean. It was time to get the truth out of her before she drank more.

"Why exactly did you follow me all this way, Mrs. Pearson?"

She drank another sip of wine, put her glass down, and crossed her arms, looking straight at him the whole time. "You know why. When your mother learned where you were going, it worried her like crazy. It wasn't so much that you came here, but you felt the need to go without telling her the truth about it."

"How did she find out I was here anyway?"

"Your brother figured it out."

Yes, of course, his brother. Keith was smart, and observant.

"Maybe I didn't tell her and Keith where I was going because I didn't want her to do something crazy, like, say, sending you to follow me."

"I didn't come to bring you back. That's not what your mother wants either."

"She doesn't?"

"She knows you. She knows you will do what you want. She knows how damn grown up you are. Hell, kid, you've always been ahead of your time. Look at you— across the Atlantic and in the middle of this place, all by yourself!"

He had never heard her say "hell" before. Or thought of himself as grown up. Or drank wine with her. He liked drinking in her presence—it made him an equal.

"Your mom wants you to know, well, everything there is to know about yourself. But she knows going on a trip to a strange place can bring a lot of stress, and we both know you have a problem with stress."

He had never spoken about his "stress" problem with Mrs. Pearson. It was like a big purple bump on his face—plain to see but no one is rude enough to acknowledge. But now she had said it out loud.

"It's not a problem with stress. It's panic attacks—feeling stress when it's not there, that's all."

"But a little stress can trigger it. That's how your mother described it."

"My mother doesn't know what it's like, and I don't need you telling me what it's like either." Owen dropped his fork and got up. He sat down near the campfire the Australian tourists had built. Mrs. Pearson followed and stood next to him.

"It was your mother's idea. She thought going to a strange place like this was bad enough, but then to see your father..."

"I don't have a single memory of seeing my father's face. But then I see his name in the newspaper. He's real, and I'm sitting at home doing nothing about it. You want stress? That was stress."

She said nothing.

"You're not my mom. You can't tell me what to do and you can't make me go home either. I'm 18 now."

"Funny, that makes you sound like a kid."

Owen scowled at her.

"Sorry," she said. "But no, your mother didn't send me here to make you go home. I'm not here to get in your way. I'll be here if you need me. I know the terrain; I know the people. And I know this Mubego character. He's slippery."

"So, you're here to help me?"

"Is that such an awful thing?"

Owen stood and turned to face her. The light from the fire and disappearing sun made her skin glow, like a ghost. "Let's make a deal," he said. "You stay out of my way, completely out of my way, like I don't even see you around, and you don't have to go home."

"That's not much of a deal for me, Owen."

"I can't make you leave, but I don't have to listen to you either. This place is different, and things are different. I don't need your help or my mother's help."

"You don't know your father."

Owen waited for her to say more, but she simply stared at him, her thin lips pursed.

"Yeah, and? That's why I came over here."

"And ... you may find out you wish you never came."

"I guess I'll find out as soon as we get out of this zoo and back to Kumbata and I finally get inside the damn prison."

"You are a lot like your father, I'll tell you that."

Her comment made him angry and proud at the same time.

"Here's the deal, Owen. Your mom and I, and your

brother, we all think you should come home. We think you'll be better off at home. Your mom, she's thrilled you came out of your room, but maybe this wasn't the best way to do it."

She drank down the rest of her wine.

"So, she wants you to know she found a great school for you, a college, where she thinks you'll be happy and she'll pay for it and you can go there as long as you need to. And you can live there, or at home, your choice. It's a great opportunity."

"A college?"

"Well, it's more like a prep school."

"Come on. I know what's going on. She already tried this. My mom wants to send me to a mental institution. No way."

"Oh, please, Owen, it's just a school."

"No way."

"So, what? You sit and wait for the fat Colonel to let you see your father rotting in prison? Then what? What kind of plan for life is that?"

"It's not a plan. I have no plan. I plan to sit by the fire and drink wine the rest of my life. Tell her that."

"And you will sleep out here every night? With lions and bears and whatever all around you with nothing but a thin tent to protect you? How's that going to work, Owen? You have to deal with your reality. You have a problem, and you can't fix it overnight."

"Maybe not, but I can fix it without your help."

She sighed. "So be it. I tried."

The camp was in full darkness now, and the only light

remaining came from the bonfire, the camp store's light and more stars than Owen had ever seen in his life. Out on the savannah, the lions began their evening ritual of warning other lions away from their territory and calling any stragglers in their own pride to come home. From several directions, nervous and excited tourists could hear male leaders of prides bringing forth great rumbling bellows, followed by short punctuating grunts: "*Uhhhhhhhh! Uh. Uh. Uh. Uh.*"

Guidebook and wine glass in hand, Mrs. Pearson gathered her shirt to her chest against the coming chill and stood. "Please don't resent me, Owen."

"Don't give me a reason to," he said as he stood and headed for the camp store.

A half-hour later, he was drunk. The store stocked plenty of semi-cool beers they sold to him without asking for an ID. He wasn't sure what the drinking age was anyway, or if there was one. He drank four beers while sitting on a crate by the fire listening to two Australians talk about their day spent looking for leopards. He was already an experienced drinker of beer. Keith had supplied him with it sometimes, and after he shut himself in his room, Keith had brought him beer one night when their mom was out, to coax him to the basement. It didn't work. He made Keith leave the beer outside the door so he could fetch it and drank it all in his room.

To the light of the fire, Owen studied the bottle. It was Tusker, a local brew. There was an elephant with huge tusks on the label. *Fucking elephants are even on their beer.*

Why the hell does she have to know so much about his panic problem? His mom shared too much with her. And even if she does, she should pretend not to and keep her nose out of his business. She followed him across an ocean to babysit him?

Owen sat at the bonfire with the Aussies, the last of the tourists still awake. It was easy to position himself with strangers in the dark, easier still after four Tuskers. Maybe beer was better than the medication for calming him down. He felt stronger, bolder. He ran his fingers through his hair, sticky from the day's sweat. The evening air was cooler. A mosquito buzzed around his ear and he slapped it away. He lay back on the hard-packed soil and watched glowing sparks from the fire float toward the sky. Away from the oppressive glow of the city, he could see stars he never knew existed. Funny how you can see more with less light.

Unless something went wrong with the bureaucrats above Mubego's head, he would see his father soon. And that was all that mattered. He had gathered the courage to come this far, and a nosy, self-assured, 5-foot-5 lady would not change anything.

A tourist sitting by the fire played a guitar. Owen felt himself slipping into sleep, but he caught himself and got up to get to the safety of his tent. He saw the glow of a cigarette next to the tents. It was Manish, his dark face only visible when he brought the cigarette to his lips.

"Do you know which tent is mine?"

Manish pointed with his cigarette to the one right next to him. "Your friend is kind of bitchy," he said.

"She can be a problem."

"I had plenty of bitchy people in the back of my cab, but her ..."

"She might hear you."

"Let her."

Owen crawled into his tent and lay down on the low cot, pulling off his shoes. Manish kept talking to him through the tent. "Do you think they will let you see your father?"

"Yeah, I do."

"It's never that easy in Africa."

The tent was spinning a little, but Owen gripped the sides of the cot.

"Even for a white man, it's never that easy," Manish added, and walked away.

Owen lay looking outside the tent for a while, watching the tourists slowly abandon the dying fire.

He spied Wanjeri coming toward him, holding a towel. She caught his eye for a moment as she got close enough to see him in the shadows. She seemed ready to say something to him, but she only smiled and disappeared into her tent.

The lions sent their signals: "*Uhhhhhhh! Uh. Uh. Uh. Uh.*"

23

Wanjeri couldn't sleep. She left her tent and headed for the communal campfire where a half-dozen resilient Australians remained awake, beers in hand, one strumming a guitar. She stood near the fire and listened to a song she did not recognize. It was getting chilly; the fire felt just right.

She looked at all the white faces glowing in the light of the fire. Most were quiet, enjoying the moment.

White people will say anything. Wanjeri still could not decide if it was a flaw or a virtue. They hide little of their opinions and tell you how they feel about anything that comes to their minds. Wanjeri saw it in whites in Kenya, and again in London and America.

On the one hand, *wazunga* sounded so whiny sometimes. Every little setback seemed to bother them. Even when they came from freezing wet Europe to the pleasant, sunny weather of Africa, surrounded by hospitality, some of them found reasons to complain. Was it just that they were used to pampered lives?

Wanjeri thought that was the case until she went to study in England. There, she learned that not all whites are rich. She saw rows of modest slums full of modest people, and she even witnessed white people begging in the streets! She had seen plenty of beggars in Nairobi but almost never a white beggar. Perhaps only the rich whites had the wealth to come vacation in Africa and whine about things. Or perhaps the ability to share your feelings so easily was part of something larger.

Maybe it was freedom. After all, white people shared their joy as readily as their irritation. She had seen plenty of both from Mrs. Pearson that day, as she marveled at the sight of so many colorful birds, but then treated Manish like a dog.

Wanjeri was stunned to hear the low whistle call of an African Hoopoe bird right behind her. "Hoop-hoop-hoop."

She turned to look, and there stood Julian, smiling mischievously.

"That's a good imitation," she said. "You had me fooled."

He sat down next to her. "I thought you were sleeping," she said.

"I thought I was too."

"I was just looking at the stars. You can't see them as well in the city. In London you can hardly see anything except the full moon."

"It's funny you had to go all the way to England to learn about elephants that are right here, don't you think?"

"Yes, I noticed that. I was considering founding a new education center here to change that."

"Uncle Mubego could help you do that."

"I can do it without his help." A little too much contempt in her voice.

"He means well."

"He doesn't like elephants anyway, because they hurt Uncle Abasi," she said. "And maybe he doesn't like me either, because I was with Uncle Abasi when the elephant did that to him."

"He doesn't blame you for what an animal did to Abasi."

"Perhaps I am to blame though. If it weren't for me ...."

"No. It wasn't you. I don't blame you either."

If only he knew what had really happened. But she could not say the truth. Abasi, their uncle, tried to rape his own niece? It would shame Abasi—if Julian and Mubego even believed her.

"Look, it's Keith!" said Julian. He pointed to Owen's face among those gathered around the fire in the darkness. Julian was showing off that he knew about Owen using his brother's passport. He was also, Wanjeri thought, probably warning her that Owen was there, within earshot. It was just like something Mubego would do, to hint he was one step ahead. Julian was learning too much from Uncle Mubego, she thought. Mubego will ruin him.

They both got up and took seats next to Owen by the fire. "Did you enjoy the day?" she asked him.

Owen turned to see her face and then turned back to

staring into the fire. "Most of it, yes. Manish made great food."

"I thought you went in your tent."

"The music woke me," Owen said.

Wanjeri wondered why Manish was chosen as cook—to humiliate him further? Or why they were on this safari, for that matter. Or why her uncle asked her to join the safari, since Julian could handle the job of guide well enough on his own. And why did he ask her to listen to what everyone said, implying she would report back to him? Her presumed role as his spy made her even more uncomfortable about asking this young white man anything about himself or why he was here. But perhaps talking to Owen would reveal what her uncle was up to.

She resolved then to be direct, like a white person. Even with Julian listening.

"I have a question," she announced.

"Alright," Owen said.

"You aren't a tourist."

"That's not in the form of a question. But no, I'm not really. You want to know why I'm here?"

Yes, I do, she thought. No, I want to confirm what I already know.

"My uncle is a mysterious man," Wanjeri said, carefully in front of Julian. "He is always up to something, and never quite telling me what it is. I'm used to that. He has his business, and I have mine."

"Alright."

"My sister was just wondering," interjected Julian,

"what a young man your age was doing here, alone. It can be dangerous out here."

Julian seemed concerned she had taken control of extracting information from Owen. But she pressed on.

"He's not alone," Wanjeri said. "And when I was his age, I was out here in the bush all alone sometimes."

"You had Abasi with you though, until those dirty beasts stomped on his head. I don't know what you see in them." When Wanjeri did not reply, he stood without a word and went back to their camp.

"See, he blames me. He is angry at me about Abasi," she told Owen, "because I was there when he was hurt. Even if he says he doesn't, I can tell."

"You were there? How could it be your fault? It was the elephant's fault."

"It was a very unusual incident. The elephant suddenly attacked, and he thinks I could have stopped it."

It hurt her to keep up this lie, and to blame it all on her beloved elephants, but that was the only thing she could think of when it happened, and now it was too late to change her explanation. No, all she could do is stick to the story—and to hope Abasi never recovered enough to speak about it.

Wanjeri felt a strange, disturbing power that moment. It was the power of knowing a secret important to someone else. Then the feeling made her ashamed—it was the same feeling Uncle Mubego thrived on.

"I know elephants can be, well, unpredictable. That elephant that nearly attacked me on the way here,"

Owen said. "Coming from the airport, I mean. I was outside and it charged me." She noticed beer on his breath.

"It was just warning you."

"I guess."

"If it wanted to kill you, it would have."

"I guess. So, Abasi is your uncle too?"

"Yes."

"And so is Mubego?"

"Yes. And Julian is my younger brother. Uncle Mubego took us both in when our parents died. Julian is learning things from Uncle Mubego, like he was his own father."

"Do you remember your parents?"

"Oh, yes. I remember many things." They both stared at the fire for a while.

"I remember almost nothing about my dad, and he's still alive."

"I hope you'll see him soon."

She was about to tell him she knew his father too, but she let it go. Another deception she must live with.

"Are you going to be okay in the tent? With the animals around?" she asked.

"Why do you ask?"

"That lady, Mrs. Pearson—she said you might go crazy in the night from the animals. Don't worry, they never go inside tents."

"I should be OK." With beer and his pills, he should be OK, he meant.

Owen grabbed another beer and downed it inside

his tent to knock himself out before he could prove Mrs. Pearson right and run terrified into the night. He wrapped himself in the sleeping bag, head to toe, and crawled under the cot to pass out.

24

"Don't go near that guy."

It was the plainest and most resolute Mrs. Pearson had ever heard Danvers speak. Danvers was such a careful diplomat, always talking around things and saying as little as possible with as many words as possible.

"What's wrong with him?"

"He's trouble. His name is Mubego, and he's hard to pin down. His name shows up in just about every squabble in Kenya over the years, and somehow he always comes out ahead no matter whose side he's on."

Mubego was from Kenya? Mrs. Pearson sized him up. He looked like all the other two-bit African strongmen and strongmen-to-be in the room—tight-fitting white uniform weighed down with medals. Like so many of them, he had the polished look of someone whose life had started out poor and hot and tough, but had fought his way to money and power. Still, his name sounded familiar. And he was a bigshot in Kenya. Maybe he could help her.

These international conferences were affairs where minor third-world potentates were supposed to pretend they cared about what western powers wanted so they could keep sucking grants and investments out of them. They played along, barely hiding their discomfort. But Mubego seemed to enjoy it all. He was smiling and laughing.

"Now, Danvers, you know I'm attracted to trouble." she said. Mrs. Pearson felt the hair on her neck stand up. Maybe that was true.

Danvers frowned the most disapproving frown he could muster. "This is supposed to be a conflict prevention conference, so don't start one."

"Ah, no, my dear friend, I believe this is a conflict *resolution* conference. You can't resolve conflict before you start one." She winked at him. "Don't worry, I won't cause trouble; I'm going to meet people who will help us end conflict. Like you're supposed to be doing."

Mubego couldn't have been kinder. "So pleasant to meet you," he told her. "I hope you are enjoying the weather on our continent." He took her hand and bowed slightly, formally, like they were at a ball, which she kind of liked.

"It's wonderful, thank you." It was actually horrible.

"Good. Have we met before?" he asked suddenly.

"I don't believe so."

"No? But your name, it is familiar."

"I can't imagine why."

She saw him searching his memory. "You have had some business, some correspondence, with the Kenyan government?"

"Why, yes, but not in an official capacity. I recently inquired about a prisoner held there, an American."

"Ah, yes."

"Do you know anything about that case?"

"No... nothing. But I think your letters may have crossed my desk, that's all."

"I see."

"In fact, I believe they are still on my desk. And I might be able to help you after all. I'm always eager to help my international colleagues who are equally eager to help me."

"I would be interested in discussing it further," she said.

"Then we will." Mubego gazed across the room for a moment, searching for someone, and then looked down at her. "So, tell me, Mrs. Pearson, have you resolved any conflicts at this conflict resolution meeting yet?"

"None, I'm afraid. Have you?"

"Not today. But I have resolved a few in my time. In my own special way."

"And what way is that?"

"By winning them, of course."

She understood then why Danvers feared Mubego. But she liked him. He was dry and clever, like she was. He was probably mean as hell and lying through his teeth, but she liked him nonetheless.

"Hmm. Do you always win conflicts?"

"One way or the other."

* * *

Wanjeri's uncle took full advantage of the spoils of his new job as head of the prison. He bought a house in Kumbata and brought prisoners in to improve it. They painted it inside and out and built a lovely courtyard around some banana trees, creating a little green oasis stretching all the way between the walls. But Wanjeri was still surprised to see this prisoner at her uncle's house. Instead of working on his house or acting as a servant like other prisoners sometimes did, this man was sitting with Mubego at the table in the courtyard. They were both drinking Tusker. No other prisoner enjoyed such treatment.

They both stood when she entered the courtyard. Her uncle wore his uniform, and the prisoner sported the simple grey shirt and pants all the prisoners wore, but Mubego introduced him like an equal. "Wanjeri, my dear, this is Karl. He is an old friend." Karl shook her hand.

Karl's face betrayed a few years in the sun. His body filled out the standard prison outfit well. He was fit and able despite the prison food. His hair was cut very short like a military man's.

And he was white.

"Very pleased to meet you, Mr. Karl." And she took the seat Mubego offered and the glass of juice his butler brought.

"Give her a beer, Mubego," said Karl. "Come on."

"Wanjeri does not like the taste of beer much," said

Mubego. "I already knew that. I'm always one step ahead of you, Karl."

"You like to think that."

Wanjeri had never heard a prisoner talk to her uncle like this, or anyone else. She wanted to know who this strange *mzunga* was and why he was a prisoner, and an "old friend," but she knew enough not to ask such questions directly of her uncle.

"Actually, I'd like a beer, please."

"Ho! This is my Wanjeri—always finding a way to make me wrong!"

"See, you're not ahead of me," said Karl. "Wanjeri–very pretty name, by the way–what made you change your mind?"

"I saw how much fun the both of you are having with your beers."

Mubego motioned toward the house. Wanjeri watched as another of Mubego's prisoners, an Indian man with deep black hair, came out of the doorway. "Three beers, Manish," said Mubego. The man went back inside without a hint of change in the expression on his face.

"We've had a great deal of beers and a great deal of fun with them," Mubego continued, "over the years."

"True, but I've had a few more beers and a lot more fun because your uncle can't hold his beer without passing out."

This was too much. Who was this man, a prisoner who could boldly make fun of the fierce Mau Mau hero?

"You have a very unsteady memory, my friend! I

believe you were drunk at the time so you are not a reliable witness of events."

"How long have you two known each other?" She wanted to ask Karl the question, but it was safer to open it to them both. But Mubego let Karl answer.

"We fought together. Many years ago."

"Yes. And fighting begets drinking. And drinking begets stories."

"Can I hear one of those stories?"

Karl took a long drink of his beer and finished it. "I don't have any stories from those days suitable for a lady's ears," he said.

"Oh, Wanjeri is no innocent. She's an educated woman. She's at university in London."

"Really? What kind of education?"

"Zoology. I am studying elephants."

"Is that so? There is a very, very large elephant who has taken an interest in me," said Karl. "He comes to visit me almost every night, at my window, in my current place of residence."

Wanjeri took a sip of her beer. She really didn't like the taste of beer much. "Your elephant sounds like an older male, past mating age."

"How do you know?"

"The young males go out alone and stay to themselves unless there's a female ready to mate, all of their lives. The females stay together but the males go it alone. It's a lonely existence. When the males get old, they stop roaming, and sometimes they seek companions again."

"That sounds about right. This old elephant and I

have a lot in common." Karl looked down at the table, and Wanjeri saw a little sadness in his eyes. Mubego was smiling at him, with a face she had never seen on her uncle before. It was strange to see him so excited about someone. It was so personal. Mubego's wife had died so long ago, before independence, when Wanjeri was a little girl, and he had never remarried. He had no children of his own. Wanjeri had watched him build a wall around himself as he rose in power, making him more distant and unapproachable, intimidating, even to his family. He still smiled and laughed as usual, but talking to him felt more and more difficult. The further he rose, the lonelier he became. Yet this white American, this prisoner in rags, made her uncle happy, even a little vulnerable. It pleased her to see the effect this man had on him even if she did not understand it.

And the *mzunga* prisoner seemed satisfied with it too, for a prisoner. He was obviously a likable fellow, but her uncle wouldn't fetch just any likable fellow out of a cell and into his courtyard, only to let the prisoner insult him for laughs. They must have been good friends long before prison. Perhaps she would never completely understand this strange pairing, but she decided that she could like Karl too.

"I have a story for you," she said to Karl. "Not a drinking story. An elephant story."

25

They rode back to Mubego's house mostly in silence. Manish sulked; Owen mentioned he had a hangover to excuse his own unresponsiveness. He had drunk a few beers in his life, but he was not yet as experienced in hangover recovery. That left Julian to point out new animal finds along the road and Mrs. Pearson to listen. Owen closed his eyes and concentrated on relieving his budding headache before the road got bumpier. The ride lulled him to sleep, but he almost jumped when he heard Wanjeri call out an animal sighting.

"Elephant."

The Jeep had turned a curve around a large *kopje* ringed by trees and stopped. There stood a huge, nearly black bull elephant smack in the middle of the road. Two pristine white tusks thrust from the creature's skull, their tips almost touching. His belly was round but his legs were massive bales of muscle. He showed no sign that he cared he was blocking traffic.

"It's a lone male," said Wanjeri.

A lone male like the elephant that nearly trampled me on the bus trip, thought Owen.

Flapping his giant ears to cool himself, the elephant was completely at ease. He cared nothing about lions or other elephants or Jeeps. He was sleek and majestic—and he was crying. Mrs. Pearson saw the "tears" first. Sure enough, under each eye was a streak of wet. Wanjeri laughed. "Those are not tears! He is in musth," she said. "It means he's ready to mate. Be careful, Julian."

"I know," he replied. He backed up the Jeep a little.

The giant rummaged through the low-slung trees, stripping leaves and stuffing them daintily in his mouth with a swing of his trunk, completely ignoring his audience. They watched every massive movement, from the pounding stomp of the foot to the delicate, facile picking of choice leaves with the remarkable trunk.

"Males in musth can be very unpleasant," Wanjeri said. "We need to be careful."

The Aussies apparently were not aware of this. On their way out of camp too, their vehicle pulled up behind. Apparently, they had seen this big fellow before, or were too cool to be bothered with him. They waited a moment, then pulled around and sped quickly past the beast, behind it. With only narrow clearance between the animal and the trees, they almost touched him.

Too late to do any damage, the great bull spun around toward them in fear, getting only a face full of dust. Then, as if taking his frustration out on Owen's group, he turned right at the Jeep and let out the loudest noise Owen had ever heard. He trumpeted, with his chin up and trunk coiled out, and the sound seemed to fill the entire sky. It was a sound you feel, not just hear. It echoed from the hills that were barely visible on the horizon. Owen remembered how the sound of the elephant that nearly attacked him outside the bus echoed the same way.

The elephant was nodding its huge head up and down, back and forth, the tusks threatening to shear apart anything near them. Its ears waved in distress.

Owen opened his door and got out.

"What the hell are you doing?" he heard someone yell. Owen looked the elephant in the eye and cursed it.

"Go to hell, you fucking animal! Get the fuck out of here!"

He shooed it with his arms. The animal trumpeted again, making Owen jump involuntarily, but he still stood his ground.

"Fuck you! Fuck you! Fuck you!" Owen spit the words and every muscle in his body tensed.

The elephant stood still for a moment, as if it was unsure what to do next, and then it turned and ran into the bush.

Owen took a deep breath and walked back to the car with a swagger, staring directly at Mrs. Pearson the entire time. "Are you crazy?" she was saying. "Are you crazy?" He glimpsed Wanjeri's face. She was smiling.

He squeezed back into the vehicle and said nothing. Yes, Owen thought, I'm crazy. But for the first time in a long time, he felt the opposite of crazy. He felt confident, and in control, and calm. Confront your fears! No, he wasn't going home to some special school for nutcases, and he wasn't going home to live in his room forever.

26

"I learned an American phrase once," Mubego said. "It is: 'I have good news and I have bad news.'"

Owen watched as Mubego puffed on a cigarette. He had summoned Owen to the courtyard where he sat adorned in a neat white shirt—comfortable in the heat, yet formal enough, in the African style. Julian brought everyone gin-and-tonics, including Owen, but he wasn't interested in drinking now. Owen rubbed his hair, happy to be clean after spending a day in the heat of the savannah without a morning shower, and wondered what the bad news was.

"The good news is I have secured the approval for you to visit your father at Kumbata Prison," continued Mubego.

Mrs. Pearson knew what was next. She stepped into the conversation from her perch on the stone bench under the banana trees, clutching her drink.

"What does he have to provide for the privilege?"

"I am afraid it will require a payment of cash to my

superior in Nairobi. I tried to prevent this, but I was unsuccessful."

"I'm sure you tried." She mixed in enough sarcasm for Owen to understand but not to offend Mubego. Owen got the meaning: the Colonel not only did not object to the bribe; he probably will get a cut. Or maybe he will get all of it, and Nairobi will hear nothing about the whole affair.

"It is a rather large sum, I'm afraid," Mubego continued. "My superior demands $200 U.S. cash."

Owen swallowed a laugh at Mubego's idea of a "rather large sum." And for once, Mrs. Pearson kept it to herself too. If Mubego knew how low it was, he might increase it. It was a great deal of money in Kenya though.

"I don't have that kind of money with me," said Owen. It was technically true.

"That is understandable. You can get it at a bank in Nairobi. There are no banks in Kumbata that would be capable of giving you that much in U.S. funds."

"I have to go back?"

"My superior will allow you to visit your father while someone else fetches the money, if you are willing."

Nobody spoke.

"I have an excellent solution," Mubego said. It was clear this was where he'd been leading all along. Mubego leaned his ample weight back in his chair so it creaked. "Our friend," he said, twisting his thumb toward Manish without looking at him, "is someone you trust who knows this country. He will go. I will even compensate him for his effort. And to keep an eye on him to assure he returns with the money, and provide him with transportation, he will travel with you, in your car," he said, turning to Mrs. Pearson. He stood quickly and went inside with Julian at his heel before anyone could disagree.

"That would be fine," she said, even though he was already out of earshot. Then to Owen and Manish: "My driver is camped out in the back, and he should be ready to go any time."

Owen stared at her, amazed. "You have a driver... camped out this whole time?"

"Certainly, dear."

"And you were paying him the whole time?"

"Of course."

"Is the United Nations paying for ..." but she cut him off.

"Owen, you're good at math. You got straight As in algebra, right? The driver and car costs eight American dollars a day. Eight for both car and driver, for a whole day. It would cost more to take a bus and stay in hotels, or rent a car and drive it myself at the crazy prices the foreign rental car companies charge."

Owen said nothing. He hadn't thought about it like that.

"I know my way around. I'm off to pack and then your friend and I can have a lovely drive to the bank and you can find out what your father is like and go home." She pulled a silk scarf from her handbag and covered her hair as she turned to go inside.

"Thank you for doing this, Manish," Owen said.

"It is no problem. It gives me transport back home

to see my wife, at least for a while, and some money to show for the trip so she will not beat me with her tongue."

"You don't mind being in a car with her?"

"I'll manage her fine," he said. "As long as I can leave this place for a while."

"I wonder if Mubego will take some money."

"He does not care for money," said Manish, opening his arms to the grand house as evidence. "I doubt he even told anyone in Nairobi about you. He is sending me for the money because he wants me away from you. Me, and perhaps her as well."

"Why?"

"He wants control. He was using the safari to spy on you, to check you out, and now he wants to have you on your own."

"That's okay with me," Owen said. "I came here on my own. I can handle myself." It felt great to say those words out loud.

"I am sure. I only hope no wild animals come too close to you. For their sake." Manish gave Owen an awkward wink and squinted his brown eyes against the sun.

"Don't worry, Manish, there won't be any wild animals in the prison."

"Don't be so sure," replied Manish, without the wink this time.

***

Kumbata Prison felt strangely placid. The plastered walls, the high ceilings, and the open-air design gave it the feeling of a remote vacation spot. And though it shared a name with the bustling little town, the prison was a mile from the town center, in a patch of humble foothills harboring a few trees overlooking the scratch-dusted plain. He could have walked there the first day if given the chance.

Only the short wall topped by a high iron fence surrounding the front courtyard, joining the building at the corners, gave it away as a prison. In the back, there was no fence or wall, only a stretch of bare ground between the building and the forest edge.

A guard saluted and stiffened as sharply as he could manage as Mubego's car entered the front gate, dust slapping the guard's stoic face.

That was when Owen's excitement about the meeting yielded to doubt. Was he really ready for this? In his haste to get on the plane, he had packed little but a few clothes and the newspaper clipping mentioning his father. No pictures of Mom or his brother; no care package for a prisoner. He had not planned what he would say. Owen had never imagined actually meeting him. He dared not.

To Owen, the building seemed smaller than it looked from the outside. Perhaps it was the wide empty spaces inside or the flow of air. Mubego led Owen up a set of stairs and down a hall to an office on the second floor with a concrete floor and the word "Administrator" painted on the door. Though the windows stood open, the sun streamed into the room and made it hotter than in the hallway. The room held nothing more than a cheap desk with a few papers, a cabinet, a decaying black sofa and a mini refrigerator. If Mubego spent much time there, it wasn't to work.

Mubego motioned for Owen to sit on the couch and pulled two bottles of water from the refrigerator. A man in uniform put his head in the door, spoke to Mubego in a strange language and then left. The Colonel's huge wooden office chair creaked under his weight. The water was nice and cold.

"This prison only holds 34 inmates, though we could fit 110," he said. "Most of the ones here are convicted of special crimes that need my extra attention."

Owen took another drink of the cold water, and then the man returned and spoke more in the strange language. Mubego gestured to the man to lead Owen away, and Owen followed the man back down the stairs into a bare room exactly like his office but with only an empty table and a few chairs to decorate it. In one chair sat the man in the photos of his father.

"God Almighty, I will never forget that face," the man said.

Owen was confused. "You know my face?"

"It's not your face I see, it's your mother's. You ever see this face before?" He lifted a ragged finger to his cheek.

"Only in pictures."

"Exactly. Because when you look in the mirror, you see your mother's face, not mine. You got it. Good thing, too, don't you think? You wouldn't want mine."

Owen studied him. His dark brown eyes dove deep, like he could move things with them, but they did not threaten. He wore his hair in a short military-style cut, revealing the rigid muscles reaching from his cheekbones to his skull. His shoulders and chest expressed his military bearing though his body had worn thinner than his prime days. He sat with both hands on the table, palms down, as if ready to stand up at any time. He sat still, but tightly wound. Owen knew he was in his late 50s, but he looked no older than 35 or 40. Only the tough, weathered backs of his hands hinted at his true age.

Owen thought he looked a great deal like his father.

"Happy birthday."

"Thanks."

"I didn't forget."

"You forgot to send a card."

"Damn, you're sarcastic like me. I like that."

Owen didn't know what to say.

"You're 18 now, right? You could sign up for the military. You ever think about a career in the military?"

"No."

"Yeah, you probably shouldn't. Didn't do much for me, did it? Hey, how far did you come to see me?"

"It was 17 hours flying time altogether."

"I meant how far, how many miles. I think in miles. Do the math."

The question took Owen by surprise, but his father just stared, waiting for the answer. He was serious. So Owen quickly picked a few numbers and multiplied 17 by 500 miles an hour in his head. Owen could do figures under pressure. But here, it made him feel like a kid in boot camp quizzed by a drill sergeant.

"About 850 miles, I mean 8,500."

Karl Dorner let out a broad smile, his first, and slammed his left palm on the table.

"Good miles! I, on the other hand, have traveled 196,000 miles by air, and 117,000 by land. I've walked, ran, crawled, or marched 4,000 miles in Africa alone."

He was looking at Karl Dorner's hands, which still lay neatly on the table, palms down. He realized he was still standing, so he took the other chair and scooted far back enough to look into this man's eyes comfortably. This was going to be stranger than he expected.

"I've kept up with you, Owen. You're as smart as your old dad. You skipped a grade in middle school, right, because you were so damn smart?"

"Yes." How did he know that?

"Did you know in most languages, the word for an animal and the word for the animal's meat are the same? You just eat pig, or chicken. In English, the animal is a chicken, but the meat is poultry because the French ran England after the Norman Conquest. The English tended to the lambs, but the French ate the mutton."

"I didn't know that."

"Of course not. You don't know shit, you're a kid. You should read history instead of comic books or whatever kids read. Maybe you shouldn't have skipped a grade. Say, Mubego should be keeping you by now. How do you like that house of his?"

"It's … great."

"He's an odd fellow, Mubego. He has his own staff followed sometimes, but he'll let you walk around his house while nobody's home. And God knows you can't be trusted, especially now, after you've talked to me."

Owen didn't want that to be true. Instead of asking why, he gathered himself and started asking the questions.

"Do you want to know about Mom?"

"Oh, she didn't want to know anything about me, so I think it's best if we leave that alone."

"Did you try to contact her after ...?"

"Not exactly. But people contacted her on my behalf, without my permission. That was after she sent Old Lady Pearson to check on me. I guess she didn't give me a glowing review."

"Mrs. Pearson came here to visit you?"

"Yeah. A year after I landed here. She sat in the same chair you're in now."

Owen swallowed and tried not to show any reaction to that bit of news. Mrs. Pearson met him here? Before Owen did? She had never mentioned a word to him. But Karl Dorner must have read his face.

"Did she tell you about me?"

"I didn't listen." Karl Dorner did not know she was here in Kenya now, and Owen wasn't interested in talking about her. This was his time, not hers. Owen changed the subject back to his mother.

"Mom never married again or even tried to divorce you, you know."

"No, I don't know, because she did try to divorce me, but she's obviously not telling you everything, so let's preserve the illusions she gave you."

"Maybe ... maybe she didn't tell me everything. Or lied

to me. So what?" Owen was trying to think about what she might have said.

"Sure, so what? How about you, ever lie about me?"

"I told kids in school you died in a war."

"Ah, very good. There you go. And you told them I was some big hero, right?"

Owen didn't reply.

"Of course you did. So things are better that way. Why dig too deep? Reality is a bitch."

Karl Dorner finally relaxed. He leaned back in his chair, locked his muscular fingers behind his muscular head, and let out a deep sigh. He put his feet up on the table. His rough-skinned toes stuck out at odd angles from simple rubber sandals, worn and bent from all that walking.

"Are you mad at her for that?" asked Owen.

"What right do I have to be mad at her? I'm the traitor, remember? And back then, being a traitor meant so much more. It's lost its aura today. You just can't find good old-fashioned traitors."

Owen suppressed his impatience. He would not let his first, and perhaps only, meeting with his very own father be ruined because the man chose to irritate him or toy with him or not take anything seriously. So Owen changed the subject again.

"What do you do in here?"

"Eat, drink, shit, piss, jerk off, talk to elephants, smoke cigarettes, sleep. Same crap I did out in the bush as a soldier. Oh, and hunt. Now I hunt smaller game though—spiders and centipedes mostly."

Talk to elephants? Owen didn't ask.

"Oh, and sometimes I tell elaborate stories to all the sweaty convicts I live with about my adventures as a great white game hunter, mercenary for the African National Congress, Chief Executive Officer of AT&T, and ice fisherman in Minnesota. They buy it all. Did you know most Africans have never seen ice? Ice cream or an ice cube once or twice in their life, but never a real chunk of stick-to-your-tongue ice. You get the occasional prison guard who's used a freezer or worked in an ice cream store. There's an old guy, must be 150, who says he climbed Mt. Kilimanjaro specifically to see the glaciers. Freaked him out. I told him sticking his dick in solid ice for an hour makes it get harder. It's true, isn't it? It's not technically a lie. He's a lifer—killed somebody in a bank robbery—so he won't see ice ever again, but I'll bet he's told some friends out in the world, and they're all walking around sticking their cocks in snow cones right now!"

Owen's father let out a healthy laugh. He seemed to enjoy being a heartless, evasive jerk when Owen needed him to be the opposite.

"You know, the Africans think we're as crazy for living up north as we think they are for stewing in this pile of dust."

Owen was suddenly angry. "Why haven't you asked about Keith and mom?"

Karl put one hand on his cheek. "I already know what …"

"You don't know anything about us because the letters always come back unopened!" Owen was surprised by the outburst.

"I don't ... I don't get mail here. Mubego's orders." But Owen could see it was more than that.

They both sat in silence. Owen didn't know what to say. It seemed such a waste of time, to sit with his own father after all these years but say nothing.

Karl broke the silence. "Did your mother ever try to come visit me in person, like this?"

"No."

Karl didn't ask why. Owen didn't offer a reason.

"What do you mean, you talk to elephants?" asked Owen.

"What?"

"You said you talk to elephants."

Karl Dorner paused, taking back control. "They come to visit me. Out back." He jerked his thumb toward the rear of the prison house.

"And you talk to them?"

"Sure do. I speak their language. I've had plenty of time to learn it. I'm a fucking Tarzan."

"What do you say?"

"I mostly say 'thank you,' because they do all the talking. They tell me all the secrets of the elephants. Like elephants are stronger and better than humans. And I say 'thank you,' because they're right, and I needed to know that. Keeps me from slipping up and having too much respect for people. People basically suck."

The elephants talked to him? Was he crazy or pretending to be?

Owen suddenly felt hopeless in the situation. There

were only two possibilities. Either his father would live up to his dreams, or not. If he didn't, Owen would wish he'd never jumped on the plane and rushed across the globe without thinking things through. If he did, Owen would wish he could take his father out of prison and bring him home. There was no way to win.

No, there was a third possibility—he could keep Owen guessing, which would leave him where he was before he came here.

"Are you sure you never thought about joining the military, son?"

Though he called Owen "son," it was more like an older man using it with a younger man to remind him who is in charge.

"No."

"Good. Don't. There's no future in it. Look at me."

Owen struggled for something meaningful to talk about. What exactly do you say to the father you meet for the first time, in prison? "I could ... is there anyone you want me to tell anything to? Back home? Any messages?"

"Well, your mother doesn't want any messages from me, that's for sure. But maybe she goes to weddings or funerals, and old buddies ask about me, and she says I'm dead or whatever story she made up. And you could jump in and tell them that before I died, I told you a story.

"So here's the story, and it's true," he said, rubbing his hands through his short hair.

"A large herd of elephants was crossing the plains. It's the dry season, and the matriarch—the old female who knows where to go for food and water and minerals in the earth and protection—is leading them to fresh food. She knows what's in season and where to find it. She's over 50 years old, and she's teaching her daughters all her routes and tricks, like digging deep in the ground or through the middle of a giant Baobab tree for water. To get there, the herd has to cross a rather large river.

"Now, this matriarch is very wise, and the rains have been good, and the territory is safe because the humans haven't come to shoot them for meat or to get them out of the way so fat-ass tourists in Fort Lauderdale can have pineapple juice for their piña coladas. And in these good times, the herd has produced many babies. The herd crosses the river, but as they're about to continue on, they hear an agitated trumpeting behind them."

He pulled a cigarette out of his pocket and put it in his mouth, but did not light it. It bobbed between his lips as he spoke, like a conductor waving a baton.

"There was one elephant, a juvenile born the previous year, who was scared to cross. The other elephants started to walk away, but the little guy didn't cross. They trumpeted back at him, urging him on, but he still couldn't bring himself to get in the water. He would stick his trunk in and pace back and forth on the bank, but no dice. The water wasn't deep, and smaller elephants, babies even, had made the crossing. It was some kind of fear. Two adults crossed back over and tried to lead the youngster in. They pushed and cajoled and walked back over a few times. Nothing.

"After a few hours of this, the entire herd headed back over the river, and went off in a different direction.

They refused to leave the little guy alone. The will of an entire herd of gigantic animals was changed by one of the little weak ones. This wasn't even the decision of the matriarch, mind you. The entire herd knew what they would do, and they crossed back over, and they found another place to go."

Karl stood up. "Think you'd ever see a herd of humans do that? All of them? Nope. Like I said, people basically suck."

His eyes were as determined as ever. Owen watched them move beyond him and then realized why he had stood up. Someone had appeared in the hallway behind Owen.

"Colonel says the visit time almost over," said the guard. "He says you can come back later."

"The Colonel wants to count his money," Karl Dorner replied.

Owen couldn't wait for another visit, if there was going to be another visit. "I have to ask you one more thing."

"Of course you do."

His habit of knowing everything before Owen told him, or at least pretending to, was infuriating him. It was too much like Mubego.

"Did you really ... did you really do what you were charged with?"

He chewed on the cigarette and waited a long time to answer.

"Owen, Owen. Do you know what the ultimate sacrifice for your country is?"

Owen thought for a moment. "It means you die. You die in battle."

"Wrong!" He banged his fist on the table, making Owen jump. "Bzzzzt! Wrong answer."

Owen waited for the answer, but his father said nothing.

"What is it, then?" Owen finally demanded.

"Go find out, godammit. Ask Mubego. He won't tell you, but you can go to the American Embassy in Nairobi, on Kenyatta Avenue, and ask the military attaché there. Name is Hentoff. He's one of those old buddies I told you about. Maybe he'll tell you."

"And you can tell the Colonel I said that!" he added, for the guard.

"Mr. Dorner, we must go now," said the guard.

"Which one? We're both Mr. Dorner. Can I leave? I'll get my stuff. Ha!"

The guard took Owen's arm and led him out.

"Sayonara, son. I'll ask the elephants about you. Can you come see me again?"

Owen said nothing. He didn't want his father to hear he was holding back tears.

For the first time since he had read the newspaper article with his father's name in it, he felt like a stupid, helpless kid again. He wanted to run home to Mom and cry in her lap, but it was too late for that.

There was one thing left for him to do.

27

First Grandmother led the herd back to the marsh with the soft food and cooling mud. The little one remembered it from the last rainy season, halfway past the time when new little ones were born to the young adult females in the herd, including his mother. First Grandmother now had another little one, his small sister, to teach new things and new places. This was his sister's first visit to the marsh, and all the young ones played in the mud together.

They spent the night in the marsh after covering their skin with mud and eating the soft marsh grass, which was easy to chew, but not as tasty as the good leaves on trees. The next morning, one of the older grandmothers, whose children were all mothers themselves now, stayed behind in the marsh to eat the soft plants. The rest of the herd left for the river.

The woman followed them.

When the sun was high in the sky, they reached the river. Though the rains were still far off, they had already swelled the river, and the water was grinding against the steep earthen banks that had baked hard during the dry season. First Grandmother led them to the best crossing spot, a well-beaten path where the river widened and became shallow, and the banks were not as steep.

The herd crossed quickly and confidently through the swift gray water. A few lingered to sweep water over their backs, but most feared crocodiles and the growing power of the current enough to move straight to the other side. When they had crossed, First Grandmother looked back to see that all were together.

But they were not. The smallest one, the one she had given so much knowledge to the day before they left on their journey, was still on the bank. He was desperate to join the rest, and made feints toward the water, but stopped himself in fear each time. He bellowed a whinnying cry to his mother and grandmothers.

His mother and a few others went back across the river to help him. They tried to lead him across, one in front and one to his side, but he would not follow. They gently pushed him from behind, urging him on, but he was too fearful to enter the water. First Grandmother moved ahead to keep the rest of the herd together, and then she went back to the river, but still the little one would not cross. So First Grandmother crossed back over and stood next to the shivering child.

"Little one, why don't you cross with us?"

"I'm afraid! I have never seen water moving! I will die!"

"Little one, you will not die in the water. Did you not

see the rest of us cross without dying?"

"But sometimes creatures die in the water, don't they, First Grandmother?"

She did not want to answer, but he had asked. "Yes, sometimes, but rarely."

"And they go back to the earth, like the bones in the marsh?"

"Yes. How do you know about this?"

"I heard young ones and sisters speak of it. A sister saw many dead wildebeest in the water after they crossed. They said the water takes them when it moves, or the monsters that live in the water, the crocodiles."

"Ah, I see. And now you are afraid of the water."

First Grandmother sent the little one's mother and sister back across and waited. Then she asked the little one, "If we wait here together for a while, do you think you might stop fearing the water enough to cross?"

"Yes, maybe."

So they waited. Some elephants on the other side continued to urge him to cross, but First Grandmother just waited silently for him to stop shivering. Then she asked him again, "Can you cross now?"

The little one summoned courage and moved toward the water, but when he reached the edge, his little legs gave way in fear and he began to slide in. He scrambled and screamed and whirled around, and First Grandmother grabbed him by his trunk and pulled him back out. He cowered next to her and pushed his hide against hers.

"Little one, will you not cross the river?"

"No!"

"Alright."

The little one looked up to her. She shaded his entire body from the sun with her outstretched ears.

"First Grandmother, will my mother come back over the river to be with me?"

"No, little one. We will *all* come back over. Like all of us, you are a child of the very first grandmother, and you are all there is. We will never leave you, and we will never leave each other. Never."

They would have to walk for several more days to reach a place upstream where the river ran softly and shallow and the whole herd could reach the other side without crossing swift water. But they would reach it, because First Grandmother had the knowledge to find that place, passed down to her all the way from the Spirit.

28

Owen heard the broadcast from the town's mosque calling Muslims to Morning Prayer. Manish had told him what it was. He was used to the sound now. He closed his eyes to the rapidly growing brightness, and Wanjeri's face appeared in his mind. He would have liked to see her again, but he wanted to be on a plane by day's end. He lay awake for a while as the sun rose higher, and as soon as he heard someone stirring in Mubego's office, Owen got out of bed and opened the office door.

But it was Julian.

"Where? Where'd he go?"

"The Colonel went to Nairobi while you were at the prison," Julian replied. "He had business to attend."

"Spending my money? Well, he better bring it back here first. I want my $200 back."

Owen could see Julian's face give away his shock at Owen's plain-spoken demand. He didn't care. He was as fearless as he had felt in many years.

"I don't believe it was refundable, and if it were, it would go to your friend Mrs. Pearson, since she provided it."

Before Owen could respond, Julian picked up a piece of paper from a machine on Mubego's desk: a fax.

The thermal paper stuck to Owen's damp fingers.

> Dear Mr. Dorner,
>
> I am finding it hard to express in words my sadness that your friend Manish has been seriously injured. He was a victim of hooligan thieves in Nairobi. I have left directly from the police station for Nairobi to investigate this unfortunate incident. Julian will make any travel arrangements you desire. My greatest sympathies.
>
> Col. M. E. Mubego, Commander
>
> Kumbata District Special Police Force

He had known Manish for barely a week. What travel arrangements was the Colonel talking about? Did he expect Owen to go to Manish's bedside? Surely his family would come to his aid. But what if his family needed help? No, he owed nothing to Manish.

He was too deep into all this. He had seen his father, and that was a disaster, and now it was over and time to go home. He wished he had never come. He wished he had never left the safety of his room. The fearless feeling, the triumphant feeling from when he stood up to the elephant in front of the Jeep, was slipping away.

"I want to go home," Owen said. "I just want to go home."

"I will drive you to the airport in Nairobi," said Julian.

"Where is Mrs. Pearson and her driver?"

"She has left too."

He wondered why she had suddenly left, but he was relieved she was gone. Going home with her would be totally humiliating. It would be surrender.

Owen thought for a moment about the name his father had mentioned, Hentoff. He had told Owen to go talk to Hentoff, off in some other town, to learn more. But Owen was done with this business. He wouldn't let his father send him on a wild goose chase when the whole trip had been one. No, it was time to go home.

As Julian loaded his bag into the trunk of the car, Owen saw a figure in the back seat. It was Wanjeri. She was dressed in a short blue skirt and white blouse. The clothes made her look girlish, almost demure. But as before, she moved and spoke with authority.

"What did you think of our country?" Wanjeri asked as they drove away from Mubego's house.

"It's very beautiful," Owen replied politely.

"But also very poor," added Wanjeri, filling in the blank.

"Yes, it is."

"It doesn't have to be this poor. We could have better education and better public works."

"Yes." He wasn't in the mood for this conversation.

"Sometimes I wonder if we weren't better off with the British."

"Wanjeri! Your grandfather was a Mau Mau, and you say things like that," scolded Julian. "Talk softly so he won't hear you from heaven."

Owen remembered Manish saying almost the exact

thing to him as they talked in their beds at Mubego's house.

"Grandfather can't hear me," said Wanjeri. "Anyway, he knows I only say things like that to make you mad." She smiled at Owen, a signal it was okay to laugh at their rivalry.

"Well, if grandfather doesn't hear," Julian added, "Uncle Mubego might. He was a Mau Mau too."

"How would he hear?" she asked. "Is he hiding in the car somewhere?"

Julian left her question unanswered.

"There are many well-meaning Kenyans who work hard to improve our country," she said. She seemed to be talking to Owen as much as Julian. "And there is no question we have the right to rule ourselves. I don't want the British back. I want us to live up to the promise of independence. I want us to live up to what our grandfather and uncle fought for."

"And I think you spent too much time in London," said Julian, "and your kind of talk could be dangerous, too." That put an end to the conversation.

They were moving steadily through town now, until the car got stuck behind a man, shirtless and glistening with sweat, pulling a cart in the middle of the road like an animal. As in the Jeep, Julian wasn't above passing on the shoulder to the left, but everyone had the same idea in Kumbata, and several other vehicles had appropriated the shoulder as another lane of traffic. Once clear of the town and back on the road north, they hit one of the abundant rough stretches of road, and Julian was forced to go almost as slow as in town.

Owen looked over at Wanjeri. Her long hair, straighter and wavier than most black women's hair, swayed in the wind from the window as they picked up speed. She was gazing out onto the plains, perhaps at the distant mountains on the horizon.

"What's a Mau Mau?" he asked.

She turned to him, her smooth face serious but open. Her broad lips looked smoother and more moist than his felt. "They were the rebels who fought for independence. Our grandfather took the Mau Mau oath when he was 16 years old. When the British found out and tried to arrest him, he hid in a cave at Mt. Kenya until they discovered it and bombed it. He escaped, but he was caught later and held in a prison camp for two years."

"Col. Mubego was also a Mau Mau," added Julian, even though he had already said it.

"What does it mean? Mau Mau?"

"It means 'get out.' Get out of our country."

"And they won their revolution?"

"No, they were crushed," said Wanjeri.

"But the movement made the British realize they must go home, so they went home," said Julian. "Even after the Mau Mau were defeated, they won victory anyway, and Kenya gained independence in 1965."

"It's the same as most of the rest of the empire," she said. "Now all we free Kenyans have the right to be as poor and incompetent and corrupt as we like."

Julian turned his head back so he could be heard. "My sister tries to sound smart." Owen wished he would keep his eyes on the road. "She likes to say things that could get her in deep trouble," he added, as a warning. But she persisted.

"The government thinks it is expensive to maintain the roads," said Wanjeri. "They don't know how much it costs not to maintain the roads."

"See, she is trying to sound smart again. She went to university in London, now she's so smart."

She whacked him on the back of the head playfully and he ducked to avoid the blows. "I am older than you so I am smarter than you!"

"You're not very smart, saying such ridiculous things out loud. Have you no love for your country? What we paid to be free?"

"You really are angry, aren't you?" she said. "Don't worry, my brother, I still love Kenya better than England. England is too cold."

Julian seemed to accept her answer and drove on in silence. He slowed the Jeep for traffic ahead. After a few minutes they reached the source of the delay—several stern-looking policemen poking their heads in cars and eyeing passengers on buses. They had set up a crude steel tire-puncturing device to prevent escape around the blockade.

"It's no problem," said Julian, and pointed to a sticker on his windshield as he approached the blockade. The policeman instantly waved them through.

"What are they looking for?"

"Oh, someone who robbed a bank. Or perhaps someone who escaped from prison."

Owen saw Wanjeri looking at one of the uniformed men glaring at every vehicle. She stared back, deep in thought.

"My bus was robbed, on the way to Kumbata," said Owen. "They made us all get off the bus. Then policemen came out of nowhere and rescued us."

Wanjeri turned her stare to Julian, who said nothing.

"That must have been frightening," replied Wanjeri, still looking at Julian.

Past the blockade, the short trees that held their ground on the sand-colored plain appeared less and less frequently as they moved north. Owen could see lone ostriches prancing in the distance. Further out, plumes of swirling dust formed mini-tornadoes, like an apocalyptic wasteland, only with ostriches. Though they seemed far from any town, more and more people appeared along the highway, selling fruit or driving goats.

Owen's thoughts turned to Wanjeri again, and his musings about being with her. She could lead him, protect him, in this strange land full of creatures and poor people and criminals on buses. She was tough, yet so sweet. Such a strange combination in a woman that he didn't know could co-exist. His mother was sweet; Mrs. Pearson was tough. He hadn't seen them together in one woman before. It hurt a little to think he was going home and leaving Wanjeri behind.

They had reached the suburbs of Nairobi. The area was more prosperous than Kumbata, and Owen closed his eyes for a moment, pretended he was back home, and opened them to see if the real world outside could join the conspiracy of his imagination. For brief moments, it could, until an improvised shack or crumbling lean-to broke the string of modest industrial buildings and walls hiding better houses. At first it was comforting to dwell on the security of home, but soon the repeating shocks back to reality tired him, and he gave up on the game and kept his eyes closed.

The car got stuck behind a fume-spewing truck and they rolled up the windows. To the right Owen saw a sign: "Nairobi National Park Entrance."

"Stop here, at the park," said Wanjeri.

"Why?"

"I want to show him the tusks."

"Do we have time for that?"

"Plenty of time. Turn here!"

Julian had to press hard on the brakes to do it. He pulled into the entrance, and the suburbs disappeared.

"This is a plains reserve with many of the big animals we saw in the Mara," said Julian to Owen. "It is small, but very close to the city. Good for a day trip. But we are not here to see animals, so I don't know why my sister has brought us here."

"I want to show him the tusks. Stay in the car, it will take only a few moments."

"There's not much to see of those tusks," said Julian.

"It's still worth seeing. Just for a minute. Drive us to it please."

After winding their way a short distance through a forest, the bare road opened to large grassy plains dotted with hillocks. There was a park headquarters, and on the far side of the plains, warehouses stood beyond a tall fence.

Julian saw Owen looking at the warehouses. "This park is right up against the city. It is the only wildlife park in Kenya surrounded completely by a fence."

Then Owen spied a modest pile of grey stones directly ahead. Wanjeri led Owen out to it while Julian sat in the driver's seat, engine running.

The stones were not stones. A large photograph posted in front of the pile revealed the truth. It showed the same scene, but with the pit full of elephant tusks, aflame. A ring of people in formal clothes gathered around it like a bonfire. It looked to Owen like a funeral pyre.

"These are the ashes of elephant tusks. The government burned them as a symbol of a commitment to end poaching. Trade in ivory was banned the same year, worldwide."

She squatted and picked up a bit of burned tusk.

"To see an elephant, right here in Africa, one must work harder and go further today than when I was a child. That makes me sad. This place reminds us elephants are part of the African family. White people are always coming to tell us or beg us to save this animal or that, but we Africans have to decide. We are the ones crowding elephants into tiny spaces. We are the ones shooting them when they eat our crops, or shooting them to eat their meat, or shooting them for money for food. But do you eat your own family? Do you eat the family next door? When you kill an elephant, you kill a member of a family. I have no doubt."

She stood and dropped the chunk of burnt tusk. Her black hair blew gently into her face. It was a cooling breeze.

"When I was a little girl, I wanted nothing but to know more about elephants. I grew up in Nairobi so I didn't see the animals much, but then I was sent to boarding school in the north, and there I saw them, patrolling the edges of the farms nearby. They were waiting for nightfall to raid the farms and eat the bananas and pineapples. The farmers, naturally, hated them, and would beat sticks on trees to scare them off, or even burn bits of dung and throw it at them. Now it is such a problem that the elephants aren't scared and they are hungrier because the farms have encroached onto elephant territory much more, so the farmers use fences. And rifles. And sometimes hungry people shoot them for meat, or poor people shoot them for ivory."

Wanjeri looked out at the plains, toward the distant fence.

"I could see them out of the school window, the elephants, and I wanted to go see them closer. But the teachers said they were dangerous, that they would eat me. Can you imagine? Maybe they were trying to frighten a little child, but I think some of them might have believed it. They saw the elephants as monsters because they were so big. I thought something so big couldn't possibly want to harm me or fear me. They seemed so gentle."

Owen imagined her as a smaller version of herself, in a schoolgirl's plaid shirt and white blouse, wading her way through a field of pineapples toward the giant beasts, teachers screaming after her. She could pass for a schoolgirl now, save a few inches. He wished he was her age and not still a teenager.

"I went off to university, but to study elephants I had to go to London. Imagine—the elephants are here, but you have to go a thousand miles away to study them. And then they send you back here to do field work, of course."

"Is it true elephants never forget?" Owen felt stupid as soon as he asked it. But Wanjeri did not laugh.

"They never forget what they need to know. Elephant families are led by matriarchs, the oldest and wisest grandmother. The matriarch has a map in her mind of the whole territory, and a calendar telling her when to go different places for food or water. The map can cover thousands of square kilometers. She must teach everything to the next matriarch to pass it on. They even remember their dead. Elephants have been observed handling old elephant bones, gently and with reverence. A whole group will do it. They pick them up, taste them, and smell them. I have seen it. They mourn."

"You make them sound human."

"No, they're better than humans."

"Better?"

Wanjeri turned to face him. "Elephants do everything good that people do. They think, they look out for each other, and they miss the ones that die. But elephants don't have wars or take slaves. They don't betray each other."

Owen remembered his father's words: "People suck."

Wanjeri's eyes, bright white against her dark skin,

fluttered and rolled slightly, as if she were fainting, or dreaming.

"Once I came back home to set up an elephant research center here, I thought about everything I knew about elephants and biology—everything I learned from books, everything I knew from watching them from my school window. And I decided evolution doesn't go in a straight line from lower animals to primates to humans. We aren't the only line of the family tree reaching toward the top. Why should we think we are? Crows and ravens, dolphins and whales, octopi, apes, elephants—all very intelligent, as intelligent as they need to be. Biologists used to define intelligence as the ability to use tools until they saw chimpanzees and then birds using them. Then it was language, but they listened more closely to whales and birds and learned how advanced their communication is. Eventually they will understand humanity doesn't have a monopoly on intelligence."

She must have seen something in his face. "I'm sorry for the biology lecture."

Wanjeri spied a bit of scorched tusk fallen from the ring. She picked it up and tossed it back to its grave. "Someday, maybe they'll discover animals have souls and recognize good from evil. I believe that."

Owen heard Julian honking the horn beyond the trees. He turned to walk back to the car, but Wanjeri grabbed his sleeve.

"I need to talk to you about why you are here, away from Julian. He does not approve of talking about these things as much as I do. Also, he does not know everything I know, and it is best this be left alone. He can only suffer from knowing, no matter what he does about it. He is of two families now."

"You want to know why I am here? You know why I came to Kenya, don't you?"

"To see your father, in Kumbata prison."

"Do you know why he's there?"

"He didn't tell you himself?"

"He didn't tell me much of anything," he said.

"I don't know why he is in the prison, but I know how."

"What is going on, Wanjeri? Why did your uncle keep me at his house and send me off on a safari and put up roadblocks? What happened to Manish? What is all this strange stuff?"

"I will tell you all I know, but then we must go back and you must not say anything in front of Julian."

She turned away to look out at the plains as if Julian could read her lips through the trees.

"My uncle knew you were coming. He found out from someone as you were coming here. He knows people everywhere."

"I figured that out already."

"I heard Julian and my uncle talking about the bus robbery. When your bus was robbed on the way here."

"They knew about it?"

"More than that. The bandits were prisoners, from the prison. He used them. I think he let them escape and sent them to the bus. That's why the police were waiting there to rescue the bus. But something went wrong. Perhaps they didn't know Manish was on the same bus."

Owen looked down at the ashes, trying to fathom it all. "What does this have to do with my father?"

Wanjeri met this with silence.

"I need to know everything you know," Owen said. "You're both not telling me everything."

More silence.

"Wanjeri."

After a moment, she answered.

"Your father is in danger because he knows something about Uncle Mubego. I don't know what it is, but it could hurt my uncle. He is afraid your father tried to tell you and you will tell others. He had control of the situation—until you arrived."

"Then why did he let me talk to my father in the first place?"

"I don't know. My uncle likes to play games, use people against each other. He was probably listening to your conversation the whole time. Maybe he wants to use you to find information. But your father probably knew he was listening. He couldn't say anything directly. Your father may have tried to tell you something some other way, with hints."

Wanjeri took Owen's hand to lead him back to the car. Her hand felt soft, yet dry, with strong muscles bounded by supple skin. It felt good to hold her hand, to connect, when he was so off balance. He pulled on her hand to stop her before they reached Julian.

"Wanjeri, you said my father couldn't come out and tell me everything because Mubego was listening."

"He was probably listening, yes, through a

microphone, or from a room next to yours, or his spy was."

"You don't know what your uncle's secret is?"

"No. All I know is what I've heard here and there, that your father is definitely not in prison for the crimes they say he committed. We have to go."

"He's not?"

"No, I don't think so. We have to go." She pulled on his hand.

"How do you know so much about my father?"

"We have to go."

They reached the end of the path and she dropped his hand.

"We're going to be late," Julian said.

* * *

They drove in silence through downtown. Owen barely knew Nairobi, but his mind was already piecing together a rough map and finding comfort in familiar streets and buildings. He knew enough now to see what made this city different from Baltimore or any city back home. The sunny pleasant heat; the crowds of people rivaling the biggest rush hour crowds on New York's avenues; the begging children kicking up dust with their bare feet on corroded fragments of sidewalks; the helmeted guards posted outside banks with stern faces but slouching bodies; the street merchants hawking sunglasses and trinkets to a sprinkling of white tourists.

And now that he was about to leave, Owen had the luxury of seeing the city the way it is, rather than shutting out the imperfections and traps and dead ends and ignoring the people crouching in alleys or

234 *Rick Hodges*

lying in the sidewalk wearing rags and stumps for legs. He would soon escape. He had a day and a night to spend in a hotel in Nairobi, courtesy of his brother's credit card, and then he would get on the airplane and back in his clean and ordered world. Until then, he resolved not to turn away from things that made him feel unbalanced, but to face them, to walk among them. He would go out of his hotel and walk around, without a destination. He would dwell on the heat-baked earth, give begging lepers his money and let the other beggars see it and mob him for more. He would walk over an earthen parking lot with a few crumbling chunks of asphalt worn by the rain and the traffic of sandals and bare feet, and never replaced. He would wallow in this decay, embrace it as his own, and control its grip on him without fear, and then tomorrow he would walk onto an airplane and slip away from it forever and forget he ever had a father.

They stopped in front of the hotel. As Julian pulled Owen's bag from the trunk, Wanjeri retrieved a roll of paper from her bag and placed it in Owen's hand. "Here, you will learn more than you think from this."

"What is that?" Julian asked, eyeing the paper. Julian would report back to Mubego, that much was clear.

"It's my thesis from university. He wanted to know more about the elephants. Don't read it now," she told Owen as she closed his hands back around it. "It will make good reading material on the airplane, to put you to sleep." Julian snickered. Owen stuffed it in his pocket and picked up his bag. "But look at it before you leave," she added. "Please."

"*Kwaheri*," said Julian as he pulled away. "Goodbye."

29

"Change money? American dollars?"

"T-shirts, very nice! I have a bargain for you!"

"Cassette tapes, inexpensive! Come see!"

It didn't take Owen long to stop bothering to shake his head "no" and keep walking. He had a simple map of the city in his pocket the hotel staff gave him for when he got lost, but he tried to make his way without it. He wanted to wander for a while, with no goal. It helped him think.

From his downtown hotel, he started with Nairobi's business district, with the largest, most modern buildings. He read the street names: Kenyatta Avenue, Wabera Street, Kuanda, Mama Ngina. Past a bank, then a movie theater with a poster for "Die Hard."

The movie theater made him think of Manish. He was here somewhere, in the city, perhaps laughing and bragging about a narrow escape. Owen wondered if he would ever know what happened to Manish. He wished he weren't such a serious kid. He should go home and rent "Die Hard" and act like a normal 18-year-old.

He passed minibuses loading up white tourists in ridiculous canvas safari suits headed for catered adventure. Back to Kenyatta, with its low barbed wire fences barely discouraging pedestrians from stepping on the brown-dry grass in the median but giving the avenue a harsh look, almost like the prison. Up Muindi Mbingu Street, walking behind several ragged children who didn't spot him. He ducked around the corner because, he had already learned, if they saw him, they would mob him to beg for change. Past a stunning building, elaborate and out of scale, which he determined was a mosque. Past a leper in the street, stumped fingers reaching out for money. It was the first leper he saw in Africa, or anywhere.

Past a stall full of cassette tapes advertising its wares with blaring, bouncy African pop music, attended by a man with thin white hair over a black scalp who looked too old to like the music he sold. The smell of something frying in oil met his nose, and then he saw the enormous wok with some kind of white root gently sizzling inside, right on the sidewalk, as a woman wrapped from head to toe in bright red and yellow cloth sold the fried root things wrapped in newspaper. A neat line of oranges lay in front of the wok. The frying lady smiled at him, her tongue shining through gaps in her front teeth.

He helped an Asian man push his car out of a pothole so deep it had swallowed the entire right rear tire. Thankfully, the predicament had played out in the shade of a tall bank building across the street. In front of the building, outside its tall iron fence enclosing an empty grassless lot of dust, was a market full of dried spices, fresh fruit, cheap toys, and perfume laid on crude stands hinged together with scrap wood. He walked past one of the many gift shops hawking animals carved from wood and stone. Another woman in a colorful *kanga* with something in Swahili printed on its edge selling paltry fruits and vegetables lay on the ground along the street, next to two barefoot children.

Back to Kenyatta and west, across the traffic-choked Uhuru Highway to Uhuru Park. Voices singing in the distance became louder, and he followed. Up the open hill past a few overburdened trees to find a chorus singing African melodies in an amphitheater. Back down to Kenyatta Avenue, past a hotel courtyard where white people sat with drinks at tables around a huge tree with scraps of paper pinned across its bark. He read a few— they were messages, apparently from tourists to other tourists trying to get in touch.

A right turn onto Moi Avenue to a train station, another quaint colonial remnant. Cars in the parking lot shared the last bits of shredded worn blacktop with people selling small, grimy fruits laid in the dust. Back from the station along Moi to the traffic circle at Haile Salassie Avenue. With the map, he navigated using the Hilton hotel and the tall Parliament House looming in the sky.

He saw an open lot littered with stone rubble ahead, and as he approached, he saw the back section of a large building with a hole in it. A pocked and worn sign of stone with metal letters still clinging to it gave the place a name: "U.S. EMB S Y." It was the remains of the embassy damaged by a terrorist truck bomb a few years ago.

The embassy his father had told him to visit, to meet the Hentoff fellow.

Was his father playing more games? Had he somehow not heard about the bombing of the embassy? Owen had forgotten about it himself. It was possible Karl was cut off from the news in prison, but he seemed so well-informed otherwise. Perhaps he had meant a temporary embassy somewhere else. But then Owen remembered—his father specifically said the embassy on Kenyatta Avenue. Maybe the temporary embassy was also on Kenyatta. Or maybe the embassy building still had some useable work space. Another look at what was left standing dispelled that idea. Though the damage was not severe, the building was clearly not in use. Construction workers were busy patching it up, and it was no place for bureaucrats to operate. No, his father was playing more games. He had said to go to the embassy on Kenyatta. It was a taunt; a wild goose chase.

But he had also told Owen to tell Mubego he sent Owen here. Was that meant as a signal to Mubego? That he was not revealing anything useful to Owen? Or was the rubble the message? Was it a hidden message? Had Owen missed the message? He tried to play the conversation back in his head and scour it for clues as he walked.

The crowds were thick on Moi. He turned north up a narrow side street, Luthuli Avenue, but the crowds got thicker. A hawker came after him with sunglasses for 10 U.S. dollars. "Please, please?"

His father had mentioned ultimate sacrifice, military talk, and some story about elephants crossing rivers.

An old grizzled beggar brushed his leg. Owen looked around to see if there were others nearby, and seeing none, he gave the beggar a few shillings. He couldn't do this forever or he would be mobbed and out of money. He turned down Mfangano Street, which seemed more quiet, to let his tired mind work.

His father was involved with Mubego, somehow, before he ended up in the Colonel's prison. But how? Was that why he could not say everything he wanted?

It was less than 24 hours until his plane ride home. Julian had secured a last-minute ticket for him. But the feeling of freedom from this country and its entanglements he felt all day had disappeared, replaced by a dread rising in his stomach like water bubbling up through a leak in a boat, slowly pulling it downward. He was still bound to this place he knew nothing about, and in leaving, he would leave questions unresolved. Owen's legs became light and weak and shivery, and he pushed his feet down harder onto the pavement as he walked so he could still feel his own weight bearing down on them.

He found himself in front of a decent-looking Indian restaurant. He had only discovered Indian food at home a few years ago, when his mom forced him to try it, and he was glad she had. It was delicious. It was the kind of thing he was ready for, now he was an adult.

He ducked inside and breathed the cool air. After a

week in Africa, he had already forgotten the feeling of entering a dense blue block of chilled indoor air on a hot day. It took his breath for a moment, like dropping into cold water. But it also felt modern and safe. This place was a refuge from the strange, dry, rugged continent outside, just when he needed it.

A short waiter argued with another in low tones at the back of the room, stopping only to bring him his food. He ate roti, then fish in a rich spicy sauce that warmed his stomach. He thought about Manish again. He was right—the Indian food in this country was the best choice. The break from the street and the welcoming food would be enough to restore him. He felt his legs stiffening from the rest.

Owen remembered the paper in his pocket—Wanjeri's thesis. He pulled it out to read with his meal. But every page was blank! There was only a handwritten note on the front:

> 532 Gambia Street

There was no mistaking her message. She had disguised it as her thesis to pass him a note right under Julian's nose. Was she to meet him there? When? Or was it really a message? Could it be a mistake? Would it be another bombed-out shell like the embassy? And what reason could he have to do anything but go to his hotel, hope for hot water for a shower, wake up tomorrow and get on a plane and declare himself fatherless once and for all? It would be good to see Wanjeri alone, yes, but that would probably make leaving a little harder. That was not something he wanted, not now. It was turning into too much.

He paid the bill and dove back into the sunlight and the stream of black and brown bodies and the hawkers and money-changers and lepers. He left Wanjeri's paper wadded up on his table next to a plate smeared with spicy fish sauce.

It was difficult to hail a cab in this town. Perhaps all the ancient cabs had finally broken down for good, all at once. After a few minutes of failing to get a cab, a black man in shabby pinstripes and absolutely no hair approached. "Ride a *matatu*," he said, gesturing out to the street. "A bus. Cheaper." And as if conjured, a battered white van about half the size of a Baltimore city bus, though stuffed with the same number of passengers a Baltimore city bus could hold, stopped in front. Owen followed the man on board, thinking he was taking the last spot, yet three people followed behind him and shoved in. So he had but three people to push past and jump off the *matatu* when he spied a street sign: "Gambia Street."

What was the number? 532? Why had he left it back at the restaurant? He could at least look at the house without going in.

But he did go in. The house was small and humble, but the exterior, whitewashed brick harboring a small courtyard, promised cool cleanliness inside.

Parked outside, he saw Mrs. Pearson's car and driver.

A small Indian woman who seemed to possess strength beyond her size ushered him into a bedroom as if she was expecting him. "He is getting better," she announced, half for information and half to will it into truth. There in the bed lay Manish, asleep, his face swollen and bandaged. The Indian woman, he realized, was Manish's wife.

Wanjeri had sent him to see Manish. Why?

Manish looked terrible. "I'm sorry this happened, ma'am," is all Owen could think to say to his wife.

"Thank you for your kind wishes. He told me about you, that you were a new friend from America. He liked America. He invited you to come here for supper. I would very much like to have you for supper, someday."

This was the wife Manish had joked about. She was kind and caring, and he saw now he must love her greatly despite the jokes.

Manish's wife put her hand on her husband's head and stroked his hair. It was the first time Owen had seen that hair move.

"He told me you were looking for your father. He admired you for that. He is proud of being a father himself. We have only one daughter, Adya. She fears what will happen, of seeing him die. I tell her he's not going to die, but she is not used to this kind of thing."

"He won't die," said Mrs. Pearson. She and Owen watched as his wife stroked his hair. Then she left them without a word.

Thank God he is asleep, thought Owen, so he doesn't see the look on my face. The parts of Manish that were not hidden from view by faintly stained linen bandages were purple, a mix of bruises and his brown skin. He had been deliberately hurt, it was clear, for what was done to him took time and effort far beyond the necessity of a simple robbery.

"I owe you a big tip, Manish," said Owen.

"How well do you know him, exactly?" Mrs. Pearson asked.

"I didn't know him well, but I liked him so it felt like I knew him better."

"I thought so."

"We're talking like we're at his funeral already."

She sat next to Owen. Her skin was flush with the heat of the house, and her hair laid in sweaty strands against the side of her head, the usual hair bun consigned away. She was finally allowing this continent to get to her.

"He's not going to have a funeral any time soon. I pulled some strings and called in some of the best doctors available."

"How long have you been here?"

"Two days."

He looked at her face again, at her clothes. She must have been sleeping here too. She sensed his surprise.

"Every once in a while, I can care about people, you know."

Manish breathed out heavily and seemed to smile in his sleep. Was he hearing their voices? More likely he was dreaming of the movies.

"It's been a long time since I tried to care about someone." She was staring right through Manish to some distant, precious memory.

"Why didn't you send him to a hospital?"

"In some countries, a hospital isn't a place to go if you want to get better. Besides, we thought it was best for him to keep a low profile right now."

"Why? What's happened to him?"

"He met the wrong guy in an alley. That's all I can surmise."

"That's not a reason to keep a low profile."

"Well ... true, Owen. The fact is we don't know what happened."

"Was it because of me?"

"It's not your fault. But it might be a message for you."

Owen looked at Manish's swollen eyelids. He could still detect Manish's eyes fluttering underneath. He decided this was a good sign.

"I imagined him sitting at the table with his family with a cast on his arm, laughing," said Owen. "I would have come right over if I had known he was like this."

"He's not as bad as he looks. And don't worry, the doctors are the best available on this continent. I'm having them flown in from Johannesburg."

Her hands lay in her lap, humble and moist. She had found a way to use her skills in phone calls and plane tickets and wire transfers to help someone, up close and personal.

"I didn't even know where to find him except for ... somebody slipped the address to me. I didn't know he was here."

"Then if this is a message to you, maybe you got it too soon."

They sat silent, watching Manish breathe, and then she put her hand on his.

"My father said you came to see him in prison a long time ago," he said.

She said nothing and kept her eyes aimed at Manish.

"He said my mother sent you," he said.

"Yes, she sent me, like she sent me this time. But I didn't get in to see him. He refused to meet with me. I found out he was refusing to see anyone who could help him. No military lawyers, no State Department people, nobody. It was almost as if he wanted all this to happen to him."

"Maybe he was insane."

"No, I knew him pretty well. He was passionate—is passionate—but not crazy."

"Well, from what I saw, maybe he's crazy now."

"I don't know, Owen. I can't say."

"Why didn't you tell me you came to see him?"

"Because he didn't let me meet with him. I didn't want you to give up."

"Isn't that why you followed me over here? To get me to give up?"

"Is that what you think?" She breathed in deeply and let it out. "I have to go back soon, and I'll see your mother. What do you want me to tell her?"

"About him?"

"About you."

He turned to her. Mrs. Pearson's pale, mild color was gone, supplanted by a vivid flush. Her hair, blacker still with moisture, was now fully pasted onto her pink cheeks.

"Tell her everyone tried to keep me away from my dad. Tell her that pissed me off more and I'm not leaving until I figure this out."

He stood and went for the door, turning for one more look. She was holding Manish's hand, like a mother comforting a sick child or a wife willing a dying husband to recover.

"Tell her I'll be out of town for a few more days," as he walked out the door.

"Passionate," she said, with only a sleeping, swollen Indian cab driver there to hear it.

"What?"

Manish was awake.

She put her face to his ear. "Manish? Don't move, you were hurt. Let me get your wife."

He grabbed her sleeve. "No." His breath was still difficult, and he struggled between words. "No, wait. Something to ... tell you."

She brought her face back to his. "What is it?"

"I had ... a message."

"A message? For who?"

"For ... opposition."

She knew who he was talking about. "In Kiliathra? In house arrest?"

"Yes. A message."

"You were headed down there to deliver your message, on that bus, right? But Mubego wanted to stop you. That's why he had you beaten up."

"He did it?" Manish's face grew pale.

"Well, that's my theory."

"Good theory. He got me away from his house ... you ... then ...."

"He couldn't act with Owen and me there, yes." She squeezed Manish's hand. "I'm so sorry, Manish."

"No. You ... didn't. My fault."

She could see how it hurt him to talk. "You don't deserve this."

"Deliver the message. Will you?"

She sat up. "Of course I will. It will serve that fat arrogant Colonel right. What is it?"

"Asians. General strike. We will ... support."

"The Asians? That would bring this creaky little economy to its knees." She clapped her hands together suddenly and shocked herself with her own reaction. "My dear Manish! You and your friends might just bring the fat Colonel down!"

"My wife."

"Yes, yes, let me go get her. And then I'm getting you and the family out of here. Out of the country. To get you to a decent hospital, and for your safety."

"Is... Owen...?"

"Owen is on a mission, too."

* * *

Owen tried a shortcut to Moi Avenue, but he got lost and ended up in front of the ruins of the embassy again. He walked around the far side of the high chain-link fence topped with barbed wire.

At an opening in the fence stood an American soldier in fatigues, guarding the pile of bricks from further attack. Owen asked him where he could find the embassy now.

"The Hermes Hotel, sir," he answered in a vague Southern accent. He pointed across the traffic circle to an elegant old building, out of place in the drab capital.

The lobby of the Hermes housed several American tourists (so easy to spot) milling around with papers and passports in hand. There were more armed guards. A piece of paper taped to a pillar read "USA embassy" and listed several functions and their locations. Owen picked "Information in General" and found Room 203. What "information in general" did he want? He didn't know what to ask, only who to ask for.

The door was open, and a warm breeze from a ceiling fan greeted him. Two American *wazunga*, an elderly couple, walked past on their way out, looking confused.

The room was a regular hotel room with a bed and tiny desk where a thin white man with a shiny head and round glasses sat. Papers and files stacked on the bed left only a small space for anyone else to sit, and a black boy no older than twelve in a crisp collared shirt occupied it. The man was filling out a form and didn't even look up at Owen until he finished.

"May I help you?"

"I'm not sure. I'm trying to find records on prisoners."

"Prisoners in Kenya?"

"Yes."

"You'd have to consult the Kenya government for that."

"The prisoner is an American."

"You'd have to consult the Kenya government for that."

It was hot in the room. Owen wiped sweat from his face. "You know nothing about an American in prison here?"

The man took off his glasses and cleaned them with his tie. Around and around and around on each lens.

"Unless we worked through this embassy to help him with legal advice, we wouldn't have any records. You'd still have to go to the government."

"I don't know if you helped him or not."

"I'm afraid I can't help *you*, then."

"Can't you look him up to see if you have a file?"

The man put his glasses back on. The breeze pushed the curtains up from the window behind him. He picked up his pen.

"What is the name, please?"

"Karl Dorner."

He put down the pen.

"Michael. *Maji!*"

The boy jumped up and left the room. The man in the glasses stood up and closed the door.

"Karl Dorner? You're looking for Capt. Karl Dorner?"

"Yes."

"Hmm. Well, our files are in extreme disarray following the bombing. Many were destroyed."

"I understand."

"If there is a file, and I can't say there is, it was probably sent to our consulate in Mombasa. We are only performing essential functions here now."

"Where is Mombasa?"

"On the coast. The train takes you there overnight."

Owen considered it. He could take the overnight train trip to Mombasa, with the unlikely chance he would find a file that may or may not exist, in a pile somewhere, half burnt. Or he could read the messages everyone was sending and go home and tell everyone he couldn't find his father or that he was dead.

Maybe the beating of Manish was a message to him too. Maybe Wanjeri was trying to warn him he faced the same threat. But did she want him to leave, or to be careful? Did she mean to scare him away, or simply strengthen his resolve?

The man was on the telephone. Owen turned to go, but then he had one more idea. "Is there anyone who might remember the case? Someone who works for the embassy?"

The man put his hand over the mouthpiece to answer.

"There was. But he was killed."

Owen stared.

"In the bombing."

"Oh yes. Sorry." The man held his hand to the receiver, waiting to see that Owen was leaving. With his hand up, Owen could see a long scar on his arm. He had survived the bombing.

Owen recalled his father had mentioned the name of someone to seek in the embassy, but he couldn't remember the name. No matter. It was probably the man who had been killed anyway. Another dead end on a dead-end trip.

It was over. Time to go home.

"Thank you."

The boy, a bottle of water in hand, squeezed back into the room without looking at him.

The walk back to the Hilton was only a few blocks, but the heat—from being indoors, not out in the warm, but pleasant, streets—had wrung the energy from him. He trudged up the stairs to his room on the fifth floor, as the elevators were all broken, and laid in the bed. The room was like a modest hotel room at home, except for the mosquito net hanging over the bed.

Then his stomach forced him back out of the bed. He vomited, and then slept, and vomited again, about every two hours, all night. For the first time since boarding the airplane to Kenya, he really, really missed his mom.

In the morning, he felt well enough to drink some water from the bottle beside the bed. He was still delirious though—he saw Mubego sitting across the room. Then the hallucination spoke, and Owen dropped the water bottle.

30

"Do you think I'm an evil man, Mr. Dorner?"

Owen was too weak to answer even if he had known what to say.

"It is easy to get sick in Africa. Many diseases. You cannot visit long without getting sick. I have called a doctor. He will be here shortly."

He got up and picked up the water bottle, handing it to Owen. Half the water had leaked out.

"I am not an evil man, young Mr. Dorner," Mubego said, answering his own question. "I have treated you well, and I've treated your father well." Mubego's gold tooth flashed under his lips as he spoke.

Owen still couldn't summon the strength to talk. He sucked water from the bottle instead.

"Have I not provided you with hospitality? Did I not bring you to see your father?"

The water cooled his throat enough to answer this time.

"Yes. Yes, you..."

"Did I not express my condolences for the tragedy that befell your friend Manish and am I not working right now to find the criminals who did it to him?"

He was leaning over the bed, looking straight at Owen. His face was neither threatening nor angry, but the intensity of Mubego's eyes, so white and deep against his coffee-black skin, set Owen off balance. Mubego's tone was chastising, like a mother to a child, but also calculated and restrained. Mubego had the power to demand what he wanted much more directly, and that he did not demand it made Owen nervous, and Mubego knew it.

"Yes, Colonel," Owen finally said. "But I don't think you're evil, and I don't think you did anything wrong." Did he really care what Owen thought of him? Not likely.

Mubego sat back down.

"If that is true, why do you go to your embassy and ask questions? Why don't you ask me the questions? I will tell you anything you wish to know."

Now he understood Mubego's anger.

Mubego seemed to know every move he made. Did he have spies in the embassy? Did someone follow Owen around the streets of Nairobi?

"I'm sorry."

"You are sick," Mubego said, ignoring his apology. "You ate something you shouldn't have. The doctor will be here shortly. And I have news about your friend Manish. We know he was beaten by three men, in a robbery. We have not found these men, but I have taken personal responsibility for solving the case."

The hotel door opened. It was not the doctor. It was Julian, holding a bottle of clear liquid.

The last thing Owen wanted was somebody in his room, let alone Mubego sitting so close and expecting him to pay attention, while he applied every ounce of concentration trying not to vomit again. Where was that doctor?

Mubego was holding his hat by its rim, and now he flipped it up and down by rolling the rim between his fingers. Up and down, up and down, like he was bored. Julian put his bottle on the table and approached the bedside with a spoon.

"How are you? I brought you something for the stomach. The doctor is coming, but I brought you something to help."

Oh, this is perfect. Who knew what kind of crazy medicine Julian had? But at that moment, Owen's belly tightened and heaved and even poison sounded good. He swallowed Julian's medicine.

"Vinegar?"

"Yes, vinegar. Good for you. Kills germs."

Owen had smelled vinegar when Manish cleaned the silverware on the safari. Perhaps he thought he would sterilize Owen's entire digestive tract with a tablespoon of the stuff. In any event, it wasn't poison, and it didn't make him sicker.

"We must make you well, Mr. Dorner, because we have business to attend to."

Mubego stopped flipping his hat.

"I invite you to travel to Mombasa."

Owen propped himself up on his elbows and looked at him. "You want me to go to Mombosa?"

"Yes. It's on the coast. A nice town, very old."

"Why?"

"To see your father's embassy file. You wanted to see his file, didn't you?"

Owen dropped back down into his bed. "You sure know everything that's happening all the time, Colonel."

This made him grin, the smile he always gave Owen when Owen spoke plainly to him. His teeth were bright white against his brown skin.

"This is true! And the things I say, they are the truth. This you will learn when you go to Mombosa. You'll see I never lied to you."

"He never lied to you," Julian interjected, drawing a stare from Mubego.

"I never thought you lied," Owen said, and dropped back down to the pillow. Actually, his stomach did feel better.

"Good."

"But I did think you weren't telling me everything." Owen surprised himself with his courage. Here he was, a lone 18-year-old, sick in a bed in a strange country who had never traveled anywhere before, who lived cowering in his room for a month just before getting on the airplane, speaking the truth to a big, powerful military man. It made him feel a little proud. It made him feel strong, like when he yelled at the elephant. It made him feel less sick.

"Well, of course not, Mr. Dorner. I deal in sensitive

issues, matters of national security. I cannot tell you everything. But I will tell you all you need to know about your father. I will tell you what you came to find out, and you will see it is true for yourself in Mombasa. The file was not lost when the embassy was bombed, nor by the bureaucrats. It is at the U.S. consulate in Mombasa."

The doctor finally came, complete with white coat and black bag.

"But I warn you that you may wish you didn't know," Mubego said as the doctor began his work on Owen. "Even your father knew enough not to tell you everything."

The doctor felt Owen's stomach, took his temperature, gave him some pills to stop the vomiting (Owen took two), ordered rest and liquids, and pronounced he would be well by the next morning. This, Owen mused, gave him 18 hours to decide whether he was a good doctor or a total quack about to let him die of some crazy tropical disease.

Mubego sat and watched the entire treatment. When the doctor left, he picked up the conversation as if he'd never been interrupted.

"You will find everything that I am about to tell you confirmed in your father's United States government file. Are you ready? Perhaps I should come back when you are well."

Mubego had barged in on him while Owen was puking out his insides and seeing double, and now, as he was about to reveal all, he was offering to leave? It had to be a tease, Mubego's way of reaffirming his importance.

"No, I'd like to hear it now."

"Very well. Julian, could you make some tea?"

Mubego sat back in his chair.

"Your father was working as an advisor for the Kenya military forces beginning in 1972. We had only recently achieved our independence from the British Empire, you know, and newly independent colonies were the subject of great attention from the superpowers at that time. Under the leadership of our great founder and first president, Jomo Kenyatta, Kenya became an ally of the United States and the West.

"Karl came here to advise our armed forces on certain tactical matters. I first came to know him then, when I was a lieutenant in the army and attaché to the Kenya African National Union. He was an independent soul, very dedicated to his cause, and seemed to love his country like no one I have seen since. I do not know what made him betray his beloved United States. Perhaps he was away for too long. He was in Africa for many years before he came to Kenya."

Julian brought Mubego his tea and he took a taste. "Milk," he said, and Julian took it back. Julian, noticed Owen, had assumed almost completely the humble bearing of Mubego's house servant, The Tea Man. Owen lifted his head to take a sip of his own tea. It helped his stomach a little more.

"One night, Capt. Dorner led an assault on a radio communications station in the north, in an attempt to seize it and broadcast propaganda. His assault succeeded briefly, but he was soon outnumbered, and he was captured in a counter assault. I led that assault, and I personally assured he was not killed. I wanted to ask him, face-to-face, why he would do such a thing. Before I could ask him, I learned a *coup d'état* had been planned by a Kenyan traitor, a general sympathetic to a Soviet-aligned party. The raid was planned as part of that *coup*, but it never materialized. It was discovered before it could begin. Your father was the only U.S. soldier involved; the rest were known communist sympathizers in our army.

"So I never bothered to ask him why. And I have not asked him to this day. And if he were to tell me, I would refuse to listen. He is still my friend, my good friend, and I'm happy to have him near me, but he has his reasons for doing things he doesn't share, as you know well. He can tell his elephants outside his window at the prison. They are the only creatures who will listen to his conscience. He would not confess his deepest thoughts to me, nor even to you. He is like a crazy man, talking to elephants."

Mubego took a slip of paper from his pocket and slid it under Owen's teacup. He carefully placed his own tea in his saucer and stood up, and Julian, seated near the door in waiting, followed his cue. They walked to the exit and Mubego turned back.

"I am sorry, young Mr. Dorner. I tried to shade you from this truth, but you were a persistent young man. The truth you came to find is found. Julian will pick you up tomorrow, when you are well, and take you to the train station. Go to the address on that paper and see the man whose name I wrote. It is hot in Mombasa, and the sun is strong for fair skin, so you ought not to stay long."

Owen vomited again. Two pills later, his stomach finally settled. He thought about Manish lying in bed like him a few blocks away, tended by an unlikely nurse.

Then he slept, and Mrs. Pearson stepped into his dream. She stood at his bedside along with his mother, who wore a shroud over her delicate brown hair. "Why are you wearing that on your head?" he asked her. "Because you're dead, Owen." "No I'm not." "She told me you were dead, just like your father. You're dead." She lowered her head and cried. Mrs. Pearson stared at him, her face flush and moist like it was at Manish's house. "I'm not dead, Mom, I'm just sick."

When he woke, it was still dark outside. He was not sweating, and there was no mosquito net over his bed—this hotel had air conditioning. He tried to remember everything Mubego had told him, but he could only recall, "It is hot in Mombasa."

31

The music was getting bouncier and the men more drunk. They deserved it all after 12 straight days in the bush. The tropical light was finally fading, with the African sky reaching wide open to swallow the sun. It was setting just behind the tall thin walls that defined this unlikely open-air club in the middle of a sleepy town in the north.

"They did well," Karl told the young but clever new Kenyan commander.

"I expected nothing less," replied Lieutenant Mubego. "Why don't you have a drink, Dorner?"

"I don't drink."

"I had no idea. I wouldn't have brought us here if I had known you were opposed to alcohol."

Karl grinned. "No, no. Put it another way: I don't drink anymore."

"Ah, I understand."

"I've had more than my share of beer for a lifetime.

Now I sit and watch others drink."

"The temptation isn't too much for you?"

Karl's grin became a broad smile, exposing the dimples that turned his tough soldier's can-do scowl into a boy's wicked smirk.

"If I didn't have the power to resist temptation," he said, "I'd be drunk with my face in a whore's lap in Berlin right now. But maybe I'll start drinking again someday, when I have a good reason."

It made Mubego smile too, his golden tooth catching a little bite out of the setting sun. "Well, then, enjoy this." Mubego took a deep, long swallow of his half-liter bottle of Tusker, and wiped his wide black lips with his sleeve.

"I couldn't refrain from drinking if I wanted to," said Mubego. "My men would think it strange I did not drink what they drank. They would wonder if I knew something about it they didn't, such as poison."

Karl doubted Mubego's men cared that much about whether he drank, but he made a mental note anyway.

"Couldn't you tell your men it was a Christian thing? Do Christians drink alcohol here?"

Mubego laughed a broad belly laugh, enough to make Suseko, his second in command, notice it over the music and celebration and turn to look. "Dorner, do Christians drink in America?"

"Point taken."

"I could tell them that, yes, but half of these men," he waved his can of beer at his soldiers, "are Christians. People are complicated wherever you go in the world. Hey, Charles! Charles Ngoya!"

Ngoya was one of the quietest men Dorner had trained. He was not particularly smart, but he was eager to learn, and bold. And half-drunk.

"Private Ngoya," said Mubego, "are you a Christian?"

"Yes, sir."

"Could you bless my beer then?"

Private Ngoya dipped his own can over Mubego's bottle, then across, then under, as if making the Sign of the Cross. "It's blessed, sir!" Mubego looked at Dorner the whole time, grinning.

"Now one sip will wash away the sins of all the previous drinks," said Mubego, and he took considerably more than a sip.

The unfailingly happy African tune yielded to Martha and the Vandellas. With American music in his ears and a chair under his ass, Karl felt more at home than he had since he arrived in Africa. These Africans really had learned faster than he expected, and Mubego's steady inspiration seemed to have a lot to do with it. He knew little of their language, but he could translate tone of voice. When they came to Mubego in twos or threes, unsure of what to do or how to settle a minor dispute, he could hear they were satisfied with his answer, not just because he was their commander but because they wished they could have thought of it, or had the authority to say it. And when Mubego chastised a man for messing up, every man paid attention and none resented him for it.

"Your men respect you," Karl said.

"I suppose so."

"Even though you aren't much older than they are."

"True."

"Why?"

Another belly laugh. Mubego motioned for more beer.

"Dorner, it is easy to be a hero when the enemy comes to your country and gives you no choice. Even if you are a young boy. I was 13 when I took the oath."

Karl knew Mubego had fought in the Mau Mau rebellion, but not that he had joined so young. He must have spent most of his childhood fighting.

"It's a good thing the Americans sent you to train my unit," Mubego continued. "If the British trained us, I might run into somebody I shot once. No, that's not possible—I never shot a Brit who didn't die of his wounds."

Mubego lowered his voice when he said this. Like the Americans, the British were allies to Kenya now, not rulers. British soldiers even came to this bar sometimes. With the Cold War on, the stakes were too high to let old animosities fester. The British were here to help Kenya stay strong, and firmly in the Western camp, and the Americans had sent personnel like Lt. Karl Dorner to fill in the training gaps. Mubego would lead well, his men would be trained well, and as a Mau Mau hero and member of the tribe that dominated Kenya's independent government, Mubego would probably move up in the ranks.

* * *

Two years later, Dorner was a captain, Mubego was already a colonel, they were back in the bush together, and Suseko was still Mubego's lieutenant. And Mubego was still a fierce fighter.

"Suseko!" Mubego's charcoal face was swollen with intensity, his forehead shiny with moisture despite the dry cool night air. He used the urgent barking whisper that soldiers use during night-time operations. "Set up a firing line at the opening of the forest, north and east. Private Tulana, behind me, ready to signal Suseko. Keep steady—the trick is to make them walk out, not get carried out."

Capt. Dorner kept his head down and peered through the leaves, trying to see any sign of activity at the radio station. Built in a clearing cut from the dense forest about 50 meters wide, the tiny cinderblock station, its radio tower soaring above it into the moonless sky, seemed to have just one door out. But it was dark, and the trees could hide the unexpected along with Mubego's small band of loyal men.

"Now what?"

Mubego squatted in front of a fever tree, took a cigarette from his shirt pocket, and popped it in his mouth. For a moment, Karl feared he would light it, though he didn't expect Mubego to be so stupid. But Mubego just sucked on it.

"Now, we wait. The station changes shift in an hour. We should expect to walk in without a fight."

Karl took the cigarette Mubego offered to him and took a long breath through it.

"Not quite what you expected to be doing tonight, eh, Captain?" Mubego said.

"Not quite."

"You never finished telling me why your government sent you back to see me."

"They sent me to convince you to use your vital influence in the government to move it to commit to remaining a firm Western ally, or at least non-aligned."

Mubego grinned, the cigarette between his teeth. "That's nice diplomatic talk. So, was this what you had in mind?"

"Why did it come to this, Mubego?"

"You sound like you don't approve, my old friend."

"I didn't say that. I just want to know if a rebellion is the only way to accomplish your goals."

"Oh, it probably isn't the only way." Mubego took the cigarette from his muscular lips, spat, and replaced it. "It's the quickest way, however, and the most certain. And I would think the Americans would want to support any action certain to keep Kenya firmly aligned with the West. That's what you came to ask for, is it not? The Americans seem willing to back up any treachery in Africa as long as it is pro-American treachery."

"Yes, well, we're fighting a larger war," Karl said.

Karl rubbed the sweat back over his prickly scalp. It was a cool night, but his body was damp. He heard something move outside the radio station, and everyone froze and stared, but it was only some kind of small animal sniffing its way across the clearing.

"Dorner, I'm asking you."

"Huh?"

"I want to know if your government is going to support me when I'm running this country. From you. Right now."

"Well, shit, I'm not the goddamn ambassador."

"Give me your educated opinion then."

"Yeah, they will. Commit to keeping the Soviets out, yes. Let us have bases, even better. You're in a position to control the entrance to the Persian Gulf. We want to do that, but we'll settle for keeping the Russians from doing it. So, yeah."

"Good. Let's start immediately." And Mubego pulled his side arm, an old Enfield No. 2, and handed it to Capt. Dorner. "Watch that door. When the shift comes out, tell them to surrender. They will hear your American accent. There should be two guards only, and they may be drunk. I will be on the other side. You have full command of my troops on this side if necessary." And he disappeared into the bush.

Mubego had just drafted Karl into his rebellion and slipped away without giving him a chance to respond, or even think about it. What happened next relieved Capt. Dorner of the dilemma over whether to follow Mubego's instructions or not, or even to let the Colonel use his American voice to scare the enemy into thinking they faced an entire force of American soldiers.

Dorner and Mubego and his men discovered, the hard way, that there were considerably more than two guards inside, and they were all quite sober, and they had allies stationed in a camp beyond the clearing within earshot of the sound of gunfire. Without hearing the *snap snap* of rifles near the station, the government soldiers at the camp might never have come to defend it. But one of Mubego's men, spooked at first light by the multitude of guards emerging from the station or perhaps by nothing but a stirring animal, fired his weapon too soon, giving them all away.

"They knew" was Capt. Dorner's first thought, but then changed his mind, since the loyal soldiers would have set up a better ambush for Mubego. The government did not know of specific plans, but they had beefed up security for this station, and perhaps others, in general fear of a rebellion. But now, it did not matter why.

In the dim light, men in the same uniforms fought each other, shooting wildly at whoever was shooting at them. When the soldiers from the encampment arrived just a few minutes into the firefight, officers barked desperate commands hoping to reestablish order, to no avail. Mubego's battle design was shattered and his small band fractured and confused, and soon soldiers were running into the forest whichever way their legs took them.

Capt. Dorner ran too—but not in fear. Years of military training had taught him to run *toward* the sound of gunfire, not away from it. Perhaps when he got there, he still had a chance to extricate himself and his country from the embarrassing fix in which Mubego had suddenly shoved him. But it was probably too late. He was inside a conflict he did not quite understand, among people who wore the same uniforms and the same skin color and spoke languages he could not follow, and who held allegiances to tribes and causes and intrigues and feuds and coalitions he could not discern. Yet everyone could spot him, the white man, the *mzunga* soldier, like a lame wildebeest trying to conceal an injured leg from the gaze of hungry, fiercely observant lions.

With the soldiers from the camp approaching behind him, Dorner sprinted along the edge of the clearing to get closer to Mubego and follow his escape, but he tripped and fell, and when he jumped back up, the foot he had tripped on hurt terribly, and he understood he was hit. It stung, like they always say it does. He felt blood fill up his boot and squish as he ran.

He managed to limp back into the cover of the trees, and there lay Charles Ngoya, the humble soldier he had trained so long ago. Ngoya also had a leg injury, but couldn't walk on it. As Karl pulled him up to his feet to help him along, Mubego emerged in front of them. He stared at the two of them for a moment and then pulled Karl away from Ngoya.

"We must get you out of here," said Mubego to Karl. Leaving Ngoya behind, he dragged Karl to a group of his men who were helping other wounded companions find a path away from the battle.

Karl pulled away from Mubego. "I can make it on my own. Go get Charles. He can't walk."

"Oh yes, Charles."

Mubego took his pistol from Karl and stalked back into the trees toward Ngoya. Karl heard a shot. Mubego reappeared.

"Charles doesn't need help anymore."

Karl watched Mubego holster the sidearm and push past him with a determined stroll, refusing to run like the men ahead of him. His leg brushed Karl's cheek, and it made Karl aware his mouth was hanging wide open. He closed it and swallowed against his dry tongue and finally regained his ability to speak.

"Why? Why did you kill Charles?"

Mubego kept walking as he spoke. "Charles was the one who fired without orders and destroyed my plan. I think you would have called him a 'goddamn idiot.' I like that turn of phrase." And he disappeared into the forest along with the last stray cracks of gunfire.

* * *

"Man, did you fuck up, Dorner."

The chastising from a general hurt more than his foot. It was awkward enough he could not stand at attention when the general came to his hospital room. Saluting him from his bed felt strange and uncomfortable. A salute, he had learned long ago, involved the entire body, not just the arm. It was a defiance of disorder, a reminder that men drew strength from their place alongside other men. So it hurt when he was reduced to a slouched salute from a hospital bed.

"You were in a position to stop this crazy thing. We didn't send you over here to overthrow the damn government!"

"Yes sir. But it wasn't ..."

"And then I have to fly in from Diego Garcia to patch things up. Do you understand how important it is to keep Kenya out of the hands of the Soviets? If they set up a naval base here, they could control everything coming in and out of the Persian Gulf. Our piddly little airstrip on Diego couldn't stand up against a Russian naval base on the coast. They could shut down oil supplies like *that*!" The general snapped his fingers.

"Yes sir, I understand. But Mubego would have been a firm ally."

"He would have. He's the most pro-American influence in the Kenyan government. But there's a little problem—Mubego couldn't find his ass with his own two hands. He's in no position to mount a successful rebellion. You trained with him, you should know that."

"Yes sir." He did not contradict the general in his assessment of Mubego. It was too late for that.

"That's why we sent you in."

"Yes sir."

"You fucked up." His anger vented, the general breathed deeply and let the blood flow back away from his face. "So now we have a problem."

The major behind the general cleared his throat. This was his cue.

"Sir, our analysis is the current government of Kenya would likely enter the Soviet sphere in the absence of Col. Mubego in his position as military advisor and his informal role as policy strategist, given his connections through the dominant tribe in the country. Without his presence, pro-communist elements and anti-Western sympathizers would openly embrace a Soviet alliance."

"We still need Mubego, badly," summed up the general.

"But the failed coup attempt two nights ago has severely threatened Mubego's position. And that represents a vital threat to the security of the United States." Those last words seemed contrived as if he had copied them from a document somewhere.

"Thank you, Major Black. Can you wait outside please?"

"Sir, I would do anything to fix this, to put it back," said Karl. "But I can't think of a way. I don't want to make excuses, but Mubego just turned this on me without warning. I would have died if need be to fix things."

"I know, Karl. I've always had confidence in you. And I do have a way for you to fix things."

The general paused and took a deep breath.

"It's not easy for me to ask you for it, Dorner, and it won't be easy for you to accept. But you're not about easy."

"What is it?"

"Somebody has to take the fall for this, instead of Mubego."

"I know."

"You'll face consequences. Probably prison time."

"I know."

"You'll probably be labeled a traitor."

Karl was silent.

* * *

It took Karl a day to sort things through in his mind before he opened the letter from June the general had handed him before leaving. He smelled it first for the perfume she always used to scent her letters. After he read it, he wished more than anything he hadn't opened it.

> Dearest Karl,
>
> The boys miss you, and so do I. Are you okay? Is it hot where you are? Please be careful about the mosquitoes so you don't catch a fever. I hope this trip won't last long like you promised. I'm taking

the boys to the beach house next month with Barbara. Maybe you will be there too. I know you do important work, but maybe now you can do some of it here.

Remember when you said I could ask you to stop when the kids needed you more than the country? Well, I think it's time to ask you. You don't have to put in your papers, you could find a stateside assignment, I don't mind moving. I'm sorry to ask you in a letter, but I was hoping you could do it before the kids start school so they could get a fresh start at a new school. And Owen is getting old enough to miss you. Not just to wish you were here, but to affect him, I think. He's an angel, but sometimes he acts a little sick. He worries about things. Don't worry about him, he's fine, but he's reaching the days when he really needs a man to look up to.

Please keep yourself safe for now, but come home soon. Love from all of us!!!!

June

32

Owen's stomach felt much better, but he still required one more urgent visit to the toilet in the train station. Then he found his name on the blackboard at the end of the platform to locate his car number as Julian had instructed. He bought a big bottle of water, the largest he could find, and sat on a bench to wait for his train. The station still clung to a colonial charm, an English elegance amid the wilderness, like a Mayan pyramid reclaimed by the jungle.

The arriving train was even more impressive. Along all the roads of Kenya, Owen had seen outdated equipment struggling along muddy trails and rutted roads. Broken down trucks with bush mechanics fashioning transmissions out of coat hangers lined the roads; decaying bicycles loaded with ten times their weight pushed by barefoot men. Yet here was a clean, modern, comfortable-looking machine. It was America on wheels.

Passengers streamed around him, searching for the

right entrance to the train. Black men in T-shirts, long pants, and sandals, black women in elaborate, colorful African wraps. An Asian-looking man sporting a bright blue turban and gray wax mustache. A tiny blonde white girl in cutoff jeans topped with a stuffed backpack that she could probably fit into, her companion a tall male with a rough beard and identical pack. A black man, nearly bald, overdressed in a blue pinstripe suit and alligator shoes. No beggars or cripples.

Owen stepped onto the train and found his suite, a decent-sized compartment lined with a pair of vinyl-covered bunk beds on each side, a simple sink near the window and a real toilet. Julian had booked him second class—not a private suite, but a world apart from the bench seats and hole-in-the-ground toilets he had walked past in third-class to get here. Imagine— African-style hole toilets on a moving train. It would be bad enough without lingering diarrhea.

The rest of the men in his compartment had already claimed their spots, including the shaggy backpacker he had spied on the platform. As Julian had told him, the compartments were assigned by sex because they were sleeping cars. Once the train moved, though, the little blonde backpacker appeared at the door, and with the permission of the rest of the men, reunited with him.

Owen thought about starting a conversation, but as soon as the train lurched forward, he fell into a deep sleep. He awoke to knocking on the door—a train attendant calling him to dinner. Everyone else was gone already. He led Owen to the dining car to join the backpacker couple, who he learned were from Sweden.

They gave Owen their Swedish names, which he promptly forgot. They complained about how difficult it was for them in the strong sun with their fair skin, and how they had to lug a mosquito net and take malaria pills daily because Larium, the stronger anti-malaria drug, wasn't available in Sweden. Mombasa, on the coast, was prime malaria country, they said. Owen wasn't taking any Malaria medications—there was no time to think about it before he left for Africa. He resolved not to stay in Mombasa for long.

Dinner was served on white tablecloths and china by black men in crisp white uniforms and black ties. It was probably exactly like a dining car in America, 50 years ago, he thought. The tourists, unaccustomed to such treatment and woefully underdressed, loved the spectacle. They snapped pictures of each other eating dinner. The waiters pretended not to notice, let alone resent, the ogling, and even took a picture or two for the naive *wazunga* who handed over their cameras.

The waiters made good sport of handling the real china on a lurching train. They had inherited the British intrepid formality in the face of adversity, even to the point of the ridiculous. At that moment of unexpected luxury, Owen remembered Manish's stories about his ancestors working to build this railway.

In his bunk, Owen gave thanks that his stomach handled the dinner well—curried chicken no less—and gazed at the passing landscape as the train rocked him to sleep. The train sped through a dusty brown village whose dusty brown children lined the track waving and singing "howayoo?"

He would reach Mombasa in the morning, and he would see the file about his father, and he could fly out of this malaria-infested place. The file would prove Mubego's claims that his father was nothing special, and he would go home disappointed. Perhaps staying home and nursing his hero fantasies would have been better. Still, Owen couldn't help doubting that Mubego had told him everything. Was it because Mubego seemed to care so much about it, to involve himself in every affair regarding his father since he had arrived here? Why was his finger in every pie, popping up every time Owen turned around? Was he more than a second-rate district prison warden and local police chief? Was there a reason he so carefully and expertly led Owen around the country in the service of this elaborate story?

He awoke to bright sunlight sloshing about the rocking compartment like bilge water in a rolling ship. Owen was alone. He had overslept a meal again— breakfast this time. No matter, he thought, sleep was what he needed now, not food. He splashed water on his face from the tiny sink below the window and looked out to judge the time. Then, amid the scant but robust flat-topped trees, he spied a group of elephants.

There were three of them, two large and one smaller. He was almost as close to these elephants as to the one that nearly attacked him his first day in Kenya, or the one he confronted on the way back from the safari. Yet through the window of the train, he might as well be miles away. The train passed them, and then sped through a tiny village, with more little children lined up along the tracks, waving. He might as well be miles from them too. It was nothing new for him, looking at wild animals and people in strange countries from a safe, comfortable vantage point. But now that he had walked among them, the distance felt unnatural. Owen was distinctly aware of his position as a wealthy, white, privileged person like never before. The realization was both reassuring and uncomfortable. How much more he had seen, and learned in school, than those little children waving at a train? They might never travel beyond their little villages their whole lives. Then he thought of Wanjeri, and how she must have felt traveling to his world.

He would be in Mombasa in an hour with a dinner served on real china by a waiter in a tie still in his belly. How long would it take one of those children to walk to Mombasa if they ever wanted to go? A week?

* * *

Owen had forgotten the lingering sunburn on his neck earned at Masai Mara, but Mombasa's heat reminded him again. Mombasa brought humidity that the highlands of Nairobi lacked, but it supported more trees and other tropical greenery, which almost made up for it. But not quite.

As they exited the train, a policeman stopped the emerging passengers out of respect for the Kenyan flag as it was hoisted at the Mombasa station for the morning.

Owen bought a tourist map in the station. The U.S. consulate was on Haile Selassie Road, the map said, the same long avenue that stretched from the train station to the old walled city on the coastline, next to Fort Jesus, the high stone fortress from which the Portuguese ruled this land after they wrested it from the Arabs, before they lost it to the English. Halfway down Haile Selassie stood the Hard Rock Cafe Mombasa, a great sighting that he filed away for the future, as it was likely to have air conditioning. The streets connecting to Haile Selassie seemed to have all the same names as the streets in Nairobi.

Owen looked at the note Mubego had given him to tell him who to speak to in Mombasa. "John Hentoff" he had written in his old-fashioned handwriting.

He remembered now. Hentoff—it was the same name his father had told him to seek at the embassy in Nairobi. It wasn't the same man who had died in the bombing the embassy worker mentioned.

This Hentoff man had survived the bombing, and he knew something about Owen's father. Perhaps he had even known his father. If both his father and Mubego were sending Owen to see Hentoff in search of the truth, Owen figured Hentoff either was absolutely reliable ... or a total liar.

The American accents he heard in the lobby of the consulate made Owen suddenly sick for home.

After a short wait, Hentoff found Owen in the lobby. Hentoff looked old enough to retire, but his taut frame and weathered face revealed a toughness that defied his age. His mustache drooped to his chin like it had melted down his lip, and he chewed on an unlit pipe. His hair was cropped short but was thick enough to cover his skull. Hentoff was a full six inches shorter than

Owen, but he walked and chewed the pipe like he didn't feel the least bit smaller than any man.

"They said you were coming," he said. Owen wasn't surprised to hear that. Hentoff led Owen to a room down the hall stuffed floor to ceiling with files and boxes. "They didn't tell me you were so young."

Hentoff opened a door to a small room with a single desk and a few file cabinets.

"These are the files we were able to recover from the embassy after the attack. Recovering anyone's file, especially one as old as your father's, is very difficult under these circumstances."

Was Mubego mistaken? Was this another dead end?

"But you're in luck," Hentoff continued. "I have been with the Kenya delegation for quite a while and was able to locate most of your father's file." He pointed to a thin file folder that lay on the otherwise bare wooden desk.

He pulled a chair up to the desk, motioned for Owen to sit, and slid the file toward him. Then he leaned back against the wall, arms crossed, mustache wiggling back and forth like a caterpillar as he worked on the pipe. His eyes stayed fixed on Owen. His gaze signaled expectation—to hurry up and read it, or perhaps in anticipation of what Owen would find?

The folder contained a long sheet from U.S. Army files full of basic information about Karl Dorner. Enlisted in 1960, two years at a base in Texas (Owen's mother was from Texas). Special training in tactics and weapons. Owen could only understand some of the military jargon. Time living in Germany (Owen was born in Germany). Assigned to work some unnamed jobs at embassies in

Gabon, South Africa, then Kenya, all in a year's time. Volunteered for a special security detail with a vague name. Then the record ended. A gray sheet of embassy stationery stapled to the sheet continued the story:

"The United States of America hereby waives all diplomatic and military privileges in the manner of Capt. Karl Dorner and releases him for trial on criminal charges by the Republic of Kenya. The United States further declares Capt. Dorner reverts to the custody of the United States government when and if such custody by the Republic of Kenya may end."

That was it, except for a yellowing newspaper clipping from the *Nairobi News Daily*:

> REBELS SENTENCED FOR FAILED COUP
>
> Nairobi—Three attempted rebels were sentenced to death by the Kenya High Court yesterday for their role in the plot of March last. The rebels, all secret members of the banned East Africa Socialist Revolution Party, a communist-aligned group, were sentenced after trial by a military court for attempting to overtake a communications station near Lake Naivasha in the Rift Valley.
>
> Military authorities released a statement saying the plot was part of a larger coup d'état scheme that failed to materialize after the takeover was foiled by Kenya troops and police. The two civilian employees of the station were killed by the rebels while several rebels died. One foreigner, a former U.S. soldier gone over to the Reds, was also sentenced to life imprisonment.

There was nothing to contradict, or add to, Mubego's account. Hentoff watched impassively as Owen tried to hide his heartbreak. He did not move when Owen closed the file, thanked him, and walked out into the soaking heat.

But then Owen heard a voice behind him.

"Mr. Dorner! One more thing you should know."

Owen turned. Hentoff had followed him outside.

"You really ought to visit Fort Jesus, the old fort on the bay," he said, pointing his thumb down the avenue. "It's quite beautiful, especially in the evening, around seven o'clock."

Tourist advice?

"Around seven o'clock would be a very good time for you to go to the fort. I may go there myself, and maybe we will talk more. Do you understand?"

Owen understood. It was not tourist advice. He turned and almost tripped over the carvings of elephants and giraffes a peddler had laid out on the street.

* * *

Fort Jesus commanded a high view from a cliff over a large bay and the Indian Ocean beyond. From street level, though, its entrance was just a few steps up, across the street from the old Arabian town with stone houses and winding narrow streets impassable to cars. Owen looked through a hole in the wall with an old cannon poking through it, protecting the town from invasion from the sea.

Hentoff found Owen wandering inside the fort's central plaza with various tourists. The pipe was gone, and he wore a wide-brimmed straw hat to shield from the tropical sun, or perhaps from unwelcome attention.

He greeted Owen quietly and beckoned him to a secluded place down a staircase into the lower interior of the fort. A large cannon hole, stripped of its weapon, brought a welcome ocean breeze.

"I never thought anyone would ever ask about Karl ever again," he said. "I never knew he had a family. We didn't talk about things like that."

"You know my dad?"

"Please, let me talk and then I'll need to leave. After I go, you stay here for 15 minutes and then leave through that entrance. This isn't necessarily a good idea, you understand?"

"Yes."

"Your father was a friend of mine, at least as close a friend as we could be under the circumstances. We talked about a lot of things, mostly work things, but enough for me to know what made him tick. I used to be involved in counterintelligence work in the Navy, so I know what I'm talking about. Your dad took some of the most dangerous and important work there was. He passed all his clearances with flying colors. He was no communist and no traitor. No way in hell. And he wouldn't fall for money, or sex, or blackmail or anything like that. He would have laughed at all that. There's no way your dad was involved in this. He was set up. Maybe they planned it in advance, or maybe he was just in the wrong place at the wrong time. But I don't know anyone I'd trust more.

"I never thought I'd have anyone to tell this. After Karl went to prison, the government made it plain I'd be staying in Africa for the rest of my career if I wanted a pension. On a normal career track, I'd have been shipped out of here long ago."

A couple speaking a foreign language shuttled through the room, looking out the portal at the ocean before they moved on. Hentoff waited in silence until they left, gazing with Owen at the bay.

"I think they are keeping an eye on me. And I think that's what they're doing with your dad too. They need him for something, like me. Maybe he doesn't even know why. Maybe you could go see him in prison and ask him."

"I've already seen him."

His whole body became rigid in surprise.

"You've seen him?"

"A few days ago."

"Is he doing alright?"

"He's ... surviving. He seems to be healthy, physically. But I have nothing to compare to. I never met him before that except as a little kid. I have no memories of him."

"You could compare him to yourself. You're a lot like him."

They both looked out at the ocean for a while, then Hentoff moved closer to Owen and lowered his voice.

"I would have liked to have sent him a message," Hentoff said.

"What?"

"That ... people still think about him."

"He knows that now, I guess."

Hentoff took off his hat and wiped his brow. "He saved my life, your dad did."

"How?"

"We were hunting, up in the mountains. We weren't much of hunters, but back then any idiot could go out with a rifle and shoot whatever he wanted, so there we were. We hardly found any game in the forest, and we didn't get anything that day, but we sure had fun anyway. On the way down the mountain, we got stopped by a roadblock, and two Africans with guns, big guns, yanked us out of the car. They were just kids, but people were getting killed by bandits at roadblocks left and right those days, and I was scared. Like a fool I pulled out my diplomatic passport, and they laughed. They probably couldn't read it anyway, not that they cared. One of them marched me down the road a ways and made me lie down. He was sifting through my pockets, and then he stopped. I heard Karl say something in an African language, not Swahili, one I didn't know, and I looked up and he had his hunting rifle right in the guy's ear. Behind him, the other bandit was lying face down, hogtied with his own shirt. I tell you, your dad got some kind of special training I never got in the military. He was quick and he was brave. And he was damn loyal.

"I was stunned to hear he betrayed his country. For years, I refused to believe it. It was exactly the opposite of his character and his beliefs. I guess anyone can fool anyone. But I've never accepted it. He's the last one I'd peg for doing that."

"Tell me what happened at the trial."

"There was no trial. Karl pled guilty."

"He did?"

"Yes. Not only that, he refused legal representation and all help from the embassy or the military. It was strange, like it was all planned in advance. They must have had something on him. I don't like to think about it."

"Do you know the name Mubego? Col. Mubego?"

"Of course. He's the warden up at Kumbata. A real operator. He has connections everywhere. I think it was his people who told me to expect you at the embassy. When your dad was sentenced, Mubego was at the highest level of the military here. He would have been supreme commander, working directly for the president, if it weren't for the coup attempt. He was bumped down after that. But he doesn't seem to have suffered much from it. In fact, there was remarkably little fallout."

"Was Mubego involved in the coup?"

Hentoff looked both ways.

"Sorry son, your time is up."

"Wait–how did you know I was coming? Why did he ...?"

"I have to go. Don't contact me again. This has gone too far already. Good luck. I still say Karl's a good man."

A good man. As Manish had said.

And without another word, Hentoff hurried out the passageway. For the first time, Owen felt how cool the stones of the fort were in this boiling hot town.

On the train back to Nairobi, Owen was no longer in the mood to deal with strangers, or anyone. He lay in his bunk and let the train rock him and the wind blow his hair around. He sorted through his clothes, repacking them to keep them from wrinkling any more. He folded an ancient T-shirt with a familiar stain timelessly etched across the front. It never suited his tall frame, and he had resolved to give it away many times. He picked it up, still folded neatly, and stuffed it out the open sliver at the top of the window. Some little child would soon be waving and yelling "howayoo!" dressed in an old blue T-shirt a few sizes too big.

*　*　*

"Your father wants to see you again."

Wanjeri surprised him at the Nairobi station. Despite the soothing motion of the train and the private compartment, he was groggy from a fitful night. She caught up with him in the cool passage between the platform and the street outside.

"He wants to see you again. You must come with me."

She grabbed his hand and pulled him away, like she wanted to hide them from public view. Her hand was so elegant and slim, yet with skin rough from hard work. It felt good to hold that hand, but still he yanked away from it.

"I don't want to see him, though."

"But he is your father. He wants to talk to you. It is important."

"I've seen him once; I don't need to see him again. I'm tired of entertaining your uncle and his family."

She stopped and sat on the ground where she stood, staring down at the dust, like a child refusing to move on more inch, her black hair capturing bits of the African sun.

"You think I am helping my uncle, don't you? You think I am setting you up?"

"Yes, I think maybe you are setting me up. I don't know why, but I don't care why any more. I'm tired of the games. I came here to see my father, I saw him, now I'm off to the airport."

But he could not leave her there. He could not make this his last moment in her presence. So he sat next to her on the ground, unsure of what to do next.

"Owen, I am not like other African girls. I went to England and studied and it changed me. I don't know if it made me better, but it made me understand things better. The old me would never think of doing anything that might hurt my family. But even though he is my family, I am not helping the Colonel. He has done things I would never do. I am helping you."

"Maybe you are trying to help me," Owen said, "but I still don't want it. It was a stupid idea for me to come here and see my father like he is. He's not well. He was a traitor and a criminal, and now he's insane. And Mubego plays around with me and doesn't tell me why. And even if you mean to help me, you can't beat him. Going back to prison puts me right back under his thumb."

Now she looked straight at him. Her effulgent, delicate eyes would not let go of him.

"We won't be going back to the prison," she said.

"What?"

"Owen, I spent four years in field work for my master's degree in zoology. I studied elephant behavior. It was perfectly natural for me. I followed family groups around. I named every elephant and knew everything that happened, like I was part of their family."

He was uncomfortable on the ground, but she seemed

to nestle easily into it, like a doe lying on the grass, legs tucked under.

Not back to the prison?

"I followed a large group, a very successful family, with several babies. One day, they all came upon a river to cross. They all crossed, including the young ones, except one I named Star. He was in his second year and big enough to cross the shallow river, but Star was absolutely terrified. He wanted to follow, of course, but refused to go in past his knees. The rest of the group tried for hours to convince him. Star's mother and a few others even went back over to lead him over. But Star would not cross."

Owen remembered this story. He had heard it from a crazy man who shared his name and lived in a hard, dusty prison.

When his father told him the story, it seemed pointless like his other rantings. It took a beautiful young girl with piercing eyes to make Owen sit still on the ground and understand the story had a meaning.

"So I watched as the entire group crossed back over the river and walked in another direction," Wanjeri continued, "and they went many days out of their way to avoid crossing the river. The entire family changed its destiny for the sake of one little animal. They stayed with him, no matter what."

He lost his breath for a moment. She was the source of the story! His father had heard it from her!

"Your father is no longer in prison. He has escaped. He wants to see you. He needs your help."

He sat in the sun, sweat dripping down his temple

and his leg cramping. He pondered kissing her right there, but thought again about the danger of it. She had given him the means to talk to his father one-on-one, away from the shadow of a grinning, plotting warlord. He resolved he would stay a little longer and make sense of this bewildering place before he left.

"He needs your help," she repeated. "He can speak to you freely now."

"My father told me that same story, about Star. He made me think it was some kind of ancient African myth," he said. "But it was just something you saw."

She smiled. "Every ancient African myth starts as just something somebody saw."

33

The road to Mt. Kenya was terrible, worse than the one they had taken from Kumbata south to the safari a few days ago. The driver Wanjeri had hired for the day spent much of the trip swerving into the right lane to avoid ruts and potholes. This often produced a game of chicken with oncoming traffic, usually a huge truck, which always won.

Traffic thinned as they moved away from the city, and the countryside sprung forth abruptly after they left Nairobi's suburbs. They passed a sprawling pineapple plantation with neat rows of green sprouts, each atop a single bulbous fruit. Soon they were in the foothills alongside the Great Rift Valley. Africa's sky was clearly more generous with her rain here, and massive deep-green leaves like those Owen had admired in the village between Kumbata and the Masai Mara began to appear. The surroundings became as verdant as Mombasa and the coast, but without the sticky heat. Finally, thought Owen, here was a place in Africa rich with trees but cool and comfortable—more like home than any other place he had been in Africa.

As always, people walked along the road or sat on the ground next to impromptu fruit stands, tacky carving stands aimed at tourists, or next to their broken down vehicles. Owen spotted people walking virtually every mile of the road, even where there was no sign of a nearby village for many miles. Whenever they hit another stretch of bad pavement, Owen envied the pedestrians for a moment. But not for long. Riding past people walking for what must be many miles, some carrying heavy loads, some barefoot, in a car with a driver made him feel outrageously rich, even more than on the train ride to Mombasa. In this place, he *was* outrageously rich.

"There is Mt. Kenya," said the driver. A steep, rocky summit jutting from a larger cone of land lay straight ahead. Ten minutes later, the summit was obscured by clouds, and Owen never saw it again.

"Where will we meet him?"

Wanjeri had been silent most of the drive. "It is not wise to talk now," she replied quietly, with a nod to the driver. In the quiet of their two-hour trip, Owen felt he was getting to know Wanjeri less instead of more. How little he knew about this woman bringing him on this strange adventure. Here was a woman with one foot in his world and the other in her own. He watched her staring out the window with great concentration. Does she think like an African, or a westerner? In English, or Swahili or Kikuyu? Or no language at all? Did she think in some strange elephant language, perhaps, that only she and the animals know?

They turned onto a gravel road that ran past fenced open fields. The area resembled an American farmland scene as closely as anything he had seen in Africa. Like the trees and meadows, it was reassuring. Then they reached a strip of forest at the edge of the mountain.

The driver pulled onto a dirt road with a sign leading to "Kifaru Lodge." The lodge looked like an English country house dropped into the middle of Africa. It was a two-story stone structure with a small but adequate porch. Someone had made a valiant effort to landscape around the house, but dry season means dry season. Owen spied a tennis court in a clearing just inside the trees. Were they staying here? Was his father inside? But what about the camping gear Wanjeri had placed in the trunk? Owen suppressed his questions as she had requested. She went in first.

The inside of the lodge sported dark wood paneling, a few mounted game heads advertising its origin as a hunting lodge, and a white woman serving orange juice at the door. Before he could finish his juice, Wanjeri took his arm and led him back outside. "We should not talk to anyone here if we don't have to." She huddled with him next to the pile of camping gear as the driver left them in a cloud of dust.

"We only came here so the driver would have nothing unusual to say when he goes back to Nairobi. We will leave soon on foot. I know the way. We'll leave separately so we don't attract attention as a white man and black woman hiking together. Everyone will remember that if the police ask."

He liked that she called him a man, not a boy.

"But we arrived together," he said. "Weren't we seen?"

"Yes, but I could be a tour guide or hired help for a larger group. Just the two of us together would draw suspicion, and would be easy to remember. That's why I will carry all the camping gear inside alone. Put that down."

Wanjeri had a bit of her uncle in her.

Owen dropped his bag back in the dust.

"I will tell a cover story inside. We can rest a little here, but we leave in an hour."

"Where are we going?"

"There." And she looked up at the clouds shrouding the top of Mt. Kenya.

But slipping under Mubego's gaze would be harder than they thought. As they stood outside, they saw a policeman arrive in a car and walk into the lodge. That could only mean one thing: Mubego had sent him to check out a sighting along the way, perhaps, or suspected Kifaru Lodge as a possible destination. The lodge was apparently not at the top of Mubego's list of places to check, though, since the policeman was not one of Mubego's professionals but a bumbling local. Accustomed to displays of power, he walked right in the front door in full uniform, with no attempt at subtlety, and didn't notice Owen or Wanjeri.

No doubt the first thing out of the policeman's mouth would be a request for two people meeting their description and he would come back outside. They had to leave now. Own helped Wanjeri drag their gear into the woods, out of sight, and they strapped their packs on their backs. Owen's was lighter than he expected.

No need to worry about being seen together now.

"Will the people here tell the police about us?"

"Don't worry, my family is from this region. That may serve us well for a time, but soon it will hurt us."

"Why's that?"

"It's also my uncle's family."

She led him to the head of a trail up the mountain. "We'll follow this trail so they can't tell our tracks from others, for now. Then we'll go into the forest. We must try not to meet anyone along the way, so we will leave the trail soon."

They were making a steady pace up a slight incline, and Owen was already falling behind. He wasn't in shape for climbing, or even hiking fast. Sitting in your room will do that. But he pushed himself, knowing they had to make time against Mubego's men until they were safe in the bush.

"It will be a little harder going off the trail, but we can slow down then. We will have to watch out in the heavy forest to avoid taking any large animals by surprise."

"Large animals?"

"Or snakes."

"Or snakes. Great."

It made him think of Indiana Jones and his fear of snakes, and that made him think of Manish. Was he safe now, and getting better?

As they climbed in altitude, the terrain changed quickly from the dense forest to larger, pleasantly spaced trees that allowed them to see further. A monkey let out a horrible scream to their right from high up in the forest. Wanjeri hiked in silence, and though Owen knew the quiet would suit her fine all the way up, he couldn't wait any longer to finally talk to her alone. His conversation was only limited by his lack of breath as he huffed up the increasingly steep mountain.

"What does Kifaru mean?"

"Rhinoceros."

"Are there rhinos in this area?" he asked, half interested, half alarmed. She had mentioned large animals.

"Not anymore. The Kifaru was a hunting lodge."

She had a way of explaining things with the fewest words possible.

"You're wearing jeans."

"Yes."

"You're the first girl I've seen in Africa in jeans."

"I know. I almost didn't wear them so as not to attract attention, but they are too good for walking in the forest."

"Did you wear them in England much?"

"Oh, all the time. I did many things the English way. I felt English there."

"You did?"

"Since Kenya was ruled by the English, it came naturally. We do many things like the English. Like drinking tea. Or speaking English."

"You don't drop everything you're doing and drink tea at four every afternoon like they do over there." As if Owen had ever been to England or had tea.

"Some of us do. Especially those of us who have lived in England."

"Can we drop everything and have tea right now?" he asked between breaths. "I can understand why they do it."

"No tea time today, Owen." She laughed.

Owen drank some more water from the bottle he had strapped to his waist. She hadn't touched her water yet.

"Where are we ..." He paused for a new breath. He was still a bit weak from the sickness.

"... going?"

"To a place where the Mau Mau hid when they were fighting the English. Some caves, further up."

"And your uncle, he won't, find, us, there?" he said between breaths.

"He knows the place. But he doesn't know we are going there."

That wasn't very reassuring.

"Let's rest here for a moment and listen," she said.

The trees were not tall here, but wide and strong, with plenty of space between them, almost like buildings in a city. They sheltered from all angles, yet did not hide threats, like large animals or snakes. It was cooler now too, much cooler. Though the forest had changed quickly as they ascended the mountain, the African sky was constant, half-visible through the treetops. But even the sky was obscured at the top of the mountain.

"Are we going up there? In the clouds?"

"No, not that far." He was glad to hear that.

"Are you sure your uncle won't find us here?"

"I don't think so, but it is too late anyway. Your father chose this place to meet."

Owen imagined his father hiking up this same path, much faster and with much less effort than Owen, no doubt. Was he already up the mountain? Or behind them? He didn't have the breath to ask.

They reached a small crest with a clearing just beyond it. Wanjeri sat on the ground, elbows on knees, while Owen lay on his side and breathed. The altitude was beginning to rob him of oxygen just when he needed it most. He saw little evidence of fatigue in her save a single pure stream of sweat running down her flawless brown cheek, like a tear. Her dark eyes seemed to absorb him even as she looked past him.

Owen was reluctant to talk to her more for fear it would only deepen her mystery. Jeans and tea aside, she was no English woman, nor American. He resolved instead to follow her wherever she took him and know her that way. Still, he could offer his own thoughts.

"It's interesting—the Colonel hid from the English on this mountain, and now he's chasing white people around up here."

"But I am not white."

"You'll do for now."

"I don't understand what you mean."

"Nothing. It meant nothing. It was just something to say."

He shut up as long as he could.

"You're taking a big risk doing this," he said.

"Yes."

"Why?"

"I want to do what's right."

"It doesn't matter that you are going against your family?"

She looked away. "I am doing something right for your family," she said.

"I appreciate that. I didn't before, but my head is clearer up here somehow."

She stood, ready to walk again. "Yes. My head is clearer up here too. I think … I think I don't have any family any more. Just these elephants. My parents are gone, and my Uncle Abasi is barely alive, and Uncle Mubego hates me because of what I did to Abasi."

"What you did?"

"For what happened, I mean. Because I was there."

"Oh."

They started up the mountain again.

"I think he wanted to make Manish suffer, because of Abasi. To make himself feel better. He humiliates people to remind him and everyone else who is in charge. It took me a long time to understand what kind of man my Uncle Mubego is. Not much better than Uncle Abasi was."

Owen said nothing. He didn't understand everything she was saying, but somehow he sensed it, and that was enough.

"My uncle—both my uncles—they're nothing like my father was. They use people for their own needs. Anybody. You are a tool to Mubego. He pretends to like you, and he thinks that means he is being a good man, but he is always finding a way for himself to benefit. Always himself."

Wanjeri finally wiped the sweat from her face. Owen was nearly soaked in sweat, and now he was cooling rapidly. He stopped and pulled another shirt from his bag and put it on over the sweaty one.

"So when you find the good people, it is important to cherish them," she added.

Owen sensed she wanted to stop talking about it, so he changed the subject. "Do you know the way well?"

"I have been here before," was her answer. Owen was still leery, given they were a pair of sweaty hunks of meat crashing through the territory of animals that liked to eat sweaty meat. "We must get off this trail now before we are seen."

She gestured into the forest to their right.

"We will have good guides though. This way."

"Guides?"

"Our guides know the way better than anyone."

Wanjeri led him past a thick collection of trees that hid a clearing with enough space to collect sun. She put her hand up in front of Owen, silently stopping him before he could step out into the open space. The area was dotted by tall trees and rich green grass, not the burnt brown of the plains below. It was the perfect place for loyal, intelligent, giant creatures to congregate.

These were their guides—a dozen elephants of all sizes languished among the trees, as if waiting for them. The closest was 30 meters away, yet he had not detected them until he reached the very edge of the clearing.

This was his third time coming so close to an elephant, he mused. The first time, on the bus trip, he was afraid;

the second, on the safari, courageous; and now he was content in their presence and they seemed content in his. Owen stood motionless and watched them gently pull leaves from the lower branches of the trees and stuff them in their mouths while two tiny babies, barely taller than Owen, frolicked and bumped into the legs of their kin, until Wanjeri grabbed his arm to pull him back into the brush.

"We have to wait here until the afternoon," she whispered. "Don't talk too loud. We will present ourselves, but not in a way to disturb them."

"They are going to guide us all the way to the caves?"

"Yes."

"How do they know to bring us there?"

"They will be going to a place near there. Following them allows us to stay off the trail and cover our tracks and noise, and if any danger is nearby, they will warn us."

"My father is already at the caves, isn't he? This is how you brought him here, too."

"Yes."

"You knew my father before all this." It was half a question, half its answer.

"Yes."

"You told him the story about the baby elephant that wouldn't cross the river. Star."

"I told him that story. He loved it. He loved the elephants almost as much as I do. He would come to visit us at my uncle's house."

"Mubego let him visit from prison?"

"He came before that, but yes, also when he was a prisoner. That's when I first met him."

"And you know what happened, why he is in prison and why Mubego is so obsessed with him."

"I knew a little about your father, and I knew of some things my uncle was involved in. Only after you came here have I come to understand how the stories fit together."

"How do they fit together?"

She looked at her feet. "I want your father to tell you."

"Did he tell you?"

"A bit. I thought he would have told you when you visited him in the prison. But he didn't?"

Owen didn't answer that. "When did you meet him?"

"Once when he first came from the prison, before I went to university in London. Then again after I came back and did my field research. My uncle would bring him home with him for visits."

"Mubego really let him out of prison to visit his house?"

"Certainly. He is the warden of the prison; he can do that. They would sit in the courtyard and talk. They were old friends, you know. They trained in the Army together or something. It was like having a houseguest, except when he left, he was put back in chains."

"Did your uncle tell you who he was or why he was in prison?"

"Never. But your father seemed so relaxed at the house. My uncle has a way of making anyone feel at home, friend or foe. Your father was very likeable. He asked me all about my studies, what I wanted to do. He helped to inspire me to study elephants, actually. When I said I was interested, he told me all about seeing them in the bush when he was out training with my uncle Mubego, and how comfortable he felt with them near, like they were members of his family in the same house. And I felt like that too, and so I decided to ask my uncle if I could go to London for my education."

"Is that when you told him the story about the elephant that wouldn't cross the river?"

"No, it was later, after I came back from London and did the field research for my degree. That is when I saw it happen and then told your father what I saw. He was pleased I had gone to school and done the studies. He said he wished he could go observe elephants like me. He loved being in the wild."

"Did he ever ... mention me?"

"He did not."

Owen wished he hadn't asked.

"I'm sorry, Owen. But he never said anything about his family, not to me."

Owen put his hands on his knees. He was still winded from the climb.

"When did he go crazy, Wanjeri?"

"What do you mean?"

"When did he start acting so strange? All the rambling, the bluster and lies and sarcasm he threw at me when I went to see him."

"I think perhaps you expected something unreasonable from your father. You came to him without warning, and you reminded him of something he has been trying to forget."

"Why? What is he trying to forget?"

"He can tell you. Even if I knew the whole story, I could not tell you. It involves my uncle, and he is my family. I should not speak of my own family. I have already done too much by bringing you both here."

She was betraying her family by helping him. It was no easy thing to do. In his haste to move closer to his father, he had forgotten how hard it was for her to separate from her own family, perhaps forever. What do you do after you've betrayed a man like her uncle?

"I'm very grateful to you, Wanjeri."

"Don't be. I'm not doing this for you, or your father. I have to do it. People will say going to school in England ruined me, as they've always said. Julian says it all the time. Wanjeri won't follow the authority of her father, or her uncles; Wanjeri hasn't married, she goes out in the bush alone to look at elephants. Maybe they are right. I'm not quite African anymore."

"No, no, you're as African as anyone."

"Really? Tell me, have you ever heard an African talk to you the way I do? Have you ever talked to another African the way you talk to me? Wearing jeans?"

"I guess not."

"I don't know what I am anymore. Or where I'm going."

"I guess now that's me too," said Owen.

*　*　*

Owen had dozed off with his back leaning against a tree when she woke him. The sun was drooping over the low side of the mountain, just outside the clouds. He felt his face. He had gone long enough without a shave for his 18-year-old face to sprout like any older man's. It made him feel grown up and strong.

He looked out on the clearing and saw the last of the herd heading into the forest, uphill. Wanjeri motioned at him to join her in following them. They donned their packs and walked behind, far enough not to disturb them, but close enough that they could smell Owen and Wanjeri and to know they were the same harmless humans who had spent the day following them without threatening them.

"Elephants don't have very good eyes," said Wanjeri. "They use smell and sound. Sometimes it's good to stay undetected, other times, to stay well detected. But they do see better in soft light than bright light, so keep that in mind."

The huge creatures were easy to follow, even as the forest grew darker. Their giant bodies made ample noise even as they trod single file. And if Wanjeri and Owen lost sight of the familiar rear end of the last elephant in the line, crushed vegetation and the occasional giant hunk of steaming dung kept them on track, both by sight and odor. Wanjeri stepped in some, shaking her heel off and scolding herself, and for the first time on the mountain Owen felt like her equal as he chuckled.

"How do they know where they're going?

"Elephant herds are led by matriarchs, like a wise elder. She knows from her experience the information about every route to every source of food, water and minerals, every season, and how the last drought or flood season was best handled. Everything depends on her leading the troop and passing on her knowledge to her heiress."

"Which one is the matriarch?"

"The one in front."

"Oh, well duh!"

"What?"

"Nothing."

A monkey screeched out in the trees somewhere.

"When poachers want to kill a whole herd of elephants, they shoot the matriarch first," she said. "The rest of the herd doesn't know what to do and they panic, and they can shoot them easily."

"Well, that's depressing. Don't say that too loud, the matriarch will hear you."

"Don't worry, there are no poachers around here."

Soon it was completely dark. They never would have found their way without the elephants, who blazed their trail with perfect confidence. Then they seemed to disappear into the darkness, too.

Wanjeri stopped for a moment, peered ahead into the dark, grabbed Owen's arm and led him quietly. The moon was nearly full that night, but it was on the other side of the mountain, and all it illuminated was the sky and the tops of the trees that brushed against it.

They reached the side of the mountain and then kept moving—inside of the mountain.

The moonlight disappeared, and the air cooled. Owen heard an elephant's low rumble. It sounded like a voice on a tape recorder played ridiculously slow. And he heard it echo. They were entering a cave—one so large it literally held a herd of elephants.

Suddenly, Wanjeri's face appeared in a faint ball of light. She had turned on a flashlight. Then he could see parts of an elephant's hide not ten meters away. She walked carefully over the rocks and mud at their feet, and he followed her lead. He wanted to tell her walking into a cave full of huge wild creatures meant he trusted her completely and he would follow her wherever else she took him, but he sensed speaking now could disturb the elephants. He also sensed she knew it already.

She moved the light around and they explored the cave with their eyes. The creature directly in front of them was a young one. It looked in their direction but seemed unconcerned by the light shining in its face. The rest of the elephants were spread out through a gigantic cavern with high ceilings, so big the flashlight's illumination fell short of penetrating to some parts. A few small boulders, fresh fallings from the ceiling, littered the floor, but most of the ground beneath them was soil and gravel trampled flat by the broad feet of elephants. One raised its ears at them in alarm, but Wanjeri said a soft low Swahili word, and it dropped the giant flaps down.

Owen could see narrower passages to darkness further back, which must have been other rooms in the cave—and must have held other elephants, as only five or six were within range of the light. These unlikely spelunkers were busy rubbing their tusks on the walls of the cave or collecting fallen soil into their mouths. They were eating the dirt. And just as he made this discovery and wondered why they ate dirt and whether it was safe to speak aloud to ask Wanjeri, she answered both questions.

"They are here for minerals," she said in a low, steady voice. "It is like many animals that need salt and minerals they don't get from most food sources."

"So this is one big salt lick?"

"Yes, yes, a big salt lick. Because of their weight and the way their feet are built to support it, elephants must use a great deal of energy to climb up mountains. So we know this place is important to them. They need these minerals."

"Is my father here?" Owen peered into the darkness.

"No. Another cave, very different, further up the mountain. We'll reach it tomorrow morning."

The elephants ignored them and their lights. Owen breathed easier. He could see his breath fogging in the glare of the flashlight; the air had become cold quickly.

"Why aren't they disturbed by us?"

"Because I have come here before, when I did field research on this herd. I came here many nights. They are used to the light. But do not talk too loud."

"Don't worry," he whispered.

The two tiny humans sat on their haunches inside the entrance to the palace of elephants, silently watching the creatures take up their recommended daily allowance of minerals. Owen had seen so many wonderful, terrible, and strange things in Africa, but never did he imagine he would witness an entire herd of elephants eating dirt in a cave.

"There is a theory about how these caves came about. The elephants may have dug them. They can cut through the soil with their tusks, and then the roof caves in somewhat. And of course, they eat most of the dirt. It would take a herd like this, working generation to generation, only a thousand years or so to do it."

"That's amazing. Do you think that's how it happened?"

"It is not unbelievable."

It was, he was learning, a typical Wanjeri answer. Polite, noncommittal, yet in its meaning clear enough. But she added, "This mountain is where the Kikuyu believe the world was born and they were created. Perhaps the elephants are not finished creating their part of the world."

Wanjeri turned the flashlight to a shelf of earth inside the entrance. "We'll sleep there. It's safe from the elephants and anything outside, but it still has fresh air. It's where I slept when I came here."

The cool ground felt good, and there was just enough moonlight coming in the entrance to make Owen feel snug. The shelf was narrow but long, and Wanjeri settled in with her head at his feet. For a blanket, she gave him one of the two thin square cloths she carries everywhere. He had seen many African women carry these kangas and use them for anything and everything—a dress, head wrap, baby sling, grocery bag, whatever they needed. In Mombasa, he remembered the sight of hundreds of them, of all different colors and styles, for sale on the streets.

"Tomorrow we will go to the other cave," said Wanjeri.

"It is not an elephant cave, but one where people go. It's beautiful. It is the place where the Mau Mau hid. It is where we will meet your father."

He realized his father probably saw this just days ago. He might have slept in the same spot. She brought him up here on this very same journey. What great risks she was taking for the two of them.

"Wanjeri? Are you sure about this?"

"Of course. We will be perfectly safe."

"No, not the cave. All this."

She said nothing.

He lay in the dark, breathing the smell of salty earth and elephant dung, listening to the noises of elephants shuffling and their stomachs rumbling and digesting the earth, and remembered something. In this dark, unfamiliar, confining place, filled with beasts like the one who almost killed him on the bus ride, fleeing from a dangerous and unpredictable man, his heart should be beating hard and adrenalin saturating his body and sweat sliding over his skin. But he was fine. His body had forgotten to have a panic attack for days. And now it still did not come, and he knew it would not come, and in this cave, he felt as free as ever.

He couldn't see the moon to tell how long they had lay there asleep when he was awakened by the strangest elephant noise he could imagine. Elephants, he knew, nearly always make deep rumblings or majestic, earth-shaking trumpets whose power, were it released in full inside the cave, might break his eardrums. But this noise was a tiny, shy whimper, quite un-elephant like. He turned his head to focus on the direction of the small sound.

It was Wanjeri, quietly crying.

Without a word, he twisted his body toward hers. He held her as close as he dared without offending her and wiped her tears away. Her body felt smaller and more fragile than he had judged it, and she shook as he gently squeezed the tension and despair from inside her. For the first time, Owen felt as if he were of some use to her, like he was her age instead of just a kid. They lay there silently until she grew still and drifted back to sleep.

He lay awake, uncertain of the future and what he would learn tomorrow. But tonight, he slept as houseguests of this gentle, fierce family of elephants. He was no longer afraid of them like he feared the elephant that charged him his first day in Africa. Now they protected him instead. Lying there on the bare earth, he felt a loyalty to them as strong as their bonds with each other, and somehow it was precisely the right place to be, sleeping on the ground in a cave full of elephants, warmed by a thin cloth and a herd of huge, quiet beasts.

34

"I never want to leave! I want to stay with you forever, First Grandmother!"

"You say that now, but you will want to go when it is time, just as your older brothers did."

He saw the two young males, both born several years before him, walking rapidly in the distance, toward the setting sun. He would miss them, but when he asked where they were going, and learned that he too would be expected to leave someday, it shocked him. In his younger days, when he learned that males leave, he had decided to stay instead. He tried to hide under First Grandmother's belly like he used to but, proving her point, he was no longer small enough to fit.

"Where are they going?"

"To find other bulls to live with. To find new mothers to mate with. To live as they want."

True to her word, he grew even more, and within the next two rainy seasons he was as confident and strong as any animal, elephant or otherwise. He was the largest and strongest animal of all now, with hard tusks that could tear down entire trees. He no longer needed the protection of this mother and grandmothers and First Grandmother. He feared nothing—except perhaps the sisters and mothers with young calves who warned him away as he paraded around the herd, showing off his might. Soon it was clear he, and his might, were no longer appreciated, and he found himself walking rapidly toward the sunset, just as he had seen his brothers and other young bulls do. Then he stopped and turned.

He hadn't even thought to say a word to First Grandmother. She was watching him with the same intense look as the day he was too afraid to cross the river so many years ago. Her gaze never wavered. She seemed to urge him on, knowing he was ready. He turned back toward the sun and ran fast, never looking back, until it was dark and he could no longer smell or hear the herd.

In his first night, he was consumed with sadness. He was so far from his family he could no longer hear their low rumbles in his ears or through his feet. He had never been away from them, not a single day.

Then he felt vibrations through the ground. Soon his ears detected the deep rumbles in the air. He followed their direction and saw three young male elephants gathered near a water hole, playing and flapping their ears. He was uncertain if he should approach, but then he detected the distinct smell of one of his older brothers who had left the herd just a year before.

He was no longer afraid.

When he felt the power to mate inside him, a wet stain appeared on the side of his head. The tears trickled past his eyes and over his ears. He felt stronger and more alive than ever. He was to be feared, not to fear. He broke the promise he made to himself long ago and picked a fight with several other males, even a few with bigger and longer tusks. And he won them all. Then he listened for the deep, low call of a female, and when he heard one, he ran a long distance to find her herd and mated with her.

He felt the power of the Spirit within him, the one who created the elephants from the soil of the mountain as First Grandmother had told him long ago. It felt good to have the power to fight and run and mate, and the power to do good things with his power, awesome things like create a new elephant, just as the Spirit created the first nine, long ago.

Later, he saw the mother elephant whose baby he had sired (he noticed her odor first) with her herd—and with a little youngster following her closely. The little elephant, who had a trunk that wobbled and swayed as he ran around playing with the other youngsters and tusks just beginning to grow out, paid close attention to the first grandmother of the herd. He knew the young one would learn a great deal from this first grandmother, and would find a place in the world.

* * *

Wanjeri woke with the elephants. A hint of sun lit the cave, enough for her to see them filing out. She could hear their broad feet shuffling through the dirt on the floor of the cave, and she could tell from their footsteps the size of each creature as it passed the little shelf, just inside the entrance, where she and Owen had slept. It had kept them high and safe from the elephants' feet.

Without moving, she lay next to Owen and listened to him sleep. She stroked his soft brown hair. She had never even touched a white person's hair before, not even a white woman's. It was so soft and silky, softer even than her mother's hair had been when she and Wanjeri had taken turns brushing and twisting it long ago.

Wanjeri had never had a lover or a man she cared to marry. She had thought about many boys, and men, but never really touched one. Sometimes when she thought about them, the stink of her Uncle Abasi's breath, full of whisky, clouded her thoughts. She had never stroked a man's hair like this, nor had one comfort her as he had done the night before. Stroking his hair didn't come naturally—it was only something she had seen girls do with their boyfriends on television or in a park, especially in London. But the moment she touched this young man's hair, it felt more like the hair of a child to her than a grown man. She felt like a mother rather than a lover, comforting a lost and weary little boy as he had comforted her, a lost and weary little girl.

How had she come to lie here in this cave with him? She had slept here a few times with no companions but the elephants, but this was the first time she had shared this secret place with anyone else. Three nights ago, she had led Owen's father to the very same place, but left him to find his own way to his final destination as she went back down to fetch his son.

She had not meant to betray her family this way. The things she imagined her aunts and cousins and friends whispered about her while she was out in the bush—that she was not like them, that she thought only of herself, that studying in London had made her think herself better than them—perhaps those whispers had come true. But she didn't think she was better than anyone else. She felt like she had never quite joined her own family in the first place, not since her parents died. Who had taken the place of the kind, soft-spoken father she remembered? Uncle Mubego, who thought of her and everyone else as toys to entertain him or tools to use for his designs. And Uncle Abasi, who thought the same of her, in a darker and more evil way. They had betrayed her. Her family would never see it that way, but it made Wanjeri feel better. She had stayed true to her mother and father and what they would wish for their youngest daughter. She felt her mother's presence there with her, gently stroking her hair, as she stroked Owen's.

She hadn't planned this. It just happened. These white men, father and son, had come into her world and forced her to choose between right and wrong, and she chose right. Now she did not know what to do next or how she would pay for her choice. Would Mubego know what she had done? Probably. Would he even care? Was it part of a plan he was orchestrating? She didn't have the knowledge to judge. She might go home as if nothing had happened, or it might be dangerous to even show her face in the whole country again. She might have to run and hide somewhere else in Africa, or even go to England. Or perhaps she could stay in the bush with the elephants, following them as she had many times, like she was one of them.

35

Owen woke to the sound of a stomach rumbling and soon noticed it was his own. He was hungry enough to eat dirt like an elephant. The nearer reaches of the cave were now lit by the morning sun, and he could see inside the cave. It was far larger than he had imagined. The elephants were gone.

"We should go soon," Wanjeri said. She was pulling a pile of large rocks apart just outside the cave.

He sat up and dug through her backpack, finding none of the fruit she had packed. "Is there any food left?"

"I put it outside last night, under these rocks," she replied, "so no hungry elephant or any other creature would smell it and come looking for it." She dug their breakfast from under the rocks and handed him some.

Their hunger sated with tiny sweet bananas not much larger than his thumb and a juicy oval fruit with musky reddish flesh under the peel, they set off uphill again. They neither saw nor heard any elephants. The animals had probably headed back down the mountain, explained Wanjeri, but now the destination was near and they no longer needed the guidance of the big beasts.

After trekking another 30 minutes through thick vegetation, they reached the trail and rejoined it. Nobody would be up here this early, she said. There were no camps this far up the slope for tourists to spend the night. The trail led down a steep bank to a stream. A narrow twist of sticks and wire formed a crude bridge. Crossing over, Owen heard the unmistakable rush of a waterfall uphill through the stream valley.

On the other bank, the trail turned to follow the stream uphill, toward the sound of the falls. It was steep enough for them to scramble on hands and feet for several minutes. And then they reached a clearing with a modest, yet fantastic little waterfall. The free-falling water emerged from between two looming rock ledges, 20 or more feet high, which sheltered a large clear pool fed by the falls. The clearing made a comfortable beach for this tiny ocean. Some large boulders, sheared recently from the outer points of the ledges, lay in the clearing. On one of the boulders sat his father.

He had his legs stretched out toward the water and his chin on his fist, pondering the waterfall. Owen and Wanjeri approached without speaking. Owen knew he had already detected their approach. Then he turned and looked Owen right in the eye and said the last thing Owen expected to hear.

"It's good to see you, son."

"It's good to see you, Dad," was Owen's automatic reply. Then he felt enormous embarrassment and discomfort at saying it. It was not something he wanted to say first, and perhaps not at all, but there it was already, spit to the ground, and he could not pick it back up.

"Things don't always work out the way you plan them, do they?" the elder Dorner said.

"No, they don't."

Owen sat on the beach, and Karl got up to sit closer to him. His father walked with a notable limp. This time, Owen looked his father right in the eye, but Karl Dorner did not return his gaze. He stared into the gush of water filling the pool. Wanjeri squatted far away, dipping her hands in the water and washing her face, keeping a respectful distance from their reunion.

Owen resolved to stay silent. Back home, two people sitting in silence was uncomfortable, and he would feel the desperate need to fill the space with words, any words. But things were done differently in this country. He had only been here a week, but he felt like he knew. Sitting high on this mountain and saying nothing for a while was not something to be feared. The words, when they came, would mean more. He would wait for his father to explain why he wanted to come all this way to meet, and how he managed to escape Mubego's clutch.

His father didn't take long to break the silence.

"Have you figured out what the ultimate sacrifice is, Owen?"

"What?"

"What I asked you. When you came to see me in the prison. What the ultimate sacrifice is for a soldier. Figure it out yet?"

Owen had not thought about the question. Was there really an answer he had in mind?

"No."

"I'll tell you what it's not. It's not to die for your country. I get why you would think that, but it's not. Sure, that's what they call dying—the 'ultimate sacrifice,'—but then they teach you there are worse things than dying. It's a contradiction. So, what's worse than dying?"

"Torture?"

"Think harder, Owen."

Owen thought for a moment, then offered, "Losing your honor?"

Karl turned and looked at Owen. "Exactly! Damn, you're smarter than you should be with the genes you got." But then he looked away. "Did you know I chose your name? 'Owen?' It was my dad's name."

"So ... what? What's your point? You lost your honor?"

"No, Owen, I didn't lose it. I gave it up. Or to be more precise, I made it look like I gave it up."

"It ... it was all fake?"

"It was all fake. All of it. I was never a traitor. I didn't help a rebellion. I didn't do any of those things. I didn't give up my country, I gave my honor to it. Sacrificed my good name for the greater good, just like sacrificing my life. It was a cover story. I was a scapegoat."

I knew it! thought Owen. His silly childish fantasy had turned out to be true! It was all he had hoped for by coming all this way. His lips tightened into a smile that held back tears.

"Do you see? Do you see what I gave up? Everyone

thought I was a traitor. Not just that—I gave up you and the family, and your memories, your respect. It's worse than death. I'm a soldier! A soldier will stuff a grenade up his ass and pull the pin before he gives up on what he believes in or betray what he stands for. That's his job."

The next feeling Owen experienced snuck up on him—he was angry.

"You left us for that? You let Momma think you were a traitor?"

"Yeah. Like I said … a fate worse than death." Owen heard his father choking back tears, too.

"So why the hell are you here now? What did you take me on this wild chase up a mountain for?"

"I couldn't explain myself in that prison. I thought it would be easy to chuck you out of there without feeling anything, but I couldn't do it. When I saw you, it was the first time I really regretted all this. All of it. Really, really regretted it all. And it's worse now because the whole thing is over. The Russians aren't coming any more. But I can't just say, 'never mind' and ask for a ticket home."

Owen looked into his father's eyes. His face resembled a man who had forgotten how to swim searching for someone to stick his hand out and pull him from the water.

"You've got to understand what I did. It was the right thing. I was a Judas, but Judas was necessary. What if he hadn't betrayed Jesus, and he never got nailed up? Jesus would have lived a while and then died choking on a chicken bone or something, and Christians wouldn't have any religion! Everyone plays their part in the grand scheme. I thought I was doing the right thing back then. But I got to thinking after you came to see me. The world's changed. It's not divided up into the free world versus communist hell anymore. Africa is just Africa now. It's all just one big hot hell. I wonder if it was all worth it now. I mean, family is family. A man wonders if his loyalties have been in the right place."

His voice became a little rougher, a little older.

"Remember that elephant that visits my window almost every day? He's an old bull, like me. That's why we get along. I've learned more from that old animal than any person, ever. One thing about elephants is they don't have to choose between family and nation. Family and nation are one and the same. Things are simple for them."

"Africans used to be like that, too."

The three of them turned at once to the new voice speaking from behind and above them. It was Mubego.

"We all used to be like that, my friend," Mubego said. "No need to choose between family and nation. They were one and the same, as you said."

Mubego was standing on the rock ledge above the waterfall, the perfect pulpit for the drama that always seemed to accompany his cruelest moments. Karl tensed, ready to flee. Julian appeared behind him, from the other side of the falls, armed with a rifle, and Karl relaxed again. No need to waste energy.

"Of course, we still have our families, our tribes," the Colonel continued with his lecture to his captive audience, "But the British and French and Belgians and the rest came and put a new layer on top, ignoring the lands of the tribes, and crisscrossed it with borders they drew between them for their own convenience, here and all over the continent. Oh, and then the Americans came. And I am a servant of this country now, and my tribe, and my family. It's a complicated business, but I am up to the task, don't you think?"

"You serve nobody but yourself," sneered the elder Dorner.

Mubego paused and pondered this. Then he climbed down from the rock, stood next to Julian with rifle in hand, and surveyed the scene.

"I can't believe Wanjeri thought I wouldn't find this place, even with those smelly elephants to cover your tracks. I was coming here before she was born. I tracked game here. The rebels, we hid here for months on end. The British eventually found this place and bombed it from the air. Imagine—an air raid on a few hungry men and boys hiding in the forest. Such brutality, and desperation. And we still won, in the end. You can barely see any evidence of the bombs, but I remember every inch of this place, before the bombs came down."

He turned to Owen. "Your Asian friend, Manish," he said. "You will be happy to know he is feeling better. He is on his way to a hospital in Italy on a government plane. The old lady, Mrs. Pearson, she actually had the courage to ask me for help getting him to a better hospital. I did everything she asked. Manish had no more need to suffer. I'm not an evil man, I just do what is necessary."

"You had him beaten in the first place, though, didn't you?" said Owen, feeling as courageous as his father.

"Hmm." Mubego nodded toward Wanjeri, who was

still crouched by the water. "Did she tell you that, or did you figure it out yourself? No matter. I used men who work for people in Nairobi, and they took their job too seriously. They were supposed to scare you by scaring him. I'm sorry for that. He is a pleasant little man. I enjoyed his company. But even with the bashing they gave him, you didn't frighten easily. Like father, like son."

Owen felt strange to be proud of a compliment coming from Mubego, but he was.

"And now you meet your father and learn all about his terrible deeds."

"I already know the truth," replied Owen. "I learned it in Mombasa and here today. You made him take the blame for what you did. You tried to overthrow the government, but he had to pretend it was him to keep power. You fed everyone bullshit to save yourself."

"Bullshit!" laughed Mubego. "Oh, how I love that word. What a lovely, perfect American word. I think I learned it from old Karl, a long time ago. Yes, it was bullshit. Of course it was. But bulls need to shit sometimes, do they not? That's how everyone did things back then. There were more important issues—the Russians. Your government is as much to blame. When greater issues are at stake, people don't matter. I learned that from the Brits, and the Americans after them. Your father didn't come here as part of the Peace Corps and he didn't give a damn about Africans either. The Americans came here so the Russians wouldn't come here, and they would do whatever it takes to keep them out. So neither you nor he are in a position to lecture me about politics or overthrowing governments."

"Yeah, we get it, Mubego. Why did you follow us all up here?" said Karl.

Mubego looked at Karl, but he was staring at his son. "Well, there's the matter of an escaped prisoner. He was once my friend, and he remains a valued guest in my prison. But the main reason is I couldn't miss this grand performance. You, Capt. Dorner, denied me the opportunity to listen in on a tender reunion between father and son, when he came to see you in the prison. You really flubbed that one. I was listening to every word. Are you surprised? Of course not. I needed to know what you had to say, and what he had to say, and why he was really here.

"But I wanted more. I wanted to hear which way you went, Karl. Do you keep up the story about committing treason and send your boy home disappointed? Or do you tell him about the choice you made to take the blame and live in my prison instead of coming home to him, and send your boy home disappointed even more knowing you chose this wasted life?

"But you flubbed it and didn't make a choice, and that was so disappointing. That's not like you, to lack courage like that. I was not entertained."

"Mubego, you are scum," sneered Owen. "You destroy lives for nothing." Karl smiled with pride at Owen's brave words.

Mubego smiled too, as broadly as Owen had ever seen, his gold tooth capturing and reflecting the dim light of what remained of the cave the old Mau Mau warrior had once cowered inside under the blows of British bombs.

"Ha! Now the son is the fighter the father once was," Mubego replied. "But you don't understand, young Owen. I do important work here in my country. You know that by now, don't you? Why did your father have to throw away his life for me? Because I kept this country for him and the Americans. This is a good country, full of good people, and I did what I thought was best for them. And you should be very proud of your father. He was no traitor to America. He loved his country, too. He taught me another word, a word for what he agreed to be—'stooge.' He was a stooge for his country. Kenya could have been ripped apart if he hadn't stood up to take the blame. The Russians would have been running naval patrols out of Mombasa. They could cut off the oil supply to the entire world with one phone call. Kenya was very, very important to America back then. Not so much now, wouldn't you say, Capt. Dorner?" And he laughed, too hard.

"Shut up, Mubego." Karl Dorner's face was screwed up in anger, and Julian perked up and raised his rifle a little.

"Yes, he was a hero like no other—to his country. So you should be proud."

"Shut the fuck up, Mubego!"

The Colonel let slip a little snort. "Of course, he was a traitor to his family, but what is family? Not country, not nation, not tribe. Family is not much of anything, is it, Karl?"

"Shut up!" And Karl Dorner lunged at him, but Julian held him back with his elbow crooked in this neck, the other arm still in control of the gun.

What Owen saw next stunned him though he understood it as well as anyone could.

His father breathed faster and then gasped for air. Perspiration formed on his forehead, retained there in the cool up-mountain air. He put his hands down on the earth, palms down to steady his stomach and his spinning head.

Owen wanted nothing more than to put his hand on his father's back, to rub his shoulders and tell him the attack would pass soon, that it was all in his head, a physical reaction to stress, not a lack of self-control or character. Owen wanted to tell him that panic spells did not make him a coward.

Even this man, the bravest and toughest man Owen had ever met, the man who fought in the wilds of Africa and willingly walked into a dusty prison—even he had attacks like Owen's. Owen wanted to hold his father at that moment, to hug the fearful feeling out of him, like Owen's mother had done to him when he was a boy.

But when he moved toward his father, Julian stepped forward with the rifle in hand and stopped him.

Mubego didn't seem to notice Karl Dorner's condition, or else he had seen it before and no longer cared. He turned to Wanjeri, who had sat motionless and silent on a rock next to the water, her arms around her knees, observing.

"And you. Wanjeri."

She looked up at him, small and helpless against his bulk and his power.

"You are so predictable," Mubego sneered. "You love your smelly elephants, and you lead me right to my escaped prisoner and his pathetic little son. You always do what is expected, like a good girl. Did you think the elephants would cover your tracks? I lived on this mountain for two years! I know this place better than you, and I don't need disgusting elephants to lead me around. You've always been stupid and you accomplish nothing but looking at those fat, ugly creatures. I'll shoot a few of them just for you on our way down the mountain while you watch." He laughed and looked at Julian, who smiled and lifted his gun as if aiming at one, making a shooting noise with his mouth.

Mubego was still laughing when Wanjeri calmly stood and climbed the cool smooth rock to her uncle, put her mouth to his ear and whispered. The laugh suddenly stopped.

"What?!" yelled Mubego in a rage. She ran back down the rock surface, next to the rushing water, set her feet squarely, and turned back to him.

"It's the truth. I made Abasi how he is," she said. "It was me. He tried to touch me when I was a girl, so I hit him in the head with a rock. It wasn't an elephant, it was me." She said it calmly, with determination, and not a hint of fear, but loud enough for everyone to hear above the rushing water.

Mubego was speechless with rage.

"It's the truth. Uncle Abasi deserved it. I didn't mean to hurt him, but he deserved it."

Without another word, Mubego lunged at her. Before he reached her, Karl jumped up and slammed his body against Mubego's.

Then Karl was on top of Mubego. Julian ran to the

two as they struggled, kicked Karl in the ribs enough to roll him over, pointed the gun at Karl's chest, and fired.

"No!" Mubego shouted and fell to his knees—to comfort Karl.

"This was not supposed to happen!" He was yelling at Owen. "This was not supposed to happen!" It was the only time Owen would recall seeing Mubego completely out of control of himself.

Then Mubego looked up. "Where is she?" Mubego demanded of Julian. "Don't let her escape! She saw this! She heard it all!"

Owen looked for Wanjeri, but she had disappeared into the forest.

Owen crawled over to his father, cradling his head in his lap. Blood was running down the rock toward the stream. "I didn't plan it this way, Dorner," Mubego said. "I didn't plan it this way. Why did you do that?"

But Capt. Dorner said nothing, and his life leaked away from his body into the churning water.

36

Long before the elephant appears at the window, Owen senses the animal's rich odor and the faint sound of his four huge, flat feet compressing the soil wetted by the rains that began a week ago. Col. Mubego permits the old elephant to approach the small window, though the thick stone wall and prison bars prevent his trunk from reaching Owen. Mubego's standing order to the guards is not to throw rocks at it like they do to the buffalo or baboons that wander too close to the compound. If Mubego wanted a fence to keep them all out, he could have the Nairobi authorities build and pay for it. He could even have the elephant shot. No, the prison lacks a fence because Mubego wants it to lack a fence. The only animal allowed to take advantage is the lumbering bull.

When Owen is not content to listen to the old bull's stories, he tells his own elephant tale, the one about a little elephant that would not cross a river and the family that would not cross without him.

After Owen whispers the story through the bars, the serene elephant swings his weighty head, his ears slapping against his body as a billow of dust clouds the air. Then he ambles away, his eyes half closed and his swaying body relaxed as the forest closes around his rump. Though the trees and the darkness hide his enormous body, Owen dreams he can hear his broad flat teeth shredding fibrous leaves and bark late into the night.

Mubego had wanted Owen to stay, confined at all times, at his home until he could figure out what to do. But Owen had chosen to live in the prison cell his father had occupied, breathe the same air, and sleep on the same cot.

After one month in the cell, he cannot say he understands his father's decisions or that he senses his father's nature within him. But, like his father, Owen does understand the old bull elephant is talking to him. He can detect it just on the edge of his hearing, and all around him, in the ground and the prison walls.

At nearly every sunset, the old bull emerges from the forest to visit Owen's window. His broad ears flap the rapidly cooling air across his back until under the shade of the prison wall he rests his trunk on the window ledge. His hide is rough and crinkled like an orange peel but colored dark by the rain. Beyond his peak years, he treads with deliberate and balanced steps, perfectly aligned with the passage of his weight and smothering the sound of any objects crushed beneath the soles of his feet.

Owen once saw a photo of the massive muscled

arms of a linebacker cradling a nude newborn baby. He thinks of that picture when he watches the elephant walk, with a gait that weds power with precision. This creature must weigh at least 10,000 pounds, but he can tread through the forest in nearly total silence.

How different this gentle, quiet, reassuring creature seems compared to the enraged elephant Owen met on his first day in Africa or the agitated one he confronted on the safari.

Mubego summons Owen occasionally to give him news. A letter from the United Nations—probably arranged by Mrs. Pearson—demanding his release, or letters from his mother. Sometimes Mubego even reads Owen's mother's letters to him, as if he couldn't read them for himself. She is in Nairobi, working to get him out, and trying to arrange a prison visit. Owen thinks back to the letters his mother had penned to his father. Had it been Mubego who rejected them so that they were returned unopened?

When Mubego summons Owen to his office, he does not seem himself. Owen sees stress in his eyes, perhaps even fear. Something was going on in the world that Mubego couldn't control. Events that Mrs. Pearson had put into action, perhaps, after seeing what Mubego did to Manish. She wouldn't hesitate to stick her nose into the business of an entire nation. Perhaps she had helped Manish complete his mission to organize a strike. He could sense trouble from the way the other inmates spoke in hushed tones, and in their native languages, careful not to let Mubego or his guards hear.

And Wanjeri—where was she now? Working with Ms.

Pearson, perhaps, or pleading with the right people in London to help Owen get out, or agonizing over ways to come home. Or was she simply hiding among the elephants? Mubego never mentions her, nor does Owen, but they both know she is out there, and that she knows Mubego's secrets.

Despite being the prisoner, Owen feels more in control than ever. He knows Mubego cannot kill him, nor can he indefinitely hold Owen. Mubego can only contain this problem for a short time, concocting more stories and deliberating before the pressure builds to boiling point and something explodes.

Each day, before the old bull elephant arrives, Owen stands by the window tracing his father's footsteps in the sand. Through the window, he stands as his father once did, watching swollen grey thunderheads that a week ago were only wispy clouds, the first Owen had seen in Africa's sky. Though his father is gone, forever this time, Owen finds comfort knowing his story is complete. No part of his father's life can happen anymore without Owen to witness it.

His father's sparse possessions remain in the cell. Owen cherishes them all, carefully turning the pages of each of the books neatly arranged at the back of a simple table: a *Bible* (New International Version), a *Koran* (in Arabic, though), Ken Follett's *The Key to Rebecca* (paperback, cover gone), *Unlock the Power of the Bond Market*, and *The Idiot's Guide to Knitting and Crocheting*. His father, he surmised, had gathered this eclectic collection from the prison's Red Cross library. At the front of the desk sits a fossil of a typewriter, but without a ribbon. Owen has yet to figure a use for the machine besides staring at it. He has kept a few of his father's T-shirts and pants, an extra pair of sandals made from old tires he had bought from another inmate, a pen and pad, water bottle, and some iodine pills to make drinking safe. Pride of place was a crude sculpture of his own face made from a little rain water mixed with dust swept from the floor. Owen thought it was a good likeness.

He has noticed how his African inmates—he is the only white, and the only foreigner—appreciate the few belongings they own, and reuse them until they disintegrate. Those inmates were not in awe of him, or afraid of him, or hostile to him as a white American in their midst, for he was not the first white American to occupy this cell. They had liked his father, and so they liked him.

Owen no longer carried anxiety pills. They had slipped to the bottom of his bag after the safari and were long forgotten. If the attacks returned, he would try to slow his accelerated breathing, and fight against the overwhelming feeling of panic. But they probably wouldn't come back.

This small cell—humble but sturdy like the mud and straw structures huddled inside the thorny bomas that keep lions and hyenas out—is enough for Owen. Waiting it out in his prison cell is not so different from the years Owen spent self-imprisoned in his bedroom. It serves as a refuge from the chaos of the world as he shares stories with the old bull elephant.

Few of Owen's own life stories make sense to him

now. They were merely fantasies he had created to wrap and burnish the truth, like pearls built around grains of sand. Although Africa will vastly change the trajectory of his life, Owen needs the now to be now, and the here to be here, until the rain washes away the dust that holds the last of his father's footprints.

The old bull is his unwavering friend, his tiny eye pressed against the prison bars, fearing nothing and wanting nothing to fear him. In the evening, within moments of the elephant's farewell, Owen already looks forward to his visit the next day, when he will return bearing signs of his wandering: scratches and scrapes on his side from the thick, thorny acacias to the north, skin the muddy color of the soil in the marshes to the east, and salty gray mountain soil on his feet from where the bones of First Grandmother and his ancestors lay.

37

He no longer feels the urge to follow the calls of young females that resonate through the forest for miles at a low frequency, deep below the wan capabilities of a woman's tiny, feeble ear. His scraped and beaten tusks and notches in his ears display medals from great battles, but his body is still sturdy. His teeth are not yet worn down and he can still chew the hard forest leaves.

He has been alone for a long time, but never lonely. The soil beneath his feet still feeds him. It is where he came from. It is where the Spirit lives. The soil holds the bones of his sisters and mother and grandmothers. He comes to touch them sometimes, to cradle their bones in his trunk and smell them again. He remembers the stories and paths and places his first grandmother shared with him. He remembers the sweet foods she led them to when his teeth were new and fresh. Long after he went out on his own to find mates and live his life as a bull should, he still remembered her. He remembered how she taught him not to fear being apart from the rest, because he never really was alone as long as he stood upon the soil, and tasted it, and held the ancestors' bones. And he remembered how she taught him that some women, like the one that always followed them on their journeys, were not to be feared either, but to be taught just as she taught her grandchildren.

So he was not afraid to visit the one he could barely see with his old, weakening eyes, the one who always looked back at him from inside a small hole in the rock. The woman, a male, had been there for many seasons— for as long as he had roamed the forest nearby. Only his odor had changed, oddly, to a younger, fresher smell. Somehow he knew the man wanted to learn about the world, and about where he came from, just as young elephants want to learn. Though First Grandmother said women could not learn knowledge, he would try to teach it to this one. While he was no first grandmother, he would do the best he could. He could teach this man a great deal just by standing close to the little hole in the rock, waiting.

Special thanks to Michael Neff, Susan Mockler, the wonderful people at Stormbird Press, and Audrey, Brita, and Elenor, who love books.

About the Author

Rick Hodges is a writer and author whose written works are as diverse as his life experiences.

Rick enjoys a deep appreciation for the natural world on a simple, introspective level, informed as much by digging in the dirt as a child or beekeeping as a teenager as by travels to great landscapes. A voyage to East Africa, and the experience of seeing how the people there lived in tandem with wildlife, inspired his novel, *To Follow Elephants*.

His daytime career as a writer for non-profit groups and journalist in Washington, DC, has given Rick the chance to write about a wide variety of topics and experiences. Government, politics and business issues have all crossed his desk, of course, in the form of news items, fundraising appeals, speeches and congressional testimony. But his published portfolio also includes a nonfiction instructional book for high school students about the Muslim world, an article about the best way to make coffee that appeared in the *Washington Post* Food section, a humorous essay about raising a child with a disability, an article about airline collision avoidance systems he wrote after riding on a demonstration flight involving his plane flying head-on at another, and a story about a town that united to make a dying boy's last day the best of his life, among many others.

Aside from his 9-to-5 writing, Rick has produced fictional works, including short stories and a stage play. He wrote his play, *Three Generations of Imbeciles*, based on a 1927 court case from his home state of Virginia that cleared the way for involuntary sterilization of people with disabilities for decades before the practice was outlawed.

Rick's wife, Elenor, is executive director of a local environmental organization and inspired him to work for a time as a grant proposal writer for The Wilderness Society. In his current job, Rick writes magazine copy for a national labor union. He lives with Elenor and his two daughters in Arlington, Virginia.

www.RickHodgesAuthor.com

An Invitation from Stormbird Press

Stories about our world, and our relationship with nature, have been told by people for thousands of years. It is how we share our moral tales, empower ourselves with knowledge, and pass wisdom to the future.

Our titles all passionately communicate people's reverence, wisdom, and inspiration about the places, plants and animals, habitats and ecosystems, of our shared home—*Earth*. They whisper where we've been and foretell where we are going.

Around campfires and hearths, beside streams, across tundras, under the shadow of mountains or the wide branches of mighty trees, and in the pages of Stormbird's books, people's stories and wisdom carry like feathers in the wind.

Joins us and become part of our community of eco-book-lovers.

We will keep you up to date with our latest catalogue, give you access to new releases before they arrive in bookstores, give you chances to win signed editions, and much more.

Stormbird Press

www.StormbirdPress.com

CPSIA information can be obtained
at www.ICGtesting.com
Printed in the USA
FSHW011803041119
63740FS